# Rabboni, My Love

## *A Memoir of Jesus' Wife, Mary Magdalene*

*Time Changes.*
*Everything Passes but Love.*
*Peace Abide You.*
— v'Taher Libeinu. 114

*With love and Peace*
*June Kerr*

AVIVA
PUBLISHING
New York

# June Kerr

# DEDICATION

*For David, Michelle, Henri, and Becket*

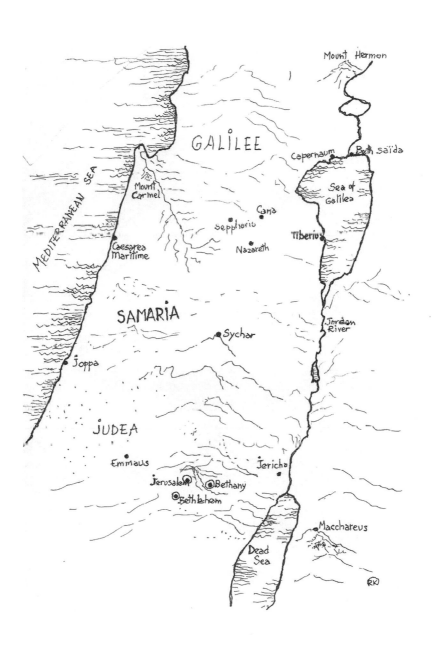

# AUTHOR'S NOTE

This is the story of the life of Jesus from a new point of view, told by his partner for life, Mary Magdalene. It explores possible connections between Jesus and the Torah (the books of Moses), the Psalms, the Prophets, as well as the history and wisdom literature of the holy books of Judaism, Islam, and Christianity. It suggests how and why four different approved versions of Jesus' death and resurrection mention Mary Magdalene as a central figure, and yet inexplicably reject her and her news. Who was she? Why was she chosen? What happened to her?

In writing this book, I have connected bits of allusions and intimations familiar to first century readers of the gospels and epistles to consider possible alternatives to traditional assumptions which have divided people, and to ask what were the relationships between the people involved, what was the back story to Jesus' reported public life, and what might have been hidden and why. For example, *Rabboni*, the word of address Mary Magdalene is reported as using when faced with a seemingly impossible alive Jesus was the highest, most respected term of address in the rabbinic school in Jerusalem two thousand years ago. Given to a select few, it means "My

Great Master." In another example, the man pulled from the crowded street to help Jesus carry the cross is reported to be from Cyrene, famous at the time for its major export, sylphium, an herb subsequently over-harvested to extinction, which prevented unwanted pregnancies. What did these allusions mean to a first century reader?

*Rabboni, My Love* offers a fresh exploration of possible answers to these questions and more in a story of the private lives of Jesus and his wife, Mary Magdalene.

# CHARACTERS IN
# *RABBONI, MY LOVE*

Chapter One:

- Joshua/ Jesus: Rabboni teaches in school of Hillel, member of the Sanhedrin (High Court), master of family holdings

- Miriam/Mary: Wife of Joshua, mother of John Mark, Joseph, and Sarah

- Hillel: Scholar, Sage, Founder of School, Former Head of Sanhedrin

- Gamaliel: Rabbon, Grandson of Hillel, teaches in school of Hillel, Leader of the Sanhedrin

- Nicodemus: Rabbi, Joshua's friend who teaches with him in school of Hillel, married to Miriam's friend Rachel

- Alphaeus: Chief steward of Olive Orchards for Joshua and Miriam

- Judas: Chief steward of money and accounts for Joshua and Miriam

- Thomas: Chief steward of animals of transport for Joshua and Miriam

- James: Son of Alphaeus, shepherd of flock on Mount of Olives for Joshua and Miriam

- John Mark: Oldest son of Joshua and Miriam, student of Gamaliel

- Joseph: Second son of Joshua and Miriam

- Sarah: Daughter of Joshua and Miriam

- John: Cousin of Joshua, widower, former priest now reformer/baptizer

- Justus: Close childhood friend of Joshua from Galilee, leader of Zealots

Chapter Two:

- Susanna: Country cook for Miriam and Joshua, wife of Thomas

- Simon: Student/servant of Joshua, brother of Joshua's friend Justus

- Martha: Sister of Miriam, wife of Simon of Bethany, sister of Lazarus

- Uncle Joseph: Joshua's mother's youngest uncle, metal trader

- Barnabas: Oldest son of Joshua's sister Anna, assistant trader to Uncle Joseph

- Thad: Student of Joshua, son of John and Dinah who died in childbirth

- Nathan: Chief steward of Jerusalem home of Joshua and Miriam

- Tobias: Nathan's assistant, door keeper,

- Rhoda: Housekeeper of the Jerusalem home of Joshua and Miriam

- Elizabeth: Wife of Caiaphas, mother of two sons, Mathias and Joshua, daughter of Annas, friend of Miriam and Martha

- Joseph Caiaphas: High priest, son-in-law of former High Priest Annas

- Mathias: Student of Joshua, best friend of John Mark, son of Caiaphas and Elizabeth, grandson of Annas and Judith

Chapter Three:

- Salome: Wife of Justus' brother Simon, Miriam's helper

- Simon: Husband of Martha, olive orchard and land owner in Bethany

- Lazarus: Brother of Miriam and Martha, scholar, olive orchard and land owner in Bethany

- Hanna: Wife of Lazarus

Chapter Five:

- Zachariah: Joshua's cousin by marriage, named for John's father

- Abraham: Founding father of faith in One God, Creator of the Universe

- Simon: A Samaritan, trader of Silphium from Cyrene

Chapter Six:

- Herod Antipas: Current puppet ruler of Galilee, married his brother's wife, fought with his brothers over Hasmonean Dynasty power

- Gestas: A Zealot who attacked Joshua

- Demas: A Zealot whose ankle Joshua healed, but who robbed Joshua

- Bartholomew: Student of Joshua, helps Judas, nephew of another rabbi

- James: Joshua's first younger brother, rabbi, member of Sanhedrin

- Joseph: Joshua's second younger brother, nicknamed Joses, scholar studying in Alexandria

- Jude: Joshua's third younger brother, manager of Bethlehem flocks

- Judith: Cook for the Jerusalem household of Joshua and Miriam

- Daniel: Assistant to Nathan in Jerusalem home of Joshua and Miriam

- Mary: Mother of Joshua, Anna, James, Joseph, Jude, Simeon, Tamara

- Zachaeus: Friend of Joshua, a tax collector in Jericho

- Abigail: Wife of Zachaeus

- Deborah: Friend of Miriam, wife of Joshua's friend Justus

- David: Anointed by Samuel, Second King of Israel, Joshua's ancestor

- Herod the Great: Hasmonean Dynasty, tried to kill baby Joshua

Chapter Nine:

- Moses: Led Hebrews out of Egypt, gave Hebrews Ten Commandments

- Miriam: Older sister of Moses, saved him from death when he was a baby

- Aaron: Moses' brother who helped him, became first high priest

- Andrew: Fisherman, disciple of John, son of Jonah, Simon Peter's brother, became disciple of Joshua

- Philip: Fisherman from Galilee, disciple of John, part Greek, part Hebrew, husband of Diana, father of Jason and Dan, disciple of Joshua

- Diana: Wife of Philip, mother of Jason and Dan, helper to Miriam

- Jonah: Boat partner with Joshua's father, Joseph, in Galilee

- Zebedee: Boat partner with Joshua's father in Galilee

- Joseph: Joshua's father, skilled craftsman of law, scholar, owner of land and flocks, investor, Nazarene

- Simon: Fisherman, son of Jonah, brother of Andrew, husband of Adah, disciple of Joshua, became known as Peter

- James: Fisherman, older son of Zebedee, disciple of Joshua

- John: Fisherman, younger son of Zebedee, disciple of Joshua

- Zealots: Rebels who vowed to overthrow Herod and Romans

Chapter Ten:

- Simeon: Joshua's youngest brother, owns vineyard outside Nazareth

- Judith: Simeon's wife

- Nathaniel: Fisherman, friend of Philip, son of vineyard owner in Cana,

- Tamara: Joshua's youngest sister, married Nathaniel

Chapter Eleven:

- Zachariah: Priest who passed Joshua on Jericho Road

Chapter Twelve:

- Peter: Nickname for Simon described in Chapter Nine

Chapter Thirteen:

- Joel: Priest, Cousin of Joshua and John

- Annas: High Priest, father-in-law of Caiphas, father of Five Chief Priests

Chapter Fourteen:

- Rachel: Wife of Nicodemus, granddaughter of Hillel, friend of Miriam

Chapter Fifteen:

- Josiah: Priest, manager, negotiator for Annas

- Simon of Cyrene: Trader of silphium, widower, rescuer of Joshua on Jericho Road
- Naomi: Widow, engaged to Simon of Cyrene, has five sisters

Chapter Sixteen:

- Omah: Mother-in-law of Peter, daughter of former head of synagogue in Capernaum
- Adah: Daughter of Omah, wife of Peter
- Jonah: Agitated, possessed young neighbor in Capernaum

Chapter Seventeen:

- Marcus: Roman Centurion, friend of Joshua from Gaul, husband of Amelia
- Hermes: Deathly ill son of Marcus and Amelia

Chapter Eighteen:

- Matthew: Tax collector in Capernaum, brother-in-law of Omah

Chapter Nineteen:

- Arrah Bar-Hannani: Head of the Capernaum Synagogue
- Daniel: Rabbi, Pharisee, School of Hillel, member of Temple delegation
- Seth: Scribe, Sadducee, School of Shammai, member of Temple delegation
- Amos: Rabbi, member of delegation from the Temple

- Samuel: Rabbi, member of delegation from the Temple

- Ben: Severely injured construction worker

- Judas: Zealot leader in Galilee, father of Justus, Simon, and several other sons, friend of Joshua's father

- Pontius Pilate: Roman Prefect of Judea, husband of Claudia, father of Pilo

- Herodias: Wife of Herod Antipas, former wife of Herod's brother Philip, mother of Salome

- Salome: Daughter of Herodias and Herod Antipas

Chapter Twenty-Four:

- Elizabeth: Wife of Caiaphas, see Chapter 2

- Judith: Wife of Annas, mother of Elizabeth and five chief priest sons

Chapter Twenty-Five:

- Solomon: Son of David, king of Israel known for his wisdom and wealth, builder of the First Temple in Jerusalem

- Claudia: Wife of Pontius Pilate, mother of Pilo, friend of Miriam

- Amelia: Wife of Marcus, mother of Hermes, friend of Miriam

Chapter Twenty-Seven:

- Jonathan Bar-Annas: Chief priest, one of five sons of Annas

Chapter Twenty-Eight:

- Judas Bar-Hezekiah: Leader of Zealots in Galilee, see Chapter 19
- Uncle Cleopas: Caravansary innkeeper in Emmaus
- Aunt Mary: Wife of Cleopas, sister of Joshua's father, Joseph

Chapter Twenty-Nine:

- Nahum: First priest who passed by Joshua on the Jericho Road
- Rachel: Favorite wife of Jacob/Israel

Chapter Thirty:

- Elijah: Prophet swept up to heaven alive, expected to return

Chapter Thirty-One:

- Malchus: Chief steward and head of guards for Caiaphas and Elizabeth

Chapter Thirty-Three:

- Jeremiah: Chief steward for Annas and Judith

# PROLOGUE

As I awoke, morning mist was lifting beyond the large entrance to my cave in the wilderness of Gaul, unveiling scattered pink clouds suspended in the deep blue autumn sky. I crawled out from the soft cushions and covers that formed my simple bed, slipped on his robe against the morning chill, and went out to revel in the sunrise, his favorite time of day. Bright golden leaves covered both trees and ground on the steep slope below me. I inhaled the quiet beauty, and thought I heard Jesus say again, "All I ever wanted was to bring peace on earth." I felt the top of my left hand warm with his touch, sighed, and shared his longing.

Still living in a world filled with conflict, I wondered what more I could do to bring peace when I remembered a psalm, "Bless God every chance you get. We live and breathe God. Together let's get out the word...that if you love life and can't wait to discover beauty and delight, you must turn your back on selfishness, do something generous, and fearlessly embrace peace. Never let it get away!"

We lived that way. Although I have written to Paul, John Mark, and others concerning Jesus' teaching and public life, I have decided to write the story that lay behind it all, the story of how an unexpected gift and an encounter with a stranger changed our lives as we discovered the power of love and the way to peace.

Mary Magdalene

Wilderness of Gaul

In the first year of the reign of Vespasian,

Titus Flavius Caesar

# CHAPTER ONE

In the beginning, in another autumn, in our mid-thirties, we were known as Joshua and Miriam and lived privileged lives in Jerusalem. A member of the Sanhedrin, Joshua had recently received the highest honor, Rabboni, for his outstanding teaching in the tradition of Hillel. His students, now rabbis themselves, were teaching others. The Sanhedrin and the rabbinic school at the Temple were torn with controversy, however, between several factions. Joshua, his friend and colleague Nicodemus, and some Pharisees followed the head of the Sanhedrin, Gamaliel, in the tradition of Hillel while others followed the old traditions of Shammai. The divisiveness in the Sanhedrin mirrored conflicts at every level throughout our land of Judea.

During the autumn olive harvest, we stayed in our nearby country home which we'd inherited. Nestled in olive groves on the mountain near Bethany, it was on the main road between Jerusalem and Jericho and offered us some distance and refuge from the political pressures in Jerusalem. One evening, James, our young shepherd, returned with one lamb missing from the small flock we kept there. Joshua, tired from teaching and discussing the current issues in the Sanhedrin, decided to go find the lamb. He went to change out of his robe and the key he wore around his neck, symbol of his authority to teach, into his old shepherd's sandals and short tunic while I went to the kitchen to get a sack of his favorite bread, cheese, olives, and ripe figs, with a skin of watered wine. We met again in the herb-filled courtyard and kissed. With food, wine, and his rather worn old crook and sling, he was rejuvenated and went out singing. He did enjoy being by himself on the mountain now and then when he could get away.

We were sending a caravan of olive oil to Jericho the next morning. Alphaeus, our burly, old chief steward, gave orders with his gruff good humor for loading the oil, for more picking, and then pressing again after the caravan left. I checked that the records were all in order with our quiet, meticulous account keeper, Judas, whose sturdy, skeptical twin, Thomas, in charge of our saddle and pack animals, would lead the caravan.

Our oldest son, John Mark, sixteen and vying for top honors at the temple rabbinic school, always had the rapt attention and devotion of his excitable younger brother, Joseph, already eleven, and his adoring little sister Sarah, just nine, when he told them stories after the evening meal. As usual, I had to remind them it was time for bed. After I kissed all three, I sent them off giggling to settle down for the night. I wrapped myself in a warm stole against the early evening chill, and went out to cross the dusty work yard, pass the olive press, and climb to the large rock in the middle of our garden of gnarled, old olive trees, perhaps alive since the time of Abraham, to wait for Joshua to return. From the rock, I could see the mountain above the trees, serene in the light of the just rising full moon.

I sat down and began to sing to myself, "The Lord is my Shepherd..." but I soon heard a muffled bleating, and Joshua's laugh. Delighted, I looked up and caught a glimpse of him, not far up the hill. Clearly silhouetted against the large silvery moon, Joshua, lamb over his shoulders, crook and sack in hand, was making his way back home. I sang, "goodness and kindness pursue me every day of my life...," and smiling to myself, climbed down from the rock, pulled up a little succulent grass, walked down around the press, and crossed the hard, packed dirt toward the mountain path.

As Joshua walked into the work yard from the path, he saw me and flashed his big, pleased-with-himself, boyish grin, which I always found so irresistible. After a quick kiss, he handed me his staff and bag, and then lifted the lamb off his broad shoulders onto the ground. The lamb wobbled, got its bearings, and then seemed very happy to be on its own four legs and safely home. It nuzzled Joshua's legs, and then mine, as it reached for the tender grass I offered. We laughed with delight as the lamb kicked up its hind legs and danced around us while Joshua, with his arm around my shoulder, and I, with mine around his waist, began slowly walking across the yard toward the fold on the olive garden's far side near the road.

"Where did you find him?" I asked.

"In the little gorge beyond our cave...broken foreleg... couldn't climb out." Joshua paused, gave me another quick kiss on my cheek. "Don't worry, Mim. I lifted him out and fixed it. It's fine now."

"You fixed it?" I asked. "I'm not worried; I'm astonished," I replied. "You never cease to amaze me."

"Still a pretty good shepherd, don't you think?" he chuckled. "Everyone fine here?"

"Double yes! You're still a wonderful shepherd!" I laughed. "And Alphaeus, Judas, and Thomas have everything ready for tomorrow. No one could have more responsible men for stewards," I said, "but James feels terrible. I'm sure he thinks he has let his father down. Alphaeus was not pleased with his son's news about the lost lamb. He's—" But I was interrupted by James, who had heard us and came running. James, greatly relieved and appreciative of Joshua's shepherding skills and stern kindness in giving him a bit of advice, led the lamb back to the fold while we headed back to the dark, thick walled coolness of our simple, old house, built around an herb-perfumed court with a large rustic table sheltered by lush grape vines hanging from a trellis above it. We paused before going on to our bedroom.

"Joshua," I asked softly so as not to disturb the sleeping household, "how do you do it?"

"Do what, my love?" he asked quietly. "Patiently question my colleagues and students, to show them that the *One True God* loves us and has created us to live in love and peace... which I was doing all morning," his eyes twinkled and he kissed me again, "or climb the mountain, find, and heal our little lamb?" Smiling broadly at my "You know what I mean" look, he persisted. "I think finding the lamb and healing it was easier. It didn't argue."

"Easy or not," I laughed, "it's unusual. Do you think you can heal people, too?"

We had reached our bedroom. Taking my shoulders in his hands, he gently turned me to face him, and with twinkling eyes, he teased, "Let me try! Where does it hurt?"

"Oh, Joshua," I laughed again.

Relaxed, he laughed too and kissed me again. "Oh, Mim, many people can heal. Remember those I wrote to you about in Borsippa? They did amazing cures."

I nodded, "A long time ago...."

He sighed, "I do have a gift, but I don't know how healing fits in with my teaching."

"It seems simple—" I started to respond.

"It should be simple," he laughed, "but nothing is simple these days, my dear." He took me in his arms. "We're surrounded by violence and distrust on every side. Divisions just get wider and wider as we accuse each other of the smallest infractions of the law. I don't know if teaching or healing can make a difference," he shrugged. "I've decided to go to Jericho tomorrow with the caravan to find Justus and John and talk again...see if we can find a way through all of the attacks and counterattacks, all of the bitterness and fault-finding that surrounds us. What do you think?"

"I think it's a good idea. You three *can* make a difference, I'm sure."

# CHAPTER TWO

An early riser, Joshua was already up, preparing to leave with the caravan, when I woke the next morning with the sun shining through the small window. I dressed and went into the courtyard where I found Susanna tending the small, clay oven from which she brought warm bread to the table laden with goat cheeses, ripe figs, honey and nuts, and pomegranate juice. I felt grateful as I began to eat, still wondering about Joshua healing the lamb, and now going to Jericho this morning with the caravan to find Justus and John.

Soon Alphaeus and Joshua, in a dull brown traveling tunic and robe, walked in from the work yard where I could hear men talking, arguing, and laughing while loading the animals with jugs of oil. The voice of Simon, the idealistic, youngest brother of Justus, Joshua's best friend whom he was going to Jericho to find, was distinctive and louder than the rest. Joshua came over and gave me a kiss and whispered, "How is it that I love you this morning as—"

I returned his kiss, whispering, "Shh!" My affectionate, handsome husband, while discreet, was not daunted by the presence of others in expressing his love to me, but I had to admit that I always delighted in the brush of his soft beard against my cheek.

"Eighteen years and counting," he laughed, as ever reminding me of how long we had been married, never taking a day for granted, which he knew I appreciated. He helped himself to some juice. "It's good to come in to a little quiet from all of that noise. Simon is defending his brother and the Zealots as usual while Thomas worries about all of the recent caravan raids." Sitting down next to me, he added with a chuckle, "Maybe I'll ask them to join Justus and me tonight if we can't reach John....Maybe they'll help us solve all of our difficulties."

"I hope so," I responded as Judas walked in and handed Joshua the leather pouch with the records, saying, "They're ready to leave shortly. Everything you need is here."

Alphaeus had men picking olives and would begin pressing again as soon as the caravan left. I planned to go to Jerusalem with the children to join my sister Martha, who was there shopping for a few days. Joshua told me Uncle Joseph was in the city with our nephew Barnabas, making plans for his next metal trading trip to Gaul, and he wanted to take John Mark, our oldest, with him; Uncle Joseph wanted to talk with me about it. At that moment, his cousin John's earnest young son Thad, whom we raised from his birth and who studied with Joshua in Jerusalem, rushed in breathlessly. "Martha just fell...her leg...can't stand. We carried her to your house...."

Joshua and I exchanged worried glances as I said I'd get the children and go immediately. "I'll go with you," he said. "Thomas can start the caravan. I'll catch them later, Mim.

Thad and John Mark can take care of Sarah and Joseph. Let's go now."

Thad, whom I noticed was growing his first facial hair, ran to find our children. I went to get our donkeys while Joshua went to tell Thomas, give him the pouch, ask him to check cinches again, and to meet at the usual caravansary outside Jericho if he couldn't catch them sooner. We quickly mounted our donkeys and were out the gate.

We soon arrived at our large, old Jerusalem home built as its neighbors were out of the golden sandstone so prevalent in the region. Our faithful Nathan was at the door, waiting as usual. He and his helper, Tobias, took the donkeys and we rushed in through the reception area to find my beautiful and capable, but now frightened, sister reclining on a bench in a small room beyond, sipping herbal wine prepared by our indispensable Rhoda, an expert on herbal remedies for any complaint, but unable to do anything except try to calm Martha.

"What happened?" I gasped, kneeling to embrace my sister. She handed me her empty bowl and told us through tears that she and Thad had been at a new weaver recommended by our friend Elizabeth; his shop was several steps above a courtyard and already crowded that morning. She had found a shawl, wanted to see it in daylight, and stepped out the door with it for a moment. The weaver began arguing with a customer and pushed the man out the door and into her as she turned to see what was happening.

"I went off the landing, trying to save the shawl," she wailed with despair. "I landed on my feet and crumbled. I can't control my foot at all. It doesn't hurt too much if I don't move it," she added as she pulled up her dress to show us and moaned, "Oh, it's worse than I thought...I'm crippled!" Joshua asked whether he could help her. She looked at me and I nodded assurance that he could. "Yes, I believe you can," she echoed uncertainly.

Joshua quietly put his hands on Martha's knee and the swelling slowly vanished. He smiled as he gently adjusted her lower leg and foot and held them comfortably. After a few moments, he said to no one I could see, "Thank you, Father." He guided her foot onto the floor and helped her stand as Rhoda and I stood by, speechless, holding our breath, witnessing the unbelievable.

Martha's eyes grew as wide as the wine bowl she had just given me. She shifted her weight from foot to foot. Without pain, she let out a whoop of amazed relief and pulled me into an ecstatic three-way hug with Joshua, babbling her thanks, laughing and crying for joy. Relieved, I breathed again, thankful Joshua could heal people as well as lambs.

"Love you, Martha," Joshua assured her. "Glad I could help, but I have to go now if I'm going to catch up with my caravan!" Kissing me, he added, "Enjoy the day, Love. Don't forget to talk with Uncle Joseph. I'll look forward to hearing about it tomorrow."

"Thanks. I'll stay here tonight with Martha and go back tomorrow. Maybe I can persuade her to stop overnight before going on to Bethany?" Martha laughed and asked how she could refuse. As Joshua went out the door, I added that I'd look in our scrolls for what Isaiah wrote about healing. He raised his eyebrows, nodded, and smiled.

I sent Nathan's young assistant, Tobias, to find Uncle Joseph and Barnabas to invite them for dinner. John Mark would be at the temple studying with Gamaliel in friendly competition with Joshua's students Thad and John Mark's best friend Mathias, the son of our friend and current high priest Joseph Caiaphas. Sarah and Joseph were studying Hebrew with a tutor. They would all come home for the mid-day meal and hear the good news about Martha.

Rhoda brought Martha and me some more thyme wine, fruit, and nut cakes on the terrace where we could enjoy a gentle breeze while sheltered from the bright morning sun by a thick-leaved palm. I had the chance to catch up with my sister's latest discoveries of merchants and traders and hear the news of friends she'd seen. While talking, Martha kept rolling her ankle around, trying to make sense of what had happened. "I was so afraid I'd hobble on a cane or crutches for the rest of my life," she sighed, "but now, I can finish my shopping. Can you believe it?" I shared her astonishment, but we went our separate ways until the mid-day meal.

In the dim light of the small room beyond our bedroom where we kept our precious collection of old scrolls, some inherited from Joshua's father and grandfather, I found the Isaiah scrolls. I carried them into the brighter light of our bedroom and then sat on the comfortable bench near the window. I looked for something I remembered about the lame walking, which seemed relevant. Scanning, I came across good news for Jerusalem, "Arise, Jerusalem, City of Peace, your light has come and the glory of the Lord shines over you. For, though darkness covers the earth, the Lord shall shine upon you, and his glory shall appear over you; and the nations shall march towards your light and their kings to your sunrise." What a dazzling vision, I thought as I continued, "Look all around, everyone comes to you; your sons shall come from far away, your daughters walking beside them leading the way."

"Daughters leading the way" was certainly not the usual image talked about by rabbis. I wanted to ask Joshua about it. I felt I was walking beside him, but I hadn't thought about leading the way. And then I found the passage, "Be strong, your God comes.... Then shall blind men's eyes be opened, and the ears of the deaf be unstopped. Then shall the lame man leap like a deer, and the tongue of the dumb shout aloud...." That was the passage I was looking for, but when Sarah and Joseph came bursting into the room full of enthusiastic questions about Aunt Martha and chatter about their tutor and their friends and cousins, it ended my inquiry for the moment.

# CHAPTER THREE

Late the next afternoon, I was back in the country, looking forward to talking with Joshua. When I heard the caravan, I went into the yard to see Thomas leading them back, but where was Joshua? I hurried to Thomas to learn what had delayed him. Thomas looked shocked. "I thought he'd decided to stay here, Miriam. He never arrived."

"Never arrived?" I panicked. "He took care of Martha and left in a hurry to catch you. What could have happened?" I could tell by his face that Thomas had no good answer.

"We'll go right back," Thomas said. "We'll need some food and fresh water. I'll have Judas get some men to check between here and Jerusalem and ask Alphaeus to get men and follow us. We didn't see anything unusual, but...." Having raised all of my fears, Thomas began giving orders, putting his plan into action.

I ran to the kitchen, found Martha with Susanna and Salome making a stew for dinner, and blurted out, "Joshua is missing. Thomas is taking the men back to search along the road. They'll need food." Almost before I'd finished, without asking a question, they dropped what they were doing and gathered fresh bread, cheese, olives, and fruit. We packed food and drink, and with our arms full, hurried into the work yard to give the fresh supplies to the men ready to mount their donkeys again. John Mark and Thad were already on their fast donkeys. Thomas saw my anxious look, "He'll be fine, Miriam. He needs to help find his father." I couldn't disagree. Our son was growing facial hair, too, now....He looked so much like his father did at that age, intense eyes, ruddy complexion, unruly hair...and I knew he was concerned and responsible, and needed to be with the men. Thomas mounted his donkey, signaled the others, and they were off.

With nothing to do but wait, I was panic-stricken and couldn't bear to listen to Martha and Susanna's anxious chatter, so I climbed again to the big rock in the olive garden. Joshua had told me many times that hopes and fears were both phantoms of my imagination, but what could have happened to him? I repeated the shepherd psalm again, trying to calm myself. Sarah and Joseph found me and wanted to do something to help; they asked whether they could go tell their Uncle Simon, Uncle Lazarus, and Aunt Hannah in nearby Bethany. I thought it would be safe, kissed them, and let them go.

Alone again, I prayed, "Father God, your name is holy. May your will be done in our lives today." Unable to imagine God's will wouldn't include finding Joshua safe and sound, I still added that plea, too with a fervent, "Help us." The sky darkened as I waited, prayed, and waited. An almost full moon rose again to light the sky and the countryside.

At last, I heard animals approaching. I jumped down and again rushed into the moonlit work yard. I was both relieved and horrified to see John Mark walking in from the road, leading his donkey, which now carried his battered and wounded father. Thomas and the others followed behind. "Joshua," I gasped as I ran to them, and then, "Thank you, God," as tears of relief and shock streamed down my face.

# CHAPTER FOUR

Joshua tried to smile through scabbed lips and reddened eyes sunk into deep purple patches in his swollen, discolored, and bruised face. Without sandals, his feet and legs were bloody, and a cloak I'd never seen partially covered wounds on his arms and chest. John Mark and Thomas eased him down and helped him into the house, and into bed, as I ran to the kitchen to tell Martha to get oil, spices, and some broth. After I helped him sip the broth, which he found difficult with his swollen jaw, and after I cleaned and treated his wounds, he took my hands and whispered, "Thank you, Love, I have a lot to tell you..." and then before falling asleep, he added, "I met a wonderful man."

The next day, he slept while I waited and watched and dressed his wounds and offered water, spiced wine, or broth whenever he woke. I wished I could heal him as he had healed Martha. That evening, he seemed better, and the next morning, he was awake before I was, as usual. His eyes were still puffy, but twinkled a bit, and despite his still swollen jaw and bruised face, he said softly above a whisper, "I love the Lord because he heard my plea and listened to me when I called him. Death entangled me and I was overwhelmed with pain, and then I called upon the Lord: 'O Lord, save my life.'"

Recognizing the psalm, I continued to wonder whatever could have happened to my kind, strong, generous, fun-loving husband as I repeated the psalm with him, saying, "Our Lord is gracious and righteous; our God is full of compassion. The Lord watches over the innocent."

Joshua confessed, "I was brought very low and you helped me, God. I can rest again for you treated me well and rescued my life from death, my eyes from tears, and my feet from stumbling. I will walk in the presence of the Lord in the land of the living."

He paused and I continued, "I believed, but in my distress said, 'No one can be trusted.' How shall I repay the Lord for all the good things he has done for me?"

Joshua solemnly answered, "I'll lift up the cup of salvation and call upon the Name of the Lord and fulfill my vows to the Lord in the presence of all of his people."

I hesitated, not sure I wanted to go on. "Precious in the sight of the Lord is the death of his servant." The psalm seemed too close for comfort.

But with determination, Joshua finished, "O Lord, I'm your servant and the child of your servant. You have freed me from my crisis. I will offer you the sacrifice of thanksgiving and call upon your Name. I will fulfill my vows to you in the presence of all of your people, in the courts of your house in the middle of Jerusalem. Hallelujah!"

"Hallelujah," I echoed a little feebly, and asked about his vows. Already tired from talking this much, he said he wanted to tell me the whole story so I could understand them, but he asked whether I would get us something warm to eat and drink first. I was glad he had an appetite again and hurried to the kitchen.

# CHAPTER FIVE

While I gently dressed his wounds again after we ate, he began his story. "After I left you and Martha, I got through the crowded streets and out the gate...past here and Bethany and on into the dry, scrub fairly quickly. Once I passed the inn, no one was in sight as I hurried the donkey down the deserted stretch toward the valley until I saw two men sitting in the shade of a big rock by the roadside. One got up and waved for me to stop. When I did, he told me his friend had badly hurt his ankle and they were out of water and needed help to get to Jericho.

"After helping Martha, I thought I could help them so I got off my donkey and took my water to the injured man... and then realized they'd been in a fight. His arm had a bloody scar and his leg, a nasty gash above his very swollen ankle. Wary, I gave him my water and offered to take care of his injuries...He muttered, 'If God wills,' so I started with his ankle, prayed, and was thankful to feel his ankle heal as I sensed tension around me, took a deep breath, and asked God to be glorified. As I moved my hands up to treat the gash, I was hit hard on the back of my head and fell flat on my face onto the rocks. I blacked out, barely knew what happened, and then struggled to get up...to defend myself...but was punched and hit and kicked as my clothes were ripped off and I was dragged out into the sun. One of them was irritated and hissed, 'Let's just kill the bastard,' but the other growled, 'No, he just healed my ankle.' Then something about orders...get the donkey and get going...and they left."

Shocked, I asked, "How could they?"

"I have no idea, or of how much time passed until I heard hoofs in the distance...from the direction of Jericho. I struggled to turn my head and saw it was a priest on a donkey. I called out, thankful for help so soon. I think he was one of my distant cousins on mother's side, but he didn't even look at me, kicked his donkey, rode to the other side of the road, and just kept going. I may have been bloody, but I wasn't dead."

"Was he blind, or afraid of becoming unclean, or of attackers lurking behind the rock?" I asked.

"I thought of that," Joshua replied. "I struggled to crawl farther into the road, away from the rock which may have frightened him, but then I became parched, fully exposed in the hot sun. My head throbbed...every part of me hurt. After a while, I heard another donkey coming from Jericho. I struggled but was too weak to wave to the rider to get help. I actually recognized him, a cousin named after Uncle Zachariah. I called his name, but when he saw me from a distance, he kicked his donkey and veered off the road...went by even faster singing a psalm so loudly I don't think he could have heard me. He went clear off the road to avoid me, Mim.... He left me to die, too."

Tears filled my eyes as he continued. "Alone again...I just couldn't believe it....If my cousins...priests even...didn't stop, who would? I guessed they were probably hurrying back to the Temple...probably returning from being baptized by John in the Jordan."

"What good did that do?" I asked. "Repent, be baptized, and then refuse to help?"

"Ironic, Mim. I agree it's strange."

"Strange," I repeated. "Didn't Abraham recognize God in strangers passing his tent? Didn't God come to Abraham, not the other way around?"

"He thought so," Joshua smiled. "We repeat the commandments to love the Lord our God and our neighbor as ourselves, but we don't seem to see the connection anymore."

"And miss meeting the real living God, where we are," I grumbled. "But what happened? Who did stop? You said you met an amazing person."

"I did, but not for a long while. Every part of me hurt...I've never hurt so much in my life, Mim. Flies started to buzz and swarm around me, and then a vulture began to circle overhead. I wondered how I'd gotten into this, and then how two cousins could go by and refuse to help...I wanted to live and thought, 'My God, my God, why have you forsaken me? Why are you so far from my cry and my distress?'

"'O my God,' I lamented, as I continued the psalm and tears filled my eyes. 'I cry in the daytime, but you don't answer....'"

"Yes," Joshua said, reaching out to hold my hand, "I felt completely abandoned, but after a while, I heard another donkey and saw another rider approaching...but as he got closer, I saw he was a Samaritan...this time not only a stranger but an enemy...and I thought I might be in more trouble....I didn't know what to do. As I watched, he slowed and seemed to look for a trick or hidden robbers, and then stopped, got down, and to my surprise, he got his skin of watered wine...brought it to me, bent down and supported my head so I could drink. I was amazed. I tried to speak, but he told me to save my strength; he could guess what had happened. He got a robe for me from his bag and helped me onto his donkey. He said he could take me to the inn. He was hurrying to join a caravan in Jerusalem."

"A Samaritan...I can hardly believe it," I said. "Someone supposed to be an enemy rescued you, not—"

Joshua interrupted. "I could hardly believe it either...I hung on in excruciating pain and bounced along...and then a cloud seemed to appear out of nowhere and protect us from the scorching afternoon sun. At the inn, the man, a trader in silphium from Cyrene he told me, got the innkeeper to help ease me off his donkey and get me settled on a clean pallet in a quiet corner. He seemed to know the innkeeper very well, paid for my care, wished me well, and was quickly on his way."

"A Samaritan?" I asked again, wiping the tears from my eyes.

"Yes, a Samaritan," Joshua said. "It's life-changing for me. I've had a lot of time to think about it. The innkeeper's wife was a cheerful, motherly sort....She cleaned and dressed my wounds and gave me herbed wine and left me to sleep. When I woke, she brought me broth and wine from time to time, but mostly I slept until John Mark and Thad came in asking if anyone had heard of a fight or robbery and found me. Thad ran back to tell Thomas while John Mark came and knelt beside me. We had quite a reunion."

"I can imagine," I said, still feeling my shock and relief when I saw them come home.

"Thomas paid the innkeeper and asked him to repay my rescuer. I want to thank that Samaritan again, Mim. He took the same risk I did to help a stranger, no questions asked, no judgment, no politics, no religion. I want to tell everyone."

When I asked where he would begin, he said at the inn he'd vowed to tell everyone the story, vowed to tell John and Justus and ask them what they thought of it. "One man chose to help me. I'll never forget him, Mim. I vowed that I'd tell everyone that we can live in peace on earth, right here and right now, when we actually love our neighbor as we say we love our God."

"Haven't we already been living that way?" I asked. "Your good influence on your students and fellow rabbis in the Sanhedrin...your fair treatment of our servants." I began to list all of the good things I saw him doing.

"Not enough, Mim. I want to tell everyone. As the psalmist said, 'I will fulfill my vows to the Lord in the presence of all of his people.'" Joshua took my hand. "To tell all of the people I know I'll have to leave our privileged life and show the way myself as well as tell the story. I don't know where it will lead, but will you come too?"

"Yes, of course, my love, I promise. I'll go with you," I said, "and help you tell your story." Joshua put his arm around me and gently pulled me to him. With my head on his chest, I felt change sweeping into our lives. I asked, "Will we go to Jericho?"

"Yes, I want to see Justus first, and then John...if the men on the road were their followers, then what they're doing won't ever bring peace or improve our lives."

"Mmm, I suppose not...you're proposing that we respond to the need of whoever we meet, and yet you were beaten and robbed when you stopped to help," I objected.

"Yes, but don't you see, God didn't abandon me as I'd thought," Joshua replied. "Instead, God rescued me through a stranger, not through my cousins."

"But what about the strangers that you stopped to help?" I persisted.

"Well," he sighed, "I honestly don't know, but I think they're probably Zealots, followers of Justus...didn't know our connection and thought they'd trick me and take what they wanted. I don't think paradise is so much about a future life after death as it is about every choice we make with whomever we meet. I think we cheat ourselves out of it or enjoy living in it right now, every day."

"Mmm...I think I'm beginning to understand," I said.

"I hope so," Joshua replied with a laugh, although laughing hurt him and was still difficult. He changed the subject to begin making plans to fulfill the vows. We talked about letting John Mark go with Uncle Joseph, then letting Sarah and Joseph stay with Martha and Simon while we went to Capernaum, a crossroads of trade in Galilee, from where we thought Joshua's ideas could spread to the world. We had a simple house in Capernaum which he had inherited from his father. Away from the pressures of Jerusalem, Joshua thought we could begin to tell others and show this way of living to strangers as well as to our servants and their families. We'd take a caravan to Jericho to see Justus and John, perhaps persuade them to join us, and then go on to Galilee and send Thomas and others back to Jerusalem to bring our children and the rest of the families once we were settled.

I was concerned for our children's education, but when Joshua questioned me, I had to admit that they were reading and speaking Hebrew as well as Aramaic. We could read the Torah and Prophets with them and help them memorize the Psalms, and they could learn Greek and then Latin to read more than inscriptions, and then mathematics, music, and art...and then I stopped and laughed.

Joshua laughed again, too, and assured me they would be fine. I said I could see he'd given this much thought when he wasn't sleeping, but that none of this could happen until he recovered. He agreed but insisted he would rest better since I had agreed to go with him, since we were planning together. I told him I would go and talk this over with Martha and get her ideas. We both laughed again. I gave him a kiss and helped him slide down into the bed to be more comfortable, gathered up bowls and what remained from breakfast, and left him to fall asleep.

# CHAPTER SIX

Simon, the youngest brother of Justus, was one of Joshua's students who lived with us. As well as being an able and serious student, he was also a very good and responsible worker, ready to help however he could, and especially good at helping Thomas with horses and donkeys. He maintained vociferous support for his brother and the Zealots and their longing to return a rightful, righteous king to the throne of Judea; the Zealots wished to replace the hated Hasmonean dynasty whose Roman toady Herod Antipas was currently on the throne and in possession of the fortresses, guards, and all of the taxes he could extract by whatever means from the entire population.

Simon was horrified both at what had happened to Joshua and the possibility that Zealots were the attackers. He asked to go to Jericho immediately to find his brother. He soon returned with confirmation...Joshua's robe, sandals, bag, and donkey. The attackers had indeed been Zealots. Simon told us his brother was furious with two of his aides, Gestas and Demas, who had participated in a raid on a large, rich caravan but were injured when they took the brunt of the fight and had gotten separated from the other Zealots who had escaped with their rewards of money, weapons, and supplies. The two pleaded that Joshua didn't look or act like an important person, didn't have a retinue or servant traveling with him, and they needed his donkey to get back to Jericho quickly before they might be caught, so when he stopped, they didn't wait to explain, but took the opportunity to take what they needed and then make sure he couldn't follow them. Joshua laughed, "I'd like to meet them again someday and forgive them. Just as I thought, they were afraid I wouldn't really help them. I'm not whom they expected....They didn't know what they were doing."

When Joshua recovered, we returned to our Jerusalem home. He went to look for his cousins who'd passed him to forgive them, and to tell his colleagues and students his story and his vow. Some rabbis were sympathetic; others were critical and told him he should ask God why he was punished, repent, and offer a sacrifice. No one thought he should leave teaching or his place of honor in the Sanhedrin.

"They sounded like Job's friends," Joshua told me that evening, attempting a little sad humor in his account of the day. "Nothing new under the sun, Mim. We still blame each other and judge in God's place. Nicodemus tried to talk me out of leaving and is skeptical that I can make a difference with my story, but he does understand my need to try. The most difficult, though, was leaving my students. Thad and Simon and Bartholomew want to come with us."

In addition to talking with Gamaliel about accepting Joshua's students as his own now, Joshua saw both our current high priest, Joseph Caiaphas, and our former high priest, who was the real power behind him, his father-in-law, Annas. Distantly related through Joshua's mother, Mary, they and their families were our good friends, and our families intertwined in three living generations. Joshua wanted to explain to them what had happened, what he'd vowed, and that, unlike his cousin John, he was not leaving to reform them, but to teach and show the way to following the commandments of love to everyone. They despaired over another frustrating sign of the violence wasting the country, and they were astonished at Joshua's decision to leave behind the prestige of his honored position to risk going into the turbulent unrest in Galilee. Both were very reluctant to see us leave Jerusalem.

Caiaphas worried about Joshua transferring his son, Mathias, to study with Gamaliel, taking John Mark's place, and he worried about John Mark leaving Gamaliel, Mathias, and Jerusalem, as well.

"They're inseparable. This is a big step for both of them," I acknowledged with a smile.

"As well as for their mothers?" Joshua asked, returning my smile. "It seems to me you and Elizabeth are very close yourselves."

I nodded in agreement, but I was determined not to look back and began packing the next day for our trip. My parents were dead, but I missed talking the situation over with Joshua's mother Mary who was currently staying in Nazareth again after her husband Joseph's death. I remembered wonderful conversations with her about how she had overcome so much adversity in her life with her steadfast faith in God's wisdom and goodness, and her simple prayer, often through tears, "Thy will be done," and trusting God to bring something good out of whatever happened or out of the risk she felt she must take. She was a beloved mentor and example of courage to me, though she could also succumb to her weakness of worrying when things didn't seem to go as she expected. But with all the children Joseph and she had been blessed with, each one uniquely gifted, pursuing his or her own path, scattered about, she was truly a nurturing mother, listening well, and responding to each one, though at times she wouldn't hesitate to gather them for a little sibling pressure and motherly guidance.

Joshua conferred with his practical brother, James, a rabbi and member of the Sanhedrin himself who preferred city life and Torah study, but offered help in an emergency. His brother Joses was studying in Alexandria. In Bethlehem, his brother Jude, who had a natural gift for breeding animals, agreed to be fully responsible for our flocks there on the slopes of the Migdol Eder. After more thought, Joshua asked Alphaeus, though not a member of our family, to take full responsibility for the olive groves, with my brother Lazarus nearby for consultation. Judas would continue to keep the records and report to us when he came with the family caravan to Galilee. Joshua made plans with Thomas for our caravan.

We helped John Mark prepare for his trip to Gaul and beyond with Joshua's Great-Uncle Joseph. Saying goodbye, not knowing when we would see him again, was a tender moment, unexpectedly difficult for us, a major passage in our lives as well as his. I wondered how Mother Mary had felt when Joshua left on his first trip with his great-uncle, and tried to focus on all of his adventures, his wonderful letters, stories, and the beautiful gifts he had brought back for our wedding. I hoped John Mark's trip would be as important and significant for him as his father's was. Perhaps he, too, would venture beyond Gaul to Britain.

As we were preparing to leave, closing down the big house in Jerusalem fell mostly to me. Leaving our servants, Rhoda, Judith our cook, Nathan, and his assistants Daniel and Tobias, we arranged with Joshua's brother James to oversee things there and keep the house open at least for Mother Mary and other family who would stay there from time to time. Our country home would be in good hands with Alphaeus and his wife overseeing the other servants. Susanna, our creative country cook who loved to combine whatever spices and herbs she could find in new ways with whatever was ripe in the garden, could come with us in the first caravan to Capernaum since she was married to Thomas and they had no children yet. Salome, married to Simon, was always anxious to help and would make the trip easier for me.

Saying farewell to my dear sister Martha and her quiet, but supportive husband, Simon, an astute investor with interests in several small jewelry workshops in Jerusalem, and a respected land owner with olive orchards outside Bethany was more difficult for me than I had imagined. So much was unknown, but I hoped we could return for the great feast of Passover. Joshua's devoted supporter, my wise and thoughtful brother Lazarus, and his adoring wife, Hannah, had prepared a delightful farewell gift for me, a bundle with sheets of beautiful papyrus from the Egyptian shopkeeper in Jerusalem.

Our trip to Jericho was uneventful, although I felt tense when we approached and passed the rock where Joshua had been attacked. We went directly to the large, comfortable home of our friends, Zachaeus and Abigail. Simon went to find his brother. Justus soon arrived on horseback with his men, Gestas and Demas. Now recovered from their fight and attack on Joshua, as vigorous and spirited as their horses, these two Zealots watched their leader, Justus, and Joshua embrace more warmly than long lost brothers. Nothing, even this mistake, could come between them. At Justus' signal to them, Gestas and Demas each sheepishly apologized, and Joshua forgave them. After they had tea with Zachaeus, Justus was satisfied and sent the two on their way while he stayed to talk with Joshua, Simon, and Zachaeus, a wiry, savvy little man, about some tax issues before going home again to get my energetic friend Deborah with the gorgeous, dancing eyes, and return for dinner. Deborah was well-matched with the dashing, high spirited Justus. We hadn't seen each other for many months, so we delighted in sharing stories of our friends and families long into the evening with the gracious, bejeweled Abigail and her adoring husband.

It rained that night, but the next morning was fresh and clear. Justus brought Joshua a horse and they rode up to the ruins of Herod's palace on the fertile Jordan valley's edge. Quite a pair, I thought, as they strode out the door...about the same height, muscular, in the prime of life, exuding energy and purpose while laughing and obviously enjoying the banter and teasing that comes from growing up together.

Reflecting on the previous evening's conversation, though, I was struck with just how different they were. Justus was competitive, always looking for an opportunity to elevate himself at another's expense. When I'd mentioned my observation to Joshua, he'd shrugged and said, "He's just insecure, Mim." Well, Justus was not a scholar and hadn't traveled out of our region of Galilee, Samaria, and Judea, but he was a man of action, was streetwise, had a strong will, a winning smile, and the ability to captivate men's imaginations, stirring them to join him in getting back at their enemies, the men who ruled them, controlled their world, and taxed them to death. But, I thought, most of all he wanted to exert his influence and power over his friend, Joshua, the one person Justus had thus far been unable to win over to his cause.

When Joshua returned that afternoon, he told me the palace, which had been as large and impressive as any he'd seen on his travels with Uncle Joseph, now lay abandoned, destroyed by a large earthquake. Joshua said they'd tied the horses and climbed through the weeds around large stones, marvelous mosaic floors, tumbled pillars, and came to the remains of a wall where they sat and talked as they looked out over the date palms of the valley below, the salt sea where we had all learned to float as children, and then to the hills beyond, to Herod's impressive hilltop fortress of Machaerus, from which he now controlled the valley and the trade routes.

To Joshua, it seemed that such power, although it appeared formidable, was actually ephemeral. Palaces and fortresses were subject to earthquake, wind, and fire; their inhabitants to jealousy, greed, and treachery. Sitting in the ruins of a palace, filled with so much pretense such a short time ago, Joshua thought how rulers don't live much longer than the wildflowers springing up in every crack. "Why would you be willing to give up your life to pursue such illusory power?" he'd asked Justus.

It was difficult, Joshua thought, to argue with the ruins on which they sat, and yet Justus did...said he believed that they could rebel with God's help, establish the prophesied righteous kingdom, bring peace. Joshua disagreed and told him he would make one compromise after another with killing and destruction, never be satisfied, and get so entangled that he would edge into a kind of self-made hell with death his only escape.

Justus had tried to assure him that they would be different, and he had said that God had chosen David and promised the kingdom to his faithful descendants. He admitted that many of David's descendants didn't have a shred of faith, but he said Joshua was different...had always loved God, and should be king, like the Wise Men, royal scholars from the East, had predicted when he was born, saying they had seen a star in the constellation for Judea announcing a new king they believed was Joshua. Justus not only wanted Joshua to be king, but he wanted to be Joshua's protector and the head of his army. "I asked if he remembered the wisdom scroll that begins, 'Love justice, you rulers of the earth. Set your mind on the Lord and seek God with your whole heart...trust God.' Justus laughed and said I was always better at memorizing than he was, but it sounded familiar, and that it was just what he meant. We both loved justice, trusted God, and were completely different from any of the Herods and their officers and commanders.

"I just shook my head and told him dishonest thinking cuts us off from God, asked him just to look at the ruins... said the use of force *does* take liberties with God's power...the power of love. I told him God loved us and brought us out of slavery in Egypt without a fight...no warrior could take credit for that."

"Well, he's as idealistic as you are," I responded, "but how could he argue with that?"

Joshua laughed, "Oh, he argued...that God loved David and David was a warrior, but I reminded him that David was also a lover and a singer and a poet. We argued back and forth for a while; I quoted another bit of wisdom, 'Don't stray from the path of life and draw disaster on yourself by your own actions...God created things to live.' I said we just couldn't achieve peace and justice while robbing and killing people."

"That seems so obvious...just think of how many other innocent people, simply going about their lives, have been attacked as you were...doesn't he see that from your story?"

"No, I don't think so. He was frustrated and asked how I proposed to stop all of the injustice...said we're little better than slaves again...."

"Oh, dear," I sighed.

"I told him we could bring change that benefits everyone and quoted the wisdom scroll again, 'Without God, men have asked for death by their words and deeds.' I propose we ask for life, love God and whoever is near us, regardless of who they are, but he shook his head, told me to be realistic, said Herod and the Romans torture and tax us to death. Their officials remove anyone in their way with trumped up charges, and wield whatever power they can grab. He asked how I could change them.

"That's the hard part, I admitted," Joshua continued. "It probably takes more courage to face a man like that with love and forgiveness than it does with a weapon, but I know he

trusts false gods who make empty promises, and who eventually reward him with disappointment and death. So I try
to remember that the true God loves both of us, and asks us
to love, not kill.

"'Well...' Justus said climbing down from the rock wall.
When I followed, he put his hand on my shoulder, 'Old
friend, you do it your way...I'll keep doing it my way. I'll try
to minimize killing...especially women and children who get
caught sometimes. We'll just have to see which way works,
see who establishes the righteous kingdom and gets you on
the throne first.' We laughed and hiked down to the horses,
arguing and making promises to keep thinking about our
conversation. We had a great ride back...and as we parted,
he said, 'I'm still so angry with Demas and Gestas...it's really
unforgivable.'

"I reminded him I'd already forgiven them and my cousins who didn't stop to help. It's a chance to put my theory to
the test, but I hope I don't have many more tests like that!"

"Well, I certainly hope you don't have any more tests like
that, either," I laughed. "You two have always been so close,
but—"

"Didn't I choose the perfect place for our conversation,
Mim? I thought the very stones would plead my case, but
Justus is sure he can set up a righteous kingdom and bring
peace and is sure God will fight with us. I think he must have
been too impressed with those stories I told him about the
Wise Men. Herod the Great was sure scared, but he scared
my parents more, and it was worse for our tribesmen in Bethlehem having their baby sons killed...but you have heard
these stories before. I guess it was all pretty exciting to two

nine-year-old boys when Justus and I climbed a mountain with our sacks of food and bedrolls and crept into a cave to start a fire and spend the night telling stories. He remembers vividly all the details of my story that night. He told me that since I was born to be king—as he puts it—I would have to take my responsibility seriously, give up this love of whomever I meet, and think of the good of the whole nation, use my position and prestige, and join them."

"How can men with such different visions remain such good friends?" I wondered aloud.

"Well," Joshua heaved a sigh, "as you said, we've been friends for as long as I can remember. We love each other, Mim. I told him God didn't need an army to get us out of Egypt, only one man who believed God. God did the rest. Maybe he'll think about it and join us later."

"Maybe he will," I tentatively agreed.

# CHAPTER SEVEN

Even though we were up early, our animals, which had stayed with our servants at the caravansary, were already groomed, loaded, and waiting at the gate. We traveled east past springs and fragrant gardens, slowly moving through the date groves toward the Jordan River, joining a parade of caravans as well as men alone or in small groups, in priestly garb or simple tunics. This was a man's world; few women could be seen in the caravans, none alone or in small groups.

Thad was nervous about seeing his father. Rather than admit this to the other men, he chose to ride alongside me in uneasy conversation. I assured him that he would be fine... that he could be baptized if he wished. I didn't think his father would refuse him. The road rose gently above the river. We looked down and saw John just ahead in the water, with a crowd gathered on both banks.

As we left the road to descend toward the river, we could hear John's voice ringing out denunciations to the men on either side, quoting the Prophets, asking why these men had come out like a brood of vipers to the wilderness, trying to avoid the judgment of an angry God. I could feel Thad shrink in embarrassment that his father looked so wild and was shouting like this. Torn with indecision, he said, "I'm afraid to go, Miriam. I'm afraid he'll shout at me, humiliate me in front of all of these men."

Joshua took the lead. He dismounted, took off his sandals and robe, and then in his short tunic, waded out into the river toward John. John, following his audience's eyes to see what might have distracted them, broke into an uncharacteristic grin. He immediately waded through the water to meet Joshua, and in an even louder voice, shouted, "Behold, the Lamb of God who takes away the sin of the world!"

"Behold the Voice crying in the wilderness, 'Prepare the way of the Lord!'" Joshua shouted back.

Neither of these shouted greetings made any sense to me, or, I suspected, to anyone else who heard them. However, the two seemed oblivious to the rest of us and were delighted with their secret call and response, which came so naturally. The two men met in midstream with a warm embrace that astounded everyone who didn't know them. Encouraged, leaving his robe and sandals beside Joshua's, Thad waded in his tunic, somewhat tentatively, out into the stream after Joshua. Sensing his approach, Joshua pulled back from the embrace with his cousin, "John, it's been a while...but may I present your son for your baptism? It's been an honor to raise him for you. He's a fine student and a responsible member of our household."

John, surprised and visibly moved to see Thad now a grown-up young man, asked him whether he wanted to be baptized. Thad, still a bit shy, responded that he did.

John then asked him whether he repented of his sins and promised to seek God's will for his life. Thad, nervous but in earnest, replied that he did with God's help, John held out his arms and said, "Then come, Thad, and God will wash away all your uncleanness." He took his son, submerged him in the river, brought him up, and embraced him as he hadn't embraced anyone before, except perhaps Thad's mother before she died in his arms soon after Thad was born. A buzz rose on the banks as men wondered what was going on in the middle of the river.

As they drew apart, John grasped Thad by his shoulders, looked him straight in the eye, and in a low, hoarse, emotion-filled voice, said, "Thad, you're my beloved son. I'm very pleased with you....Serve God and learn from Joshua."

"Yes, Father, I will," and then, "Thank you...I love you." They embraced again.

When they'd released their embrace, Joshua said, "And now, I'm next, John."

John, still overwhelmed with emotion at this unexpected encounter with his now grown son whose birth had caused him such grief, was surprised and objected, "It's I who should be baptized by you, Joshua."

"Not so, not now," Joshua replied, sympathetic to his cousin's feelings. "I was almost dead and made vows to God, John. I want to wash away anything that might keep me from fulfilling them. We can talk as soon as you can join us, but for now, my baptism. I renounce anything that might keep me from loving God with all of my being, that might separate me from God's will for my life."

"So be it," John said. He took Joshua in his arms and submerged him beneath the water. I had followed Joshua

and Thad to the water's edge and wanted to be baptized for
my vows, too, but I knew I couldn't join them, couldn't be
baptized in view of men. Women had a separate place for
cleansing.

Focused on the reunions and baptisms, I'd barely noticed a
soft cloud covering the morning sun, but as I watched Joshua
emerge from the water in John's arms, there was a flash of
lightning, and the cloud parted, focusing a dazzling beam of
sunlight on Joshua and John, as thunder pealed across the
sky. A fresh breeze wafted past, brushing us with moisture
and an extraordinary sense of vitality.

Startled, a beautiful white dove flew up from a nearby
willow and then gently circled down to rest on Joshua's shoulder, surprising me, a short distance away. Joshua seemed at
ease, his left arm still around John's shoulder, his right hand
reaching to calm and stroke the dove. I saw tears in John's
eyes and guessed they mirrored Joshua's. I felt as startled as
the dove at the strange phenomena. The cloud disappeared.
The moment passed. The intense energy dissipated, and we
were bathed again in bright morning sunlight.

That afternoon, John freed himself from the many who
had come to question, to repent, to be baptized, and with
only a couple of his men, came upstream to where we had
pitched our tents. Joshua and John wanted to be alone with
family, and so the four of us—Thad, John, Joshua, and I—sat
on rugs and cushions in the shade of a willow at the river's
edge. Joshua told John what had happened on the road to
Jericho, of his leaving the rabbinic school and Sanhedrin in
Jerusalem, of Thad's desire to come with us on our quest, of
his conversation with Justus, of how he wanted John to join

him in offering people a new way of life, changing how they lived, not just letting them feel clean by a religious ritual, safe from a distant God, while continuing a selfish life.

John was thoughtful as we quietly watched the river flow past us, little ripples, eddies, and swirls interrupting the main current here and there. "I just don't know," he began. "Your experience is very troubling. These snakes slither out here, in and out of the Jordan, without shedding their old skins. No matter what I say, they don't really repent. They remain as selfish and fearful as ever, thinking the ritual did something for them, thinking no one can see their hearts. I'm not sure even my own disciples really hear."

"I know, John. I felt similar frustration teaching in the Temple. The Torah, the Psalms, the Prophets seem so clear to me. What separates us from God is our unwillingness to risk loving and forgiving, and then to trust God for the outcome. I've forgiven our cousins who left me for dead while they hurried back to Jerusalem and the Temple, but I couldn't find them to tell them I forgave them when I looked for them around the Temple after I had recovered and got back to Jerusalem myself. I'll keep looking for them whenever I return to celebrate the feasts."

John shook his head. "But they didn't stop to help you. Ever since we were little, I tried to take care of you...the family stories about your birth and peace with God, but then that first passage I was given to read in the synagogue...about the voice crying in the wilderness. I guess that's why I led you on so many of those trips into the wilderness to learn to survive and to discover God's abundance even there."

Joshua nodded. "Remember that long, forty day trip we took?" John laughed as Joshua added for Thad and me, "Like Moses leading the people for forty years. We didn't take anything with us but some flat bread, flour, a skin of water, and cloth to make a tent. We just asked God to provide what we needed and vowed we wouldn't complain."

"I remember we got hungry toward the end, but neither of us would break our vow and complain, even though I did suggest you turn those stones into bread," John chuckled as he continued to share the story.

"And I remember telling you that man doesn't live by bread alone, but by every word that proceeds from the mouth of the Lord. You were impressed, but we were very thankful for your mother's bread and cheese and honey when we got back to Bethany."

"Indeed we were," John sighed. "I remember the long talks, the stories of your birth and the Wise Men who'd found you when you were little and brought such impressive gifts and even more impressive stories of the study of the stars and what they signified for you. You didn't need much encouragement from me to take the opportunity and go with your uncle on that first trip...to the East. I could hardly wait for you to come back. We were fascinated by their studies of the stars, and you were full of stories of fantastic buildings and sculptures and gardens and centers of scholars and learning when you returned." They both smiled contentedly at the memory.

"Yes, but even then, I remember telling you that that kind of power and opulence isn't real or lasting. I saw the ruins, too. In fact...that's what I tried to show Justus."

John nodded thoughtfully, "But remember that you were given three gifts by the Wise Men. Gold could represent being a king, but frankincense could represent being a high priest. Do you remember my fantasy that you could climb to the top of the Temple and shout, 'Listen to me!' And the priests and people would say, 'Why? Who are you?' And you'd say, 'I'm God's chosen high priest,' and they'd say, 'Prove it,' and you'd say, 'Fine. I'll jump off the top of this Temple and live. Then will you listen and do what I tell you?'"

We all laughed as Joshua replied, "And I think I remember spoiling your whole fantasy with another quote, 'You shall not tempt the Lord, your God.' No, John, neither becoming a high priest, nor a king is for me. The third gift though was myrrh...both perfume and embalming spice. How I live and die may be the way to show others the way to peace on earth and peace with God."

Breaking the silence that followed, I asked, "John, why did you greet Joshua this morning as 'the Lamb of God who takes away the sin of the world'?"

"That goes back to that wilderness trip, too," John said. "After the first Scripture I read about the voice crying in the wilderness, my father told me an old Aramaic story which I told Joshua on the trip. It seems that Pharaoh had a dream that disturbed him. He called for his soothsayers to interpret it. In the dream, he saw a large hanging balance. On one side, the scale contained Pharaoh and all of Egypt, but outweighing it on the other side, the scale contained a single lamb, the Lamb of God. The interpreters told Pharaoh that a Hebrew boy was about to be born who was the Lamb of God. In due course, he would destroy Egypt and liberate the

Hebrew people. So Pharaoh ordered all Hebrew baby boys be killed, which led to the amazing saving of baby Moses, with his sister Miriam watching out for him, and then eventually our Exodus story."

"That sounds so similar to Herod killing all the baby boys around Bethlehem when Joshua was born," I said. "I knew about Miriam guarding and saving her baby brother, Moses, but I didn't know why Pharaoh wanted to kill baby boys...the part about his dream of the Lamb of God."

"It's not told very often," John replied. "But on our trip, remembering Moses speaking with God, leading us into the Promised Land, I began to call Joshua, 'The Lamb of God,' and he has called me, 'The Voice Crying in the Wilderness' ever since."

Thad and I felt taken closer into the tight bond between these two by these explanations.

"But thinking about that dream again," Joshua said, "maybe the interpretation could be that someday the Lamb of God would liberate everyone, Egyptians included, from despotic rulers and from slavery to fear and selfishness and greed and jealousy and worship of false gods...no winners, no losers...everyone free to love others and enjoy peace...maybe love can outweigh force."

Emboldened by the warmth we felt, Thad spoke up. "Joshua, what about that thunder and lightning today? I wonder why that dove landed on your shoulder? It was really strange."

Joshua smiled, "I don't know what you heard, Thad, but I heard my Heavenly Father say about the same thing your father had just said to you, "You're my beloved son and I'm pleased with you. Continue fulfilling your vows to me.' As for that dove, well—"

John interrupted, "Thad, when I began to baptize, I had a vision of a dove descending on someone filled with God's Spirit. It actually happened today...just like it did in my vision. The cloud, the light, the thunder; didn't you feel the Presence?" We nodded. We had definitely experienced something out of the ordinary that we couldn't explain.

Reflecting on that moment, with nothing more to say, we were content to wonder quietly, watching the river, comfortable in our shared silence in the willow's shade. After a while, John asked Joshua to tell him more about his vow.

"I just vowed," Joshua began again, "to share the story of the good Samaritan with everyone I can. I'd like everyone to see that we can live in the Kingdom of God right here and right now, if we actually dare to respond to others the way we would like them to respond to us...in unselfish love."

"That's easier said than done," John laughed.

"Is it?"

"I think so," John replied. "We've had the commandment to love since the beginning of time, but men are fearful and selfish. Will the fear of judgment perhaps get them to change?"

Questions remained unanswered as Thomas interrupted to tell us dinner was ready. Rugs had been spread on the ground in the shade of a tree just outside our tents. We joined the others around bowls of stew and stacks of warm bread and entered into lively conversation with them as we savored the simple meal in this idyllic setting. With the sun edging lower in the sky, we and our world were bathed in the most beautiful golden glow as we relaxed and laughed at one story after another....

Before John and his disciples returned to their camp that evening, he agreed to hike into the hills the next morning with Joshua, after breakfast. Later when we were alone again in our tent, I asked Joshua to baptize me, early in the morning before he went hiking, with the same baptism he had experienced. His eyes twinkled and he said he'd be honored, assuring me he understood and cherished me as his partner. I remember well our tender embrace that evening as we melted again into the unity we felt.

# CHAPTER EIGHT

The morning sun's first rays streamed into our tent and woke me. Joshua was already awake and greeted me with a warm smile. "Thank you! Everything in me says, 'Thank you!'"

I smiled, delighted to begin the morning of my baptism with his double entendre, his appreciation for me and for God with this psalm. My heart and voice both sang, "Angels listen as I sing my thanks. I praise you, and say it again, 'Thank you! Thank you for your love, thank you for your faithfulness."

"Both your name and your word are beyond compare. When I called, you responded and gave me strength," Joshua answered as he slipped an arm around me.

"When they hear what you have to say, Dear God, all earth's kings will say thank you," I replied with enthusiasm. "They'll sing of what you've done. How great your glory! High above, you see far below, no matter the distance. You know everything about us." That was a comforting thought to me, especially after the Jericho Road. Joshua nodded as I continued, "When we walk into the thick of trouble, keep us alive in the angry turmoil."

Joshua smiled, calm confidence in his voice, "With one hand strike our foes; with your other hand, save us," and we joined together, "Finish what you started in us, dear God. Your love is eternal, don't quit on us now!"

"Well," I sighed, "that was a wonderful beginning. Let's go." We laughed, leaped out of bed, pulled on light, loose tunics, and gathered a couple of towels in our arms as we headed out of the tent, down to the river.

In the water, I made the same requests that Joshua had made the day before. He took me in his arms and gently submerged me in the cool, clear water, saying, "Be clean of anything that separates you from me or the Unnameable Only True God, or from fulfilling your vows." As he brought me up from the water, I felt a moment of intense energy flow through my entire body, warming me despite the water's chill and the thick mist now hovering around us. He smiled, "Your seven energy centers are open, pure, and cleansed, my dearest one." With that, midstream, we embraced again, flooded with love, overwhelmed with emotion at the blessing and unity we felt. The mist surrounding us lifted as Joshua whispered in my ear, "I'm so thankful for you...so thankful you're with me, my love."

"You can't imagine how thankful I am for you," I answered, thrilled. Completely in love, we glowed with this new connection, now joined in our vows and our baptisms. As we waded, arm in arm, into the bright morning sunshine to get our towels and dry ourselves, I felt that everything was new and fresh with unlimited possibilities before us.

Later, after savoring some warm bread, honey, and cheese, which Susanna had put out by our tent, and after John and

Joshua had gone off on their hike, I sat by the river, wrapped in my robe, drying and combing my hair in the warm sun. I relished a quiet morning to absorb my intense joy, our baptisms, the clouds, our conversations, and all that had happened so far on our journey. When my hair was dry, I went into the tent to find my writing materials, ink, and papyrus scrolls from the Egyptian shopkeeper in Jerusalem. I spent the rest of the morning writing, something few men or women could do.

I mused at the contrast between Joshua, his friend Justus, and his cousin John. Each man was so different, and yet they were so close to one another, held together by Joshua's love and admiration for them both, I thought. John had separated himself from women after his Dinah's death. He had left the priesthood with his family's status and position, taken nothing but his sorrow and disillusionment with him into the wilderness; he had worn simple, rough sandals and a rough woven tunic with a simple leather belt sometimes tied around his waist, and carried a rough but tightly woven robe of sorts which served as blanket or protection when needed. He didn't care about grooming and didn't care to attract men, but the more he castigated them and their sins, the more they seemed to flock to him for cleansing.

That afternoon, after Joshua and John returned and parted, Joshua told me John wouldn't be joining us. I could see he was deeply disappointed as he went to sit by himself at the river's edge. A while later, a couple of earnest-looking men came up the river from John's camp, asking for him, and they talked for a while.

After dinner when we returned to our tent, Joshua was ready to talk. "You're the only one willing to join me, Mim. Neither John nor Justus can stop the violence or make peace, but they don't see that they're only repeating what's failed over and over again. They're stuck in traditional solutions and won't risk radical, fearless love with me."

"But Joshua, we've just begun," I responded. "Your vow wasn't to convince Justus or John, but to tell them your story. You were attacked and left for dead by their followers, and now they're the ones unwilling to change and help, but that doesn't mean God won't send a stranger. I don't know who'll come, but it seems likely, if I understand your story, that it'll be someone we don't expect."

"You're amazing," Joshua smiled. "I guess I was lying here feeling bruised and deserted in the scorching sun again. I hadn't thought of it that way," he laughed softly.

I smiled, amused at his response. "Well, if neither Justus nor John will join us in paradise, what shall we do next?" I asked. "The psalm says, 'God has prepared a banquet for us in the presence of our enemies.' Maybe we should invite them?"

Joshua laughed and pulled me to him, "You're too much!" he said giving me an appreciative kiss. "The next step, my dear, is to pack up and travel on to Capernaum. John sent two of his followers from Galilee to help us...a little support, at least. We don't have extra donkeys, but I can take turns with them, walking and riding. They're content to come and share what we can offer."

"I can walk with you from time to time while they ride," I volunteered.

"You really are in this with me, aren't you?" he said. "You're reminding me of the psalm this morning…'Finish what You started in us.' You're already my strong tower, Mim!"

# CHAPTER NINE

The next morning, everyone was awake before dawn. Susanna baked flat bread, offering a hot round to whomever passed her fire. While Salome and I packed bags, men took down tents and loaded everything onto the donkeys. The two newcomers, Andrew and Philip, arrived in time to help. Since we would follow the river, we didn't need to fill the water jugs. Forming the caravan, Thomas began heading up to the road with the lead donkey as John arrived and gave Thad a much appreciated hug and more encouragement. He said goodbye to his students, sent them to help with a couple of pack animals objecting to the steep little incline, and then joined Joshua and me.

"Thinking about that wilderness trip again," John started, "the exodus wouldn't have happened without Miriam, Aaron, and Moses, but Miriam and Aaron had to stay out of God's special relationship with Moses. If we three play those roles, Miriam, I'm the Voice, Joshua is the Lamb...the Anointed One...and you're the Watchtower. I hope you do reach the Promised Land, and that you'll lead my son and many others into its full enjoyment. Use all of your God-given gifts,

Joshua. Be patient with us. God willing, you'll eventually bring peace on earth."

Joshua embraced John, helped me onto my donkey, mounted his, and we hurried to catch up with the caravan. While not joining us as we'd hoped, John had given us his blessing and the titles that would remain with us forever. Although few knew its origin, I treasured my title. Both Joshua and John had independently given me what would become my special name, "Miriam, the Watchtower. They'd included me in their special relationship, sealed in the wilderness so many years before.

As we headed north, I had time to think again about our journey. In a way, Joshua and I were going through a wilderness, leading our servants and those we met on the way into the Promised Land. I thought about the story of Moses and wondered whether we would have as many problems as he'd had drawing people out of the entanglements of their old lives into the freedom to love one another and just be thankful for what is.

Along the road following the river, the caravan moved in a slow, rhythmic manner, not only giving us the time to think, but to inhale the beauty and fragrance of the date palms, pomegranates, figs, and citron orchards we passed. Joshua soon took a turn at walking. He gave his donkey to Philip and walked with Andrew. When we stopped for water, he suggested I walk with him for a while and let Andrew ride my donkey.

Once the caravan was moving again, we followed without difficulty, keeping pace. Joshua asked me what the chances were that one of the two men from Galilee would be the younger son of his father's fish boat partner, Jonah of Beth-saida. I had no idea, but was surprised at the connection.

"I've known Andrew's father for years," he said, "met him and Zebedee every summer since my father died when Judas and I came to settle accounts. Andrew's older brother lives near our house in Capernaum with his wife and family. I played along the seashore with Simon and Andrew and James and John when we were little and Father brought me to Capernaum with him. If I can, I'll go fishing with them. Better than just collecting our share of the profits!"

"Absolutely! What a wonderful opportunity! Sailing...I'd like to go too, but that's another man's world. Your father gave money for the boats?"

"Yes, for a share of the profits. It seems to have worked out for everyone. Our fathers were great friends as well as partners, but I lost touch when father died, except to settle the accounts each year."

"Sad memories," I sighed, still feeling the loss of his father as much as I did the loss of my own. "Your parents were so in love, I think they adored each other as much on our wedding day as they did on their own."

Joshua nodded and we walked on, absorbed in our own thoughts. No wonder he called The Unnamable his heavenly father; his father had been such a wise, generous man. I wondered what Andrew's father and brother would be like. Andrew seemed to me a rugged young fisherman of few words, but strong, somewhat shy, and ready to help. These fishermen were different from Joshua's students in Jerusalem, I thought. Joshua's father had been unintentionally caught up and killed in one of the attack and reprisal skirmishes so prevalent in the region of Galilee these past years. He'd been trying to get back to Nazareth to protect his family. I wondered what conflicts we would face on land, and what storms Joshua might face at sea if he actually went fishing with these tough fishermen.

"Now you'll need to show you're not afraid of the conflicts on land or the storms at sea!" I blurted out loud my hoped for conclusion to my musings, but from the look on Joshua's face, I realized those words were too close for comfort and I tried a new subject. "From Capernaum, we can visit your mother when she's in Nazareth. I'm not sure why she likes it there so much. It feels too small and remote for me, too quiet."

"Which is exactly what made it ideal for my parents and what makes it such a perfect base for Zealots now," Joshua laughed with a touch of irony.

"Ah...I suppose, but I'm glad Uncle Joseph got you to study in Jerusalem, or we might not have met," I said with the urge to give him a little kiss on the back of his hand. He smiled, raised my hand to his lips to return my kiss, and said it was a long time ago. After lunch at a watering stop, he suggested I ride and asked Philip to walk with him.

I learned later when we were walking together again that Philip, a handsome, sensitive-looking young man with a weathered face, was also from Bethsaida. He had hired himself on to Jonah's boat, which was how he had met Andrew. They were both drawn to John's message of repentance since in years past, both had been wild and rebellious. Philip, whose father was Greek and whose mother was from the tribe of Dan, had married a young woman from Bethsaida, only to squander what little money he had. Needing to support his wife and two little boys, he had hired himself out fishing, and then, with Jonah's blessing and most of his wages safely left to his wife, he had gone off with Andrew to repent his former ways.

"I think there's real hope for Philip," Joshua said. "I think he's ready to hear our good news. He's tired of trying the gods of luck and gluttony and sex and only finding empty promises. I think I'll ask Jonah if I can hire him."

"And his wife and children?" I asked.

"We can find a place for all of them, can't we? Her name is Diana; she's part Greek, too. I think she may be a big help to you if you'll give her a chance," Joshua replied. "We can begin to keep our vows by teaching them and the other servants."

"I'm getting one surprise after another," I said. "I thought I'd manage with Susanna and Salome until the others came from Jerusalem, but Philip and his family may be the first to learn about our Promised Land. Who'd have thought strangers, part Greek?"

Joshua laughed. "There's something else I discovered, Mim," he continued. "Well, I knew it, but hadn't given it much thought. We'll need to speak Greek as well as Aramaic in Galilee, shift back and forth, use both languages at once. With the trade routes, Philip reminded me that he lives in both worlds even as a fisherman."

"Speaking another language is more than just words, you know," I said. "Some words can be translated, but really don't have the same meaning in another culture. We've had problems enough trying to explain our understanding of the

Kingdom of God in Aramaic. Won't they be more intense here? Let's see, to begin with, your name in Greek is Jesus, mine is Mary. Let me introduce myself," I added, teasing with a lighthearted laugh.

To which Joshua, not to be outdone, stopped, bowed, and replied, "Pleased to meet you, Mary. I hear you're called the Magdalene. My name is Jesus. My cousin calls me the Lamb of God, and he and my friend Justus sometimes call me the Christ."

"And there you have it," I said, laughing again. "How do you combine Mary, 'woman of the sea,' with Magdalene, 'watchtower'? What could that mean in Greek? What does 'strong tower' or 'watchtower' mean to a Greek?" I asked.

"And what does Jesus, 'the savior' who is a lamb, or the Christ, 'the oily head,' 'the anointed one' mean?" Joshua countered. "They have laurel wreaths and heroes who are half-men, half-gods."

"And mermaids, sirens, and jealous goddesses," I added, bemused.

"Our names, and these titles, won't be our only challenges. It all seems to have something to do with strangers and the unexpected," Joshua concluded.

"Speaking of unexpected, I've been wondering. In the exodus, the sign of God's presence was a dense cloud. Maybe we'll have to be looking for clouds like the one at your baptism...and the mist on the river at mine. They were both so unusual."

"Interesting...and then there was that cloud that sheltered me as I hung on to our good Samaritan's donkey," Joshua said as he gave my hand another kiss before letting it drop to go forward among the men in the caravan, which had come to a stop in some shade near the river where another caravan had also stopped for water. Information was exchanged, the animals watered, and then tents were set up again for the night.

The next day, we continued on toward the great lake, which upon reaching, we found to be more beautiful than ever, a giant blue sapphire set among emeralds, and yet, more nuanced in shade and hue as clouds played overhead. Even at this time of year, the hills were sprinkled with bits of color from wildflowers.

As we neared the lake, Andrew and Philip couldn't resist jogging on ahead to look for family and friends, to tell them of the baptisms, of the man John sent home with them, "the Promised One" as they put it. Stories began to fly from person to person about the miraculous baptism, the awesome signs. As we followed them through Tiberius and on to the north end of the lake, we met many curious and friendly people on our way into Capernaum, all interested in meeting the newcomers they had just heard about.

The simple, plain house in Capernaum was quite a contrast to our beautiful, large home built of golden colored stone in Jerusalem, but it fit in with its neighbors and we thought it was quite fine. Away from the lake, beyond the center of town and the major road, it was on a little street leading up the hill. Like the others, it was built of dark volcanic rocks, plentiful in the area from an ancient eruption, and held together with lime mortar and plastered on the inside. Bedrooms and a kitchen were off a large central room that opened onto the street. Our animals, a well, and a little garden were hidden behind a dark rock wall on the uphill side of the house.

When we arrived, the house was dusty and dank from disuse, but we opened it up and all of us set to work airing and cleaning before we could unpack what we had brought from Jerusalem. Settling into our new life, patience was the quality we seemed to need most. Joshua reminded me of a saying he'd learned on his trip east in search of the Wise Men. "Don't be in a hurry or you won't go very far," he said, "and don't try to shine or you'll dim your own light. Relax and don't seek power over others, just over yourself. If you push to accomplish something, you'll find it doesn't last, so just do what's in front of you, respond to the person you meet, and let go of the rest." I reminded myself of this daily as I made new friends, learned about the traditions of this new community, and answered many, many questions.

It seemed we spent each day learning Greek, learning about our neighbors, and letting go of misunderstandings, criticisms, and the demands of others. In Capernaum, we found that tradition ruled just as tenaciously as it had in Jerusalem. Sometimes it was difficult to remember we were leading people into the Promised Land when they seemed to be so firmly rooted in tradition, in "the way things are done here."

"In Egypt," I added under my breath with a smile. They seemed dissatisfied with so many things and yet everyone seemed to know exactly how things should be done.

# CHAPTER TEN

Our household contracted and expanded in the following weeks. Thomas and Simon led the caravan with dried fish back to Jerusalem and returned with a caravan of olive oil, along with Judas and Bartholomew, who helped Judas with accounts, sales, and acquisitions, and James, the son of Alphaeus, two more of Joshua's students from Jerusalem who wanted to live with us, with their wives and children, and our Sarah and Joseph. Visiting us now and then, the children's grandmother and youngest aunt, Tamara, whom they adored, came from Nazareth where Joshua, deferring to her wishes, had arranged for his mother and youngest, still unmarried sister to live with his youngest brother, Simeon, and his wife, Judith, part of the time after his father died.

Mother Mary and I had good talks as we took walks into the hills, or along the lakeshore, finding a place to sit and inhale the beauty. I asked her to tell me stories of her early married life, following Joshua's father to Bethlehem and then their flight to Egypt when they were warned about Herod's jealousy and fear after he heard the Wise Men's story of a newborn king. I learned about Joshua's grandparents and their desire to serve God, their devotion to purity of heart

and deed. After every talk, I wrote down what she told me
so I could tell these stories to my children, and someday, I
hoped, my grandchildren, too.

While staying with us, Tamara met Nathaniel, a friend of
Philip and Diana, a sturdy, curious, straightforward young
fisherman whom Joshua enjoyed and respected. Nathaniel
was from Cana and Joshua was from Nazareth; at least, he
was from Nazareth as far as the Galileans were concerned.
They claimed him as being from Nazareth since he'd spent
his early years there studying with his father, out of Herod's
sight.

Nathaniel was quite candid that he didn't think any good
could come out of Nazareth, a prejudice he shared with his
family and everyone in his hometown. Cana's inhabitants
were often punished brutally after a Roman supply caravan
was raided by Zealots, who began their raids from the aeries
of Nazareth, then ran back with their loot to hide among the
tombs, leaving the men of Cana to bear the brunt of Roman
reprisals. Nathaniel, however, decided that Joshua could be
trusted. Overcoming Nathaniel's skepticism and suspicion
was as unexpected and marvelous to Joshua as being rescued
by Simon, the Samaritan. If these barriers of prejudice and
hate could be overcome, Joshua thought any barrier could be.

In due course, Nathaniel, who was as attracted to Tamara
as she was to him, overcame his village prejudice, his family's
prejudice, and his own prejudice, to ask her oldest brother, Joshua, to consent to their marriage. Joshua consulted
his sister, their mother, and then diplomatically arranged the
marriage, admiring not only Nathaniel's candor, but also his
integrity and courage.

We were all invited to the celebration of this special, un-precedented marriage. Our whole family, including our students and servants from Galilee and from Jerusalem, con-verged on Cana for the wedding feast. We were excited to meet Nathaniel's family, friends, and neighbors, as well as to reunite with friends and neighbors from Nazareth.

Joshua thought that celebrating Nathaniel and Tamara's marriage could be the beginning of understanding and peace between the people of Cana and Nazareth. Would the Zeal-ots of Nazareth, as well as Nathaniel, his family, and friends, the men of Cana, join him in making peace?

The day of the wedding, Joshua was delighted at the large crowd who gathered around the tables that filled Nathan-iel's parents' large courtyard festooned with greenery. Tenta-tive conversation between people from the two villages soon turned into good humored exchanges as everyone relaxed with food and wine, and then cheers as the bride arrived. The vows were exchanged under a colorful, richly woven canopy with Joshua and a rabbi from Cana performing the rituals and giving the blessings.

After the ceremony, we were all enjoying ourselves with the food and wine. The music and dancing were continually interrupted as person after person wanted to make a speech or toast. Joshua, happy, had just returned to sit beside me after visiting old friends from Nazareth on the far side of the crowd when his mother approached with a couple of servants following her.

"Nathaniel's parents are running out of wine," she an-nounced.

"I'm not surprised," Joshua replied, "considering how everyone seems to want to make a toast."

"The assistant steward, here, is desperate. His helpers are asking where to find more wine. I overheard him tell Nathaniel's father that the amphorae are emptying quickly and they're doing their best to keep wine cups filled. If you had seen Nathaniel's father's face, you would know why I told the steward to follow me—that you would take care of it. After all, we are a large part of this celebrating crowd."

Joshua blanched, shook his head, and asked, "Mother, what do you think I can do about this? Where can I get more wine in Cana? He looked at me for sympathy. "How could this happen just when things seem to be going so well, not enough wine for all of the toasts?"

Responding to my husband's disappointment, I wondered how I could help. The only idea I thought of seemed too small, but I offered him the only thing I had, my cup, still quite full of wine. Joshua raised his eyebrows, and getting out of his seat, said, "All right, Mother. It's not really my place to do something about this, but since you volunteered, I'll do what I can." He took my cup along with his own and went to speak to the nearby servants. He sent them to get fresh water from the spring for the six large amphorae nearby that held water for purification. He motioned for me to join him. "Maybe no one will notice," he said quietly when I reached his side. "This is certainly not what I expected, and I don't want to draw any attention to myself, but—"

"What can you do?" I asked, baffled.

"Mim, if God can heal Martha's knee and leg through me, perhaps this water, meant to purify our hands and feet, can become wine to purify our hearts and minds." He nodded toward our cups and prayed, "Here, Lord God, is wine we've gratefully received. We gratefully offer it to you and humbly ask for your blessing of peace. Blessed are you, Lord God, King of the Universe, who brings forth the fruit of the vine." He poured a bit of the wine from our two cups into each of the six large amphorae.

The servants soon returned with water from the spring, and then returned again, actually making three quick trips to fill the large jars while the celebration continued around us. Joshua put his arm around my shoulder as we watched. When they had finished, he said to their leader, "Now draw out a tester and take it to the chief steward."

The servant looked startled at the idea, but with nothing else to do, followed orders, dreading the consequences, I guessed. To his surprise, when the chief steward drank from the tester, he looked very pleased and called to the host, "Most people serve their best wine first, but you've saved your best for last. This wine calls for the best toasts yet to this happy couple. May the Almighty bless them!" He then ordered the astonished servants to fill quickly the guests' cups so all could join in the next toasts to Nazareth, to Cana, and to the bride and groom.

That night in our room, Joshua said, "Mim, I don't know how we got ourselves into that. Simeon couldn't have brought wine from Nazareth and we couldn't have brought wine from Capernaum, even though there were so many of us. Mother thinks I can solve any problem....Offering me your cup...I thought all we could do was offer God what we have...who am I to say what God will or won't do?"

"Another unbelievable surprise! I'm still amazed," I replied. "I had nothing else to offer you but that little bit of wine, which didn't seem like it would be enough to help at all. I suppose if God could turn all of the rivers of Egypt into blood...."

"We shouldn't be surprised at a little water turned into wine to let God's people go," Joshua laughed in relief, "to free them from attack and counterattack...and endless fighting. Still, mother caught me by surprise!"

"At least your prayers were heard," I teased. "Enough wine for the toasts and no one noticed. If people knew water became wine, you'd be invited to every feast, absolutely the most popular man in the region!"

Joshua laughed. "It's certainly not how I want to be known, though I do like a good party."

"I've noticed," I laughed myself, "but no wonder. Aren't people at their best when they're enjoying themselves and celebrating? Maybe that's why God commands us to celebrate the feasts?" With his broad smile and nod of agreement, I expanded my new theory. "Isn't it too bad we don't believe God is always preparing a feast for us to enjoy? I imagine we spoil everything with our need to earn the invitation or decide who else should be invited...or sometimes we're just too busy to notice and too busy to celebrate with whomever God has invited."

Relaxed and in good humor, Joshua responded, "Probably...I appreciate Mother's confidence, but she almost pushed me over a cliff tonight, embarrassed me to death...I'm just thankful God accepted our offering..." he sighed, winding down in simple appreciation, and after a few minutes, continuing his thought, "honored the intent of our hearts. I'll try to explain it to mother."

"It really was amazing," I repeated softly, "enough for everyone...for every toast."

"Yes, enough," he sighed contentedly before falling asleep.

# CHAPTER ELEVEN

Mother and son had their talk when we brought her to Capernaum with us for a visit. Joshua explained that all we could do was offer what we have, respond to the person who comes to us by sharing what we can. As he had often said after his attack on the Jericho Road, you don't know the moment you'll leave this life, so you might as well risk generosity and live with no regrets, confident you're a child of God, curious to see what surprise will come next.

Mother Mary and I had a talk, too, going over all of the delight of the wedding, how happy Tamara seemed to be, and how we both thought Nathaniel would be a wonderful, caring husband for her, as our husbands were for us. "I didn't know what to do, Miriam," she confided, "when I saw the look on Nathaniel's father's face and realized he had no idea where to get more wine. I didn't want anything to spoil the wedding for Tamara! I panicked and thought the only person who can fix this is my son."

"I understand completely," I assured her. "I always turn to him if things seem to be impossible, and he always finds a way through them...usually better than anything I could have imagined."

A natural teacher, Joshua taught us by asking a question, making a comparison, making an observation, telling a good story. Our lives changed as we lived this way. I could feel less anxiety every day with our students and servants, our neighbors, and strangers we met in the course of our daily activities, but we were about to be challenged. Where had the year gone? The month of Nissan was approaching. We decided to take our students and servants from Galilee along with those from Judea with us in a caravan to Jerusalem for Passover and to stay for the fifty days of counting through the Festival of Weeks, the celebration of the wheat harvest.

On the three-day journey, traveling back through the fertile growth of the Jordan valley to Jericho, we made a very brief stop to see John, who was still busy baptizing in the middle of a crowd, and then went on to Jericho where we spent a night again with Zachaeus and Abigail, but we missed seeing Justus who was away. The next day, we made the trek up the mountain to Jerusalem, the dusty road now crowded with other pilgrims with whom we sang Psalms from time to time as they trudged up the steep slope on foot.

Stopping briefly in Bethany to see Martha, Simon, Lazarus, and Hannah, we were shocked. Martha was in tears again. "It's Simon," she wailed as though he were dead. "He has leprosy." I embraced her and began to cry with her, but Joshua asked in a gentle, but determined voice, "Where is he?" Lazarus, who'd just come from next door, heard all of the commotion. He embraced Joshua and answered, "Come on. I'll show you. We have him as comfortable as we can in this other little house beside ours. I've just taken some food to his door." As they started out, he continued, "It's too bad...

it's been as hard on Martha as..." and his voice drifted out of my hearing.

Martha and I continued to hold each other and cry. Sarah and Joseph, off of their donkeys, felt a little shy, weren't sure what all of this was about, and started to go find their Aunt Hannah, but let out whoops of delight when a few steps later, they met their father arm in arm with Simon and Lazarus, all laughing and talking at once. Simon called, "Come here, you two. You've grown a cubit!" Lazarus and he held out their arms to their niece and nephew, who went running into them as fast as they could.

It would take time to digest what had just happened—the untouchable healed and embraced. But we gave ourselves over immediately to thanksgiving for our safe return from Galilee and Simon's safe return from leprosy. We went to our country home to leave the caravan animals with Alphaeus and his men to unload, while we went on to the Temple on foot with those who'd made the long trip with us from Galilee.

As we approached Jerusalem, the Temple on Mount Moriah rose above the city, an awesome, dazzling white diamond set in its golden stone setting, which gleamed in the early afternoon sun. But as we entered the city and approached the breathtaking vision, we found another reality. After almost a year in Galilee, the hubbub of Temple business felt offensive to us. Eager to share again the wonder of the great Temple, we were disappointed at what we encountered as we entered it that afternoon before the evening sacrifice. I recalled a prophet saying God had asked, "Why build a dwelling place for me when the cattle on a thousand hills are mine? Rejoice in the beauty I've created, where I come to meet you every day, wherever you are." Having just traveled through some of those beautiful hills, I wondered whether God were really being honored with all of the bustling activity.

Magnificent as the building was with its massive stones and pillars, nowhere in it could one be in quiet awe of God's glory. The Temple was the center of a thriving, noisy, religious business supporting priests in richly woven robes. It was difficult to be thankful and to find spiritual healing amid the clamor of competing loud prayers, of hawking animals, birds, and souvenirs, of money-changing at a better price than a competitor.

Overwhelmed by the parade of bleating, squawking sacrifices on their way to being killed; the noise, the stench, the souvenir business, and the Temple overrun by the market, we felt dismayed. Had we forgotten? Where was the mystery, the meeting of God who simply is "I AM" about whom we read and were teaching?

Joshua felt this noisy business was an attack on his spirit, just as the incident on the Jericho Road had been an attack on his body. Feeling wounded, he uncharacteristically shouted out, "Forgiveness is not for sale! Clean out, clean up! God's love is not for sale! God's favors are not to be hawked like a prostitute's!"

These words were not well-received by those who heard them—priests and tradesmen—all of whom were in profitable symbiotic relationships. Even some passing rabbis, with whom Joshua had taught for years, were affronted by his challenge to "the way things are done." We women walked on a little further to stand at a distance from the men who were gathering around. We strained to hear what was being said in the marketplace's din.

"Calm down, Joshua," one of the rabbis said. "Be careful how you speak for God whom you know has spoken through Moses. These are the required offerings for forgiveness." Relying on authority, passersby gathered to challenge Joshua, who was no longer one of them, having left his place of prestige and wealth for a life among the poor in Galilee.

"By whose authority are you criticizing Temple worship, the way business is done?" they asked. They explained that it was the way things had always been done. Joshua should know that. Maybe it had gotten a little more commercial. They complained themselves from time to time, but people couldn't be expected to bring perfect sacrifices from the country. Joshua should know that! Someone had to make certain that the animals and birds were perfect, and that person had to be paid to examine and certify them. Joshua should know that too.

The merchants couldn't accept any foreign money, couldn't know the value. Someone had to test the money, change it to Temple money, so merchants with certified animals and birds were paid a fair price. Competition was good for everyone, so it was a little noisy, a small price to pay to get services at the best price. Joshua should know that.

Maybe the souvenir merchants were too much, but people wanted to take something home to remember their trip to the great Temple. Wasn't it better to sell souvenirs than to have bits and pieces of the Temple, or of priests' robes, or whatever the pilgrims could get their hands on, torn away and carried off? Even with the sale of souvenirs, guards had to watch for people with no fear of God who tried to take proof they had been here.

Joshua did calm down and became the teacher again, listening to these defenses as one speaker after another got the crowd's approval. He began to respond to their arguments, to remind them of the history of tabernacle and then Temple worship, the sacred place set apart to meet God. He was interrupted by a voice in the back. One of his cousins had walked up to join the group, Zachariah, the Levite who'd passed him on the road to Jericho, leaving him for dead. We had heard he was resentful of the whole episode, resentful that he was recognized and that Joshua had not only survived but told Joseph Caiaphas he'd forgiven him. He didn't appreciate it at all.

Temple society, hearing of Joshua's near death experience on the Jericho road, had buzzed for several weeks with the ethical question of what to do if you see a man in need on a deserted road. Zachariah, jealous of Joshua's wealth and position I suspect, now said in a loud, acerbic tone, "Well, I don't know what you're complaining about, Joshua; your sheep from Bethlehem bring good prices at Passover, your fine oil, too. You're part of this system." And then, not waiting for a response, he spit out, "Who has clean hands?"

Joshua started to answer, " Zachariah, I was looking for you—"

But Zachariah interrupted, "You're quick to judge and forgive, aren't you? You think you own this place, calling God your 'father,' you bastard. By our law, you don't know your earthly father, much less a heavenly one. Why are you so high and mighty, so special, that someone should risk his life to save you when you get yourself in trouble?"

Joshua started to answer, but Zachariah continued, "Well, we'll see who keeps the Law, who wins the favor of God. What right have you to come here criticizing honest men, born to be priests because we know our fathers. Who are you to criticize us for doing perfectly legal and holy business, following our laws, making proper sacrifices?"

Again Joshua started to answer, but to the embarrassment of rabbis accustomed to the give-and-take of discussion and not a ceaseless ad hominem attack, Zachariah caught his breath and continued, "Oh, you have your hand in the money. Don't pretend you don't. Hurt my reputation; don't think you'll get off easy. I'll be watching and waiting!"

Joshua, finally able to speak, said, "Good, Zach. I hope you will. Actions do speak louder than words. I recognized you on the road, though I didn't think you recognized me. I looked for you and couldn't find you to tell you I'd forgiven you. I don't think you knew what—"

"Don't patronize me! That's an insult, and I have witnesses!" Zachariah shot back. "You think you're so special. Watch your step, I'll be watching," he added in a threatening tone, and then he left, his face twisted in anger and contempt.

After this diatribe, the discussion changed and men began to drift away in twos and threes, continuing conversations. Several of the priests in the back followed Zachariah while others stayed to continue discussing the Temple, tithes, current issues, practices, and authority with Joshua, apparently glad to have him back in their discussions, though his return to his place of honor and prestige in Jerusalem had been marred with such a bitter confrontation.

# CHAPTER TWELVE

The four Galileans—Peter, Andrew, James, and John  had wanted to go and confront Zachariah immediately. When Joshua returned home, he told me Thomas, Simon, our Zealot, and Bartholomew were ready also. They were all upset by the insults and threats, as were the women who had been with me. We had quietly gathered our children and slipped past the men caught up in the confrontation to return home quickly. All of our teaching of love and forgiveness seemed to have been forgotten in a moment.

Soon after the men returned home, we gathered for the evening meal in our large upper room, which opened onto a terrace with a view of the Temple, still glowing in the late afternoon light. But now, disappointment and the confrontation hung over us like a veil, dimming the view. Joshua glanced around the large, old room, looked up at the great beams supporting the roof, and with his usual sense of humor, suggested we all might want to remove the large beams in our own eyes before trying to remove a speck of dust from someone else's. Tensions melted with laughter and we enjoyed the meal, sharing our other impressions of the day.

When we got to our room, I heard more of the story of what had happened after Zachariah left. Joshua said he'd had all he could do to calm our men down and still continue answering questions from the crowd that had gathered. "Let threats pass," he'd told them and the others nearby. "Using blame and anger to cover feelings of guilt is an old story. Adam blamed God and Eve; Cain blamed Abel. Men have blamed God, women, and each other for their own failings ever since the beginning."

"Why can't people just be honest, ask for forgiveness, accept it, and go on with life?" I asked. "We all need to be forgiven and to forgive ourselves and others every day."

"You're right, Mim, and I'll have to start by forgiving myself for my outburst. I think there's a place for righteous anger, though, don't you?"

"Mmm....well, is loving anger righteous anger?" I asked. "Anger we feel when we see someone mistreated, or cheated, or robbed, or abused? Isn't loving anger the anger we expect of God? Isn't that righteous? Didn't the prophets think so?"

"I suppose so...but what do you think about Zachariah?"

"He must have been shocked to hear you were the dying man he passed on the road...shocked you recognized him and survived. It probably would be something like looking in a mirror and not liking what you saw...certainly not the image he's trying to make for himself at the Temple."

"Probably not...."

"Well, unless he's willing to forgive himself, I doubt he'll be happy with your forgiveness. I suspect he was either afraid or annoyed with an inconvenience," I speculated, "but either way, don't you think he's embarrassed?"

"Probably. If he were afraid of getting involved with some beaten up, half-dead who-knows-who, bleeding on the road, perhaps a trap set by men to rob him, too...or...if he didn't want to get his hands dirty or bloody and be late for the evening sacrifice...either way...you're right. Somehow he'll have to face whatever it was."

"I suspect so," I said, yawning in spite of myself. "But how about loving ourselves with some sleep, Rabboni?" I asked. "It's been a very long day."

Joshua laughed, "I dream about you when I'm wide awake, but some sleep sounds like a good idea. What a morning! What an afternoon! This will sort itself out...but that unfair attack on my mother and father really bothered me. Maybe sometime I can get you to write down the whole story you and I've heard from mother and you can set the record straight at least for our children. I don't suppose attacks like this will ever stop from those who cling to Law with its jots and titles rather than Love. But then, it was my father's skill at manipulating the jots and titles that saved mother and him."

"I remember. I'll ask her to tell me again to be sure I have it all just right. I love to hear her tell it....I get chills each time."

# CHAPTER THIRTEEN

Sleep distanced us from that harsh encounter. However, early the next morning as we were crossing our entrance hall on our way to breakfast, another cousin and former student, Joel, arrived from Jericho to tell us John had been arrested by Herod. I heard the surprise in Joshua's voice as he asked, "How did you find me? We just saw him. I've just arrived." Not waiting for an answer, he invited Joel to come and share our morning meal with us on the terrace overlooking the Temple, gleaming again in the morning sun. We sat at a small table that Rhoda had laden with warm bread, honey, cheese, fruit, and nuts. After a blessing, Joshua asked Joel to tell us what had happened, and so he began.

"I was at the Jordan yesterday morning, listening to John, getting ready to be baptized," his voice hinted at another story about his personal need to repent, "when a large troop of men came marching along the road from Jericho. Disturbed, but not alarmed, we were intent on what John was saying about the rottenness of our whole society from the palace and Temple to each of us caught in the web of corruption, with our own little compromises of which we were all too well aware. We should be washed clean of our complicity, our selfishness and fear."

Joshua and I looked at each other, as he asked, "And John urged you to repent, to turn around and live without fear, make way for God in your life?"

"Yes," Joel answered after he had swallowed a big bite of bread with honey. "But the troops didn't keep marching on the road; they marched right down the bank to the river's edge where quite a large number of us were gathered. We scattered in front of them as they roughly pushed any stragglers out of the way. Their leader barked out a command to John, who was standing well into the stream, getting ready to baptize. 'John Bar-Zachariah, in the name of Herod, come here immediately.' We were all surprised, and then more so when the commander added, 'Herod commands you to come to speak with him.' The air was thick with tension. John could have made them wade into the water with their sandals and uniforms to fetch him, but he thought better of it, and moved toward them, taking a few steps in their direction. He was not happy to be interrupted in the middle of baptisms."

"It must have been quite a contrast," Joshua said, his voice betraying the sickening feeling that overcame him as Joel described the scene. "John in his rough camel's hair tunic with his wild hair and beard, Herod's guards neat and trim in their fancy uniforms, polished shields and swords!"

"It really was! And also with us, quite a motley crowd, milling around on both riverbanks, seeking safety in numbers, and at the same time, jostling for a good position to see what would happen next. I was close enough to hear John tell the commander that he and his men could step back and wait while he baptized us, and any of them who repented of their sins, and then he would go with them to Herod."

"Hmmm! No one ever said that our cousin wasn't courageous!" Joshua said now with dancing eyes and a chuckle, clear admiration for John in his voice.

"No, he was himself—John the prophet, formidable as ever, not the least bit intimidated—but Herod's officer would have none of it. John may have had the power of Almighty God behind him, but the officer had the power of Herod Antipas, and a bunch of well-armed men who looked like they would enjoy a fight. 'Come now! You're under arrest,' the leader said very bluntly. 'It will go badly for you if we have to wade in to get you.'"

Picturing the scene, I wished John had joined us in Galilee. Joel continued, "John acknowledged the threat with what seemed to me to be some kind of knowing smile. He said something like, 'Very well,' and began wading toward the officer, stopped, and motioned to a couple of his disciples, giving his own commands. 'James, bring my sandals and carry on. Continue with the baptisms today.' Then walking toward the bank, he saw me and shouted, 'Joel, go find Joshua. Tell him I'm still preparing the way. I have an invitation I can't refuse; an impressive messenger and bodyguard invite me to speak to Herod in his fortress.' And he marched away with them."

Joshua and I sat in silence for a few minutes as Joel, his message delivered, ate more warm bread with goat cheese. "John's wilderness wasn't very far away from the seat of power," I sighed, "but I didn't expect this."

"So John is in Machaerus," Joshua mumbled half to himself. I could see his mind exploring this new turn of events as Joel continued to eat. "What will Justus do when he hears this? What about Annas and Joseph Caiaphas? John left the priesthood to call for reform...more righteousness, but take him into custody, throw him into prison, that's going too far. Herod will have to listen to Annas, and release him."

Joel observed, "John preached against corruption wherever he saw it, in the Temple and the palace, making no secret about it. We priests may feel guilty and want to be baptized, but not the king or his court. They may be superstitious or frightened from time to time, but John's right—they're desperate to control and will pay any price, make any compromise, to get power and keep it."

"And now Herod wants to control John," I sighed.

"Well, it may be more complicated than that," Joel said, quietly. "It's possible Annas and Joseph Caiaphas are tired of hearing criticism from those of us who've been baptized. Maybe they're afraid that we might uncover something they want hidden; maybe John was coming too close to the truth for them, too. Maybe it would be more comfortable for them if John were locked up in prison until he comes to his senses, out of circulation for a while in a way that can't be traced to them. I wonder if they traded favors with Herod and have a deal with him?"

I saw the change that came over Joshua's face, a dawning, disappointed, painful recognition of a possible web just below the surface, frightened men, intrigue, protection, extortion. If Joel's suspicions were true, he couldn't just go to Annas and

Joseph Caiaphas. "I wonder if Zachariah yesterday...." He hesitated. "He went so far beyond...."

"Oh, my," a wave of apprehension washed over me. Joshua trusted Joel's loyalty and asked whether he would help him get John released. Joel quickly agreed and said he had well-connected friends whom he could question without raising suspicion. Joshua said he would try to approach Justus through his brother, Simon, but Joel warned Joshua to be careful as he'd seen Gestas and Demas and other Zealots from time to time when he was on duty with Annas. This might be more complicated than we could imagine.

"Justus wouldn't betray his lifelong friend," Joshua replied with conviction. "Simon will expect me to contact his brother."

"Of course," replied Joel. "Just be aware that things at the Temple are seldom what they seem. I wouldn't relish being thrown into prison, too."

Silent, I wondered whom we could believe. Joseph Caiaphas and Elizabeth lived a few doors away and were such close friends; their Mathias had been in and out of our house all of the time with John Mark. Elizabeth's mother and father, Judith and Annas, were like a beloved aunt and uncle to me. Where would this lead? I felt uncomfortable. It didn't feel like the same place we'd left such a short time ago.

"We'd all better be careful about what we ask and say," Joshua warned, as if reading my mind. "A misspoken word might not help John...or any of us for that matter."

Joel left, promising to report back within a week...better at night, he thought, as fewer people would notice. News of John's imprisonment changed everything we had planned. At the mid-day meal, we gathered the family and servants, telling them the news. Poor Thad was devastated, having thrived these past few months with his father's approval, blessing, and baptism.

Andrew and Philip volunteered immediately to go to the fortress to find out what they could. They knew John's disciples, felt sure they could find them, learn what had happened, what we might do, whom we might pay to secure John's release. We decided that they could take some first press oil reserved from the last harvest, some cured olives, and dried fish. As traders, they could gain access to information in Jericho and perhaps in the fortress itself.

Simon volunteered to go find his brother and find out what Justus knew and could do about this, but we suggested he wait until after Andrew and Philip would return, one path at a time. That seemed to satisfy him since he was reluctant to leave Joshua after the shocking verbal attack the day before.

# CHAPTER FOURTEEN

That afternoon, unsure of what to say, whom to trust, I hesitated to go out to see my best friends after so eagerly anticipating our reunions. Just as stories had circulated about Joshua on the Jericho Road, the confrontation with Zachariah at the Temple and John's arrest were sure to circulate and grow with each retelling.

Joshua, too, seemed to need time to think through the situation to which we had returned. He was sure his men would insist on staying close to protect him. Zealots were one thing, raiding and killing to achieve their goals, but merchants of religion with their symbiotic networks were something else, perhaps more dangerous. Their lives and livelihoods were threatened, and he suspected they didn't want much light to shine on their deals.

That evening, Joshua decided to gather our servants to talk again about the Temple and his understanding of the mystery of The Unnameable "I Am" behind the great veil hanging from ceiling to floor, separating the holiest place from the rest of the Temple. The Holy of Holies, he reminded us, was forbidden to all except the high priest once a year. It was the place of God's presence, the presence of Spirit without image, nothing behind the veil, unlike other temples, Greek, Roman, Egyptian, or Persian. Once written in stone, the physical Commandment stones had long since been lost or stolen in one siege on Jerusalem or another, and were no longer there in the Ark as they had been in the first tabernacle in the desert and then in Solomon's great temple, but now, he believed, they were to be written in our lives, in our flesh and blood.

I invited our close friends, Nicodemus and Rachel, to come the next evening. Though Nicodemus was still a member of the Sanhedrin, I trusted them as I trusted my brother and sister. Rachel, a few years older than I, was also well-educated by her father and grandfather. We were blessed, privileged, and enjoyed talking about philosophy, wisdom, and Scriptures with our husbands who continued to consider our thoughts as seriously as our fathers had. Of course, we enjoyed exchanging stories about our children as well. Our participation in our husbands' conversations was unusual. Other colleagues kept their wives out of their discussions. Rachel and I wondered how there could be peace on earth when one half of a God-created union was diminished rather than encouraged, educated, and embraced.

That evening during dinner, we regaled one another with stories of our experiences during the past few months. Nicodemus brought us up-to-date on the latest topics being debated in the Sanhedrin, and we told them about the amazing things happening to us in Galilee...the healing, forgiving, teaching. After dinner, our conversation turned to John's imprisonment and then to the troubling confrontation at the Temple, including the underlying problems—the Temple so commercialized by corrupt men who tolerated the terrible conditions in the rest of the country with ongoing conflicts.

"I suppose we just can't legislate love," Joshua concluded. "We're back to Hillel and Gamaliel's view that if each of us actually loves the Lord our God with our whole being and loves our neighbor as our self, we and our neighbors can fulfill the spirit of every law, live together in peace...in the paradise waiting for us to enjoy now, for which we are all longing."

"I don't know why we don't," Rachel agreed, "but we don't."

"Perhaps fear of betrayal, that the other person will take advantage of us? Our stories tell of men who've violated, betrayed, enslaved, and killed others as well as those who've loved, risked, and sacrificed. To be fully human, to risk loving ourselves and others without judging good or evil, do we need to be born twice, physically and spiritually?" Joshua asked. "Perhaps we really need to be born twice."

"How can that be?" Nicodemus shook his head. "Born twice? What do you mean?"

"Well, if not, why do some people in never satisfied self-interest, judge, abuse, and fight to dominate everyone they meet, while others unselfishly love, care for others, and share what they can without judgment? Doesn't our spirit as well as our body need to be born...to come alive and grow and mature in order to live in peace with others?"

We didn't have answers. Joshua broke the silence, "You're probably tired of hearing me, but I'm passionate about real peace on earth. I'm sure that's why I was born...and I'm struggling to find a way to make it a reality...to show it."

"I'm not tired," I smiled, sympathetic to his longing. Nicodemus and Rachel must have agreed, as we continued talking...quoting wisdom books and Prophets on the subject...one quote leading to another...encouraging him and his quest.

As talk was winding down, Joshua shook his head. "I think I'll just have to tell some good stories to show God loves us in spite of terrible things that happen...sends people for us to love and to love us. I think we need to stop trying to make the other person into our image instead of accepting the other as created in God's image. To love or not to love, that's still the choice."

Nicodemus replied, "Well, my friend, that's sometimes very difficult. How will you know if your servants and followers really understand your message of love?"

Without a moment's hesitation, Joshua answered, "I'll watch how they care for and treat each other...and strangers unlike them...how men care for women and how women care for men. I'll watch how they care for the vulnerable... children and widows, their elders, the physically and mentally ill, the crippled, the deaf, the blind, the weak, the outcasts...I'll watch how they treat their neighbors and their enemies. I'll see if they actually love, forgive, and make peace a reality wherever they are."

# CHAPTER FIFTEEN

Gradually, we reconnected with our friends. We had come to Jerusalem for Passover, and so we prepared and celebrated the feast with our large, extended family, and we did enjoy visiting with friends in the course of that preparation. With my husband's sense of humor and superb storytelling, we avoided direct questions and voicing our new doubts. However, the shadow of John's imprisonment hung over us, and we wondered how John might be released from Herod's prison and how our family and friends might be released from what seemed like prisons of their own making, prisons of anxiety and fear and selfishness.

Philip and Andrew returned from Machaerus where they had surprised John after a week of negotiating with his disciples and guards. They were allowed to be his two visitors for the day in his small cell. He told them the guards were treating him well. He'd already spoken with Herod several times and felt he was beginning to influence him. Perhaps Herod might repent, he said, reform, and rule with justice and mercy after all. John was beginning to hope that he could be more effective in prison than he was by the Jordan in bringing real change. He sent Joshua a message, a familiar quote, "'Fear not for I am with you even to the end of the age,' says The Lord." We understood it was John reassuring us again.

Cousin Joel returned also a few evenings later. He came late after visiting with Temple gossips around the dinner table. Nathan, our faithful doorkeeper, let him in and led him up to the terrace where Joshua and I were talking after dinner, enjoying the star spangled sky as we often did. Joel seemed very anxious; his news was not so reassuring. "I sat next to Josiah, who manages connections between Annas and the merchants and moneychangers. Talk of bribes and discreet favors for one or another floated about the table with someone asking if we shouldn't be more cautious, someone might have a pang of conscience. Josiah laughed and said he didn't think we'd have to worry about that now that John and his repentance talk had been taken care of."

"That's interesting, Joel, but was more said about how John was 'taken care of'?" Joshua asked, going to the heart of the message.

"No, not directly, but later there was talk about how Annas had approved Herod's marriage to his brother's wife, Herodias, and now there were some other liaisons that Herod wanted officially approved by the high priest. Annas would have to convince Caiaphas and maybe negotiate another gift for his trouble."

Joshua nodded thoughtfully, "Well, thank you, Joel. I can see this would not be a very good time to go to Annas or Caiaphas to ask them to demand John's release by Herod since John was so critical of that marriage, even if we don't know for certain yet that they actually instigated his arrest.

We'll just have to hope that Herod continues to treat John well, and that we can eventually get him released."

I had listened quietly with a sickening feeling that men were selling themselves, their honor, everyday behind closed doors for money which actually could never satisfy them, but only rearrange their misery. After a bit more conversation, Joel left, promising to continue his discreet inquiry and urging us to continue to be cautious.

While we enjoyed gathering for Passover later that week in our spacious upper room with Joshua's mother, his brothers, their wives and children, we enjoyed a more quiet celebration of the first of the barley harvest. When Jude and his family had come for Passover, he had brought us some sheaves of barley from Bethlehem. Joshua, I, and our three children took the barley sheaves to the Temple the next day along with the prescribed lamb as our offering. Sarah and I stayed back as Joshua and the boys presented the offering to the priest on duty who turned out to be none other than Joshua's vituperative cousin Zachariah.

Joshua had a broad smile on his face when he returned to Sarah and me. "Well, we got through that," he said. "I bit my tongue...probably my greatest sacrifice...and he must have bitten his in return. Anyway, we got through it in proper form as though nothing had happened between us."

"That may actually *be* forgiveness," I ventured. "Just treating another the same way you would if nothing had ever happened between you...giving like before?"

We stayed in Jerusalem for the prescribed seven days of eating only unleavened bread and remembering The Unnameable God leading our ancestors safely out of slavery in

Egypt, but it was a relief at the week's end to go to our country house to see more of Simon and Martha, Lazarus and Hannah in Bethany. With everything that had happened in Jerusalem, there had hardly been a moment to think about Simon's recovery from leprosy, but when I did think of the disease, the dying and sloughing off of a living body in bits and pieces, I thought perhaps that was what our visit to Jerusalem was about, too...Joshua offering to stop the dying off of true worship of the living, Unnameable God with acts of love that were being replaced by deadened rituals with hundreds of little rules.

Besides celebrating Simon's recovery with my family, we went over accounts with Judas, the pruning of orchards with Alphaeus, and then Joshua went back to Jerusalem with Judas to collect the proceeds from the sale of our sheep; next Joshua and Judas went on to Bethlehem to distribute wages with Jude to the shepherds who had delivered lambs from our Bethlehem flocks to the Temple for Passover.

One day, Joshua and Thomas, with Bartholomew and James, went back to the inn on the road to Jericho to learn more about Simon of Cyrene. The innkeeper remembered the incident. "Look who's here," he had called to his wife. When she came, she was delighted to see Joshua recovered, declaring, "I wouldn't recognize you if I'd met you in Jerusalem. You were so swollen and bruised, I didn't quite know what you looked like. But I remember your eyes...even your smile a bit." Wine was poured all around and Joshua had the chance to ask about Simon, the man who had rescued him. The innkeeper said, "Simon was originally from Sychar in Samaria. He often visits there on his trading trips after he delivers his precious herb from Cyrene to Jerusalem, Jericho, and Machaerus."

"Oh," said Joshua, "silphium does seem to be a treasured gift from God. We can express our love without bringing children into the world for whom we can't care."

"Yes," the innkeeper replied. Silphium is in more demand than ever. Simon stopped by again recently. He was glad to hear that you had been found by your family, and was glad to be repaid."

When Joshua returned, he said he wanted to go back to Galilee through Samaria by way of Sychar to find Simon of Cyrene if he were still there between trading trips. The fifty days after Passover had passed quickly. We returned to Jerusalem to celebrate the Festival of Weeks, the wheat harvest, and then said goodbye again to all of our family and friends and set out for Galilee. Our fishermen, except for Philip, had returned home to Galilee soon after Passover with pilgrims so we were a smaller caravan and it was easier to travel the upper road through Samaria. Thomas was very capable, and Simon had his connections to the Zealots. I suspected we were guarded by unseen eyes and ears when leaving Jerusalem, though we passed small Roman outposts from time to time. Philip, speaking Greek or Aramaic, was able to connect with everyone he met on the well traveled road, single travelers or those in small caravans.

On the day we arrived at the old, historic Jacob's well just outside Sychar, a town of substance, stone houses crowning a hill covered with vineyards, it was late morning just before the market would close for the mid-day meal. The caravan stopped under some trees near the well that gave shade to us and our animals in the hot, dry land. The old well provided water for people and animals who lived nearby and for travelers on the trade route. Far from a river, this well was the source of life.

Joshua sent Thomas and Philip into town to buy some fresh baked bread, local cheese, fruit for our meal, but mostly to see whether they could find anyone who knew Simon of Cyrene or his family. Thad and the children stayed with the others, near the animals, helping to water them while the women laid out rugs in the shade for us to sit and rest on. Local women had drawn their water earlier.

While we were waiting, resting in the shade, Joshua saw a slight, willowy woman coming out of town to draw water. Since she was coming so late, he suspected something out of the ordinary and wondered what he could learn. He got up and walked toward the well, asking me to come also. "Maybe she knows Simon. What do you think?"

"I think it's worth asking. Remember when you seek, you find; and when you make a mistake, you're forgiven," I laughed. "I'll be right over after I ask the children to give us some privacy with her."

By the time I reached the well, Naomi had already drawn water for Joshua, who had discovered that she indeed knew Simon; in fact, she kept his house ready for him when he was in town. Joshua introduced us, telling me this information so I was included in the new relationship. Naomi's dark, sensitive, sad but inviting eyes hinted at the story she began to tell us. She had endured a quite tragic life, with one husband after another dying or being killed.

She didn't want marriage again and had become superstitious after her fifth husband was killed in an accident. She didn't expect another man to take a chance with her, a widow five times! That would be too much to ask!

"But Simon wasn't afraid, was he?" Joshua asked. "After his wife in Cyrene died last year, when he was here on a trading trip, he heard of your latest loss, and was brave enough to offer to marry you, to become engaged?"

"How did you know that?" Naomi asked, surprised. "When everyone else thought I was cursed and would have nothing to do with me, he came forward. He's not my husband—yet—but he's so very kind. I'm not sure that I can risk marriage again. I gladly keep his house for him here in Sychar. He says someday I'll go with him to Cyrene, meet his sons and daughters there, make them mine."

"I'd really like to meet Simon some day. He sounds so brave and kind," I spoke up.

"Your husband must be a prophet," Naomi told me. "He seems to understand so much about me, about this well and its history, talking to me, some kind of outcast coming to the well at noon so I won't meet anyone. He asked me for water as if your servants over there couldn't draw him all of the water he would like."

"But you must be the very person we were hoping to meet, along with Simon, of course," I said. "And yes, my husband is phenomenal. I think he knew you would come to meet us when he first saw you in the distance."

"Before you met me?" Naomi asked Joshua. "You have something about you; I couldn't refuse when you asked for water," she laughed. "I hesitated, but something about you reminded me of Simon, a kind of...and then you said you could give me living water."

Joshua nodded and laughed softly, too. "I suspected that was an offer you couldn't refuse...if water is the source of life for our bodies...then love is the source of life for our spirits. That would be living water, wouldn't it? It's what Simon has given both of us. I'll tell you my story, but in a sense, we're both alive because he dared to love us."

"I hadn't thought of it that way, but I think that's true for me. You must be a prophet to understand life that way," Naomi repeated. "Where do you think we should worship God? That is the big argument that separates my people from yours, but you seem so open-minded. Which Temple? Where should we worship? Whom do you think is right?"

"I think Simon and I are both right," Joshua laughed. "You see, on the Jericho Road, Simon and I each stopped to help someone who needed help, and helping, acting for the good of another is loving them in the way I understand and use the word love. It is what we ask of God and what God asks of us. I think that's true worship. Our bodies are our true temples and true worship takes place wherever we are."

"I hadn't thought of it like that," Naomi said again.

"Nor had I, exactly," I said. "It's not the same as a mushy feeling or passionately wanting to possess someone or some-thing for our benefit, which is how we often use the word love. But that's not what we ask for when we ask God to love us," I added with a laugh as I saw our men returning with food. While Philip, with arms full of food, continued on to a place in the shade where the others waited to eat, Thomas stopped to report that there was no word about Simon of Cyrene except that he was out of town, and when in town, he was living with a woman who—

Joshua, smiled patiently, nodded, and interrupted him to introduce him to Naomi.

Thomas was surprised and gave me a "How does he do it?" look as he went on. I smiled and shrugged before I asked Naomi, "Won't you stay to eat with us? It looks like we have more than enough food. I want Joshua to tell you the whole story of his wonderful experience with your Simon, and I want you to tell your Simon how grateful I am to him. You see, if it weren't for him, I would likely be a widow now, myself."

Naomi's eyes and mine involuntarily filled with tears at that thought. She stayed to enjoy lunch and our company, and then asked whether we would stay because she wanted to go into town and bring out as many friends of Simon's as she could find, as well as members of her former families. The more she thought about it, the more people she wanted to bring out to meet Joshua. If he would tell the stories again about worshiping God in spirit and truth...and about Simon on the Jericho road, she knew they would want to hear, too.

It seemed as if Simon and especially Naomi were related to almost everyone in town. Quite a crowd came out around sundown with food, wine, and torches, all milling about and wanting to hear Joshua's stories, his questions, more stories, and then followed music, dancing, more stories, and songs. Begging us to stay, to continue the following evening, Naomi and her family and friends reluctantly returned to town as the torches began to fade.

That night, settling into our tent, and bed, Joshua and I were both exhausted and elated. Putting an arm around me, drawing me close to put my head on his chest, he whispered, "Mim, do you realize how blessed we've been again today? First Simon, and now Naomi...I think we really do understand how to worship God...it is just taking the risk to love the person God sends us. What an evening!"

"Amazing, Rabboni," I said. "Who would think this could happen in Sychar...in Samaria? Unbelievable...I enjoyed every minute, every person I met; didn't you?"

# CHAPTER SIXTEEN

After another wonderful evening near Jacob's well with
our new friends, we traveled the dry road north toward Galilee, eventually reaching the moist air of the valleys where we
passed again through flourishing fields of grain. We joined
the road that led along the great lake and as we approached
Capernaum, Joshua recognized Zebedee and Jonah's boats in
the distance, pulled up onto the shore. He rode on ahead to
see how the fishing had been for James and John, Andrew
and Simon, the last of whom we had begun calling by his
Greek name, Peter, which meant rock-like and seemed to fit
his personality, a bit rough on the edges and stubbornly hard
sometimes. The new name distinguished him from Justus'
brother, our other Simon. As we in the caravan drew close,
Joshua came back to rejoin us, laughing from his talk with his
fishermen friends, and called back to the men who were still
finishing the cleaning of the nets, "Come on with me, now;
I'll make you fishers of men!"

The four, clearly in good humor, enjoyed Joshua's invitation to escape the final clean-up of the boats and nets, gladly
leaving it to the others as they scrambled to join us. Joshua
and I dismounted, gave our animals to Philip to manage and

walked with the four toward Capernaum. On our way into
town, they told us the news, including that Peter's mother-
in-law, Omah, whom we all adored, had been very sick for
over a week. She was delirious with a high fever in spite of
everything they'd done and they were very worried. Joshua
looked at me, saying that perhaps he could help, and I responded that I was sure he could. "I won't be long. Maybe
I can help you, too," he winked, mouthing a kiss before he
turned aside to go home with Peter, and I continued home.

Joshua was home before I expected. I was just beginning
to unpack my bag, settling my clothes and cosmetics into
their accustomed places when he came into our room, happily humming, with his bag on his shoulder. As he put it down,
I asked, "Well?"

"Well," he replied, "Omah *was* very sick just as they'd said.
Adah and Peter had tried everything. I held her hand and
asked God to forgive her and cure her. I'd barely begun to
thank God when Omah opened her eyes wide and looked
around startled; it was almost like she was waking up from
a dream. 'Joshua!' she said, 'I didn't expect you! Are you
hungry? Let me get you something to eat.'"

"Oh my," I laughed. "Typical Omah!"

Joshua laughed, too. "Yes, without a minute's hesitation,
she was up and insisting that she cook. Her color, her energy,
her enthusiasm were all back. Peter stopped her, told her
how sick she'd been, what had just happened, that we'd just
arrived, and that I was on my way home. Remembering,
she simply shook her head, broke out into her broad smile,
as though it were some kind of joke, and still insisted that I
get you and the children and return for our evening meal. I

wasn't sure what Adah and Peter thought of it all, but they were amazed and relieved and urged me to accept and celebrate with them."

"Oh, my," I said again. "Is she really up to it?"

"Yes, I think so. Actually, she is. Her eyes are as bright as ever, and her energy seems even higher than usual. Do you mind? Are you up for it yourself, after our long day on the road?"

"Of course," I laughed. "It will be a real treat to see her, and the whole family."

And so we went to Adah and Peter's that night, a night that would change our lives because Omah was not only a good and generous cook, but a friend of every older woman in Capernaum. She loved to talk as much as she loved to cook, so as she went out to get food for dinner, she told everyone she met about her wonderful cure, about Joshua curing her in the blink of an eye, no pain, no recuperation. It was marvelous!

Our short walk to Adah and Peter's home that evening was down our small street where already gathered around their door was a small crowd of Omah's friends and their family members who had aches or pains or fevers. Joshua and I exchanged a look of recognition as to what had happened. He was gracious, blessing, touching, and healing each one, asking each time, "Please don't tell anyone; just thank God."

But that was not to happen. We enjoyed the delicious meal, but Omah couldn't stop talking about how wonderful she felt, how thankful she was. We couldn't bring ourselves to squelch her enthusiasm, even though we began to realize that this event, helping her recover from the dreadful fever, curing her so quickly, was an unexpected turning point for us. She had told everyone on her way to and from the market, and in the market with every purchase she had made.

More people were waiting to be cured in the street outside the door as we left to return home later that evening. Joshua stopped to listen to each one and generously respond, touching each one as he asked God to be glorified. Person after person, as we made our way home, was healed. Faces and eyes glowed, reflecting the love at the core of my husband's being.

Our children were impatient, and then curious, to know what was happening. When we did get inside our door again, their questions bubbled out. Joseph, with his ever present and persistent curiosity wondered, "Where did these people come from, Father? Why were they waiting for you? What's wrong with them?"

Before Joshua had a chance to answer, Sarah, reflecting her gentle concern for all injured creatures from the smallest bug to animals in need of help which she willingly nursed, asked anxiously, "Were they seriously ill like Omah?" Joshua put an arm around each one, kissed them both, and answered Sarah first. "Well, Sarah, I think some of them *were* as seriously ill as Omah was." And then to Joseph, "You see, son, they are our neighbors, some of whom we don't know very well, yet, and we certainly didn't know of their pain and the illnesses that they were suffering. When they heard Omah had been healed, saw her up and about again, they wanted the same for themselves or for their family or friends whom they knew were suffering. I want to help each one who asks for help just like Simon, our good Samaritan, helped me. But it's time for bed now, you two. Run along and we can talk more about this tomorrow morning. I promise to try to answer all of your questions." With kisses all around, they were off to bed with only a half-hearted plea to me to stay up a little longer and talk more.

Relieved when we finally got to our room, Joshua sighed, "I didn't expect this, Mim; when I went to help Omah, I didn't think of all the consequences. She really does love to talk as much as she loves to cook, but—"

"But, I remember John told you to use all of your gifts," and then, I admit, I teased, "but I'm not sure he would have known about water becoming the best wine."

Joshua laughed. "No, I'm really thankful no one noticed or told anyone about that. I don't want to distract people from hearing that they can live in the Kingdom of God right now."

"Do you forgive everyone? Is forgiving the way back to full health?"

"Well, I think forgiving is to the spirit what healing is to the body. I'll get up early and hike up the mountain to talk this out with God. If the forgiving-healing connection is clear, then maybe healing *is* a better way of teaching about loving our neighbor."

"The people in Sychar didn't need healing," I ventured. "They seemed to understand the spirit of God living in us when we risk loving, didn't they?" We fell asleep that night wondering.

My husband rose early, awake with the morning star before sunrise. He kissed me lightly on my forehead as he left, and I dreamt of a lush garden, walking along a path, hand in hand with him; then we came to a beautiful little stream, rushing over and around iridescent green, moss covered rocks. We followed a path through the trees along the cool stream, which sparkled as sunlight broke through openings between the lush green, leafy branches. The sound of falling water became louder. Around a bend in the path, we discovered the sound's source and found the wonder and refreshment of a beautiful waterfall. In a brilliant sunbeam, a double rainbow appeared in the mist. I caught my breath in ecstasy and turned to....But the noise of the waterfall woke me. Noise from the street sounded like the waterfall. Wide awake and curious, I jumped up and got dressed; then I went into the big room to find out the noise's cause.

The children were with Thad near the kitchen, still eating. Thomas, Judas, and Philip were talking with Peter and John near the door. "What is it?" I asked.

"The street is full of people who want Joshua to heal them," Philip replied.

"Where is Joshua?" Thomas asked. "Andrew, James, and Simon are out in the street, trying to persuade people to go home, to take care of each other."

"Joshua went up the mountain before dawn. I'll get Salome and go out to see whether we can help the women, maybe give them herbs they can use and share with others."

"Right now, these people seem focused on what they can get, not what they can give," Thomas replied with an edge in his voice. "And what they want is for Joshua to fix them."

"John, get Simon and your brother and go up the mountain to find Joshua. Peter, you and Andrew and Philip can stay here in the street and try to calm people. You must know most of them" I said. "Thomas and Judas, you can stay here at the door and guard the house. Thad can keep the children busy while I go out with Salome."

Salome insisted that I eat before going out. I asked Thad to begin teaching the children a psalm and suggested, "I bless the Lord with everything in me and don't forget a single blessing," saying a few verses for them with enthusiasm that lingered from my dream, the surprising healing of Omah, and all that had followed yesterday. I kissed them, and left saying, "God is blessing us and our neighbors, even though we don't always see it."

Salome opened the door and we slipped out into the crowded street. She carried a basket of warm bread; I carried a basket of fragrant herbs and spices used to treat various symptoms. Instantly surrounded by women wanting help, we listened and shared what we could, the warmth of the bread, recipes, herbs, and spices for remedies. Telling sad stories, many seemed to feel better because Salome and I were listening with kindness. Our caring became contagious as women with whom we talked began to share with others, listening and then passing on what they'd learned, sharing, chattering, smiling.

Working our way down the street crowded with men, women, and children waiting for Joshua, for something spectacular I thought, Salome and I stopped to talk with an older woman sitting on a step. All at once, people rushed up the street past us. I looked up, and at the far end, beyond our door, Joshua was returning. Simon, James, John, Philip, Andrew, and Peter were all with him, attempting to make a path for him through the crowd. Joshua seemed at ease, smiling, talking, healing person after person.

After giving our last bit of bread and ginger, Salome and I made our way back up the street. As I got closer to Joshua, I saw him kneel, touch, and heal someone with a broken leg. Standing again, he gently held the dangling arm of a strapping young farmer who had just taken it out of a sling. Close now, I heard him say, "I forgive you," and then restored the arm as strong as the other. The young farmer grabbed Joshua and gave him a big, warm, hug, babbling a mixture of thanks, shock, tears, and wide-eyed exuberance that his arm was as good as new. Joshua squeezed the hard muscle in the restored arm that the young farmer offered him, and they laughed together in delight.

Whenever Joshua did a more visible and dramatic healing, a little shout of awe and approval would go up from the crowd. But someone, who had been following Joshua as he moved down the street helping one person after another, suddenly shouted out, "Damn you to hell, Joshua of Nazareth!" Shocked, the crowd was suddenly silent. In a frenzied, high-pitched scream, the person continued, "What have you got to do with us? I know you. You can't fool me. You can't hide. You're the Son of God! Leave us alone! Why have you come to love us and take away our illnesses and our excuses and our crutches?"

Simon was about to grab the young man, perhaps drugged, who was flushed, waving his arms, his fist almost in Joshua's face. But Joshua raised his arm slightly to deflect an incoming blow and to stop Simon. He looked the crazed man in the eye, and in his usual, simple command voice, said, "Enough! Come out of him. Peace!" The young man dropped his arms, shuddered, and knelt in front of Joshua, mumbling, "Forgive me, Joshua. I'm sorry." The crowd began to buzz again. Joshua helped the young man to his feet, put his arm around him, and by now, I was close enough to hear Joshua quietly say, "I forgive you, Jonah; you didn't know what you were saying or doing. Go, live your life loving and forgiving others...everyone you meet needs you."

People began to leave our doorway at last, going home for the mid-day meal, and we were able to go into the quiet and relative privacy of our home again. Joshua went first to the children, gave them each a hug, and apologized for not getting back to them that morning to answer their questions as he had promised. "So many people need help," he said. "After our rest this afternoon, I'm all yours. Your mother and I would like to answer your questions and ask you some, just the four of us."

"Great!" they responded in unison. "We learned a psalm this morning," added Sarah. "We'll say it for you..." Joseph made a 'Why did you have to say that?' face, while Joshua, with an arm around each of them, chuckled contentedly and led us to the table now filled with the fish and salads, fruit, bread, and cheese that Susanna had prepared for us.

# CHAPTER SEVENTEEN

Alone in our room that afternoon, we shared our experiences, my dream and his meditation on the mountain. He told me that when he came down to the crowds, he felt as though God were giving them to him and him to them. He said it felt strange but fulfilling, the exchanges deeply satisfying.

That evening, Sabbath dinner was a welcome beginning to a day of rest after our very busy week. We had invited the four fishermen and their families to join us around a large, put-together table spread with brightly colored lengths of cloth I'd found in the market. Lighting oil lamps, blessing God three times, sharing the light, the bread, and the wine, we entered into a holy space, reminded of God's abundant gifts to us, and we were thankful to be sharing what we had been given.

We savored the lentil and barley stew, salads and sesame honey treats as well as our memories of the week, Sychar with Naomi and our new connection to Simon of Cyrene, Omah's amazing recovery, and now the perplexing new notoriety in Capernaum. We all laughed when Joshua told us he felt like he was in the middle of a school of fish this morning, reminding us of his invitation to the four fishermen. Our lives had dramatically changed, but we relaxed around the table with songs, stories, laughter, and anticipation.

Sabbath morning, Joshua and I, with our children and servants, made our way to the synagogue, greeted many old and new friends, and separated with a squeeze of hands. I went in with Sarah and the women, he with Joseph and the men. A quiet murmur spread as some heard about Omah and others being healed for the first time.

An elder read the portion of the Torah assigned for the day, a reading from the scroll beginning, "In the wilderness." The reading began with rules for people setting themselves apart with vows, similar to rules for vows taken to other gods in the region. The passage ended with the triple blessing, from Moses and Aaron, "May the Lord bless you and protect you. May the Lord's eyes light up looking toward you and grant you grace. May the Lord's face incline toward you, and give you peace."

With a Torah reading about vows and blessing, grace, and peace, I wondered what the reading of the Prophets would be. Joshua, as the very respected great master teacher from the Temple, was given the scroll. "A reading from the prophet Isaiah," he said in his full, ringing voice, glancing up to the lattice behind which I was sitting. I could hardly believe my ears when he began, "Let the wilderness and the thirsty land be glad; let the desert rejoice and burst into flower." It was the very passage I'd read after he healed Martha...opening blind eyes, unstopping deaf ears, strengthening tottering knees and feeble arms. So familiar and now so appropriate to what happened this week, Isaiah's vision unfolded in my husband's confident voice, and I felt sure healing would be a part of our future as well.

Meeting him again after the service, we exchanged the Torah blessings and took a step deeper into the stream of public life. Following ancient rhythms, the cycles of the moon, Joshua went out to neighboring villages by foot and boat, fishing, forgiving, healing, and teaching, showing the way of peace through unexpected acts of love. Then, like the tides, he returned home.

Remaining at home in Capernaum, I relished my time with the women and children. I especially enjoyed time with Diana, a bright and curious addition to Susanna and Salome in our household, and her two impish little boys who adored Sarah and Joseph and were favorite playmates of theirs. My heart broke as we talked about problems of women she knew violated by men in their families. How could the story of the good Samaritan and God's command to love change women's lives in our limited circumstances as we and our daughters were too often subjected to abuse and despotic decisions of fathers and husbands? Diana invited friends and relatives, as did Adah and Omah. Women gathered in our home. I listened, asked questions, answered questions, and told stories. They knew my relationship with Joshua was different, was one of mutual respect and partnership. I shared my stories with him....He shared his with me.

Joshua came home from one trip to Tiberius, Nazareth, Cana, Sephoris, and little villages along the way, with great excitement. He had seen Marcus, his beloved Roman friend from his trip to Gaul many years ago. They were both surprised and elated to find one another again. "Can you believe it, Mim?" he had exclaimed. "Somehow the word that there is a healer in the region came to Roman ears and got all the way to Caesarea Maritime where Marcus is stationed. He's a respected centurion and lives there with his wife and his only little son, Hermes, who was deathly ill with a fever. Marcus got a horse and came to Sephoris as fast as he could, before I would move on, not knowing who I was, but just that I could heal very sick people. Well, you can imagine our surprise and delight when he worked his way through the crowd to me. We fell in each other's arms, and then with tears in his eyes, he told me about Hermes."

"Amazing," I said, tearing up a bit at Joshua's excitement to be re-united with the friend he had told me so much about, after whom our son, John Mark, got his second name. "What did you do? Go all the way to Caesarea Maritime with him?" I asked.

"Mim, you may not believe this, but it's true...and why I love that man so much. I, of course, offered to go with him immediately...get another horse, but he said, 'No, I don't need to trouble you or interrupt all you're doing here, Joshua. Just say the word and I know Hermes will be well. I give commands everyday and send one man here or one man there to take care of a problem. I know you. I'm sure you can do the same."

"Oh, my" I said, a bit taken back by the idea.

"I teared up, myself, Mim, feeling overwhelmed at such trust from my old friend. I don't think I've met anyone else who has that kind of faith in me...except maybe you? But, I said, 'So be it,' and felt my energy flow to the little boy, and was sure he was healed. I told Marcus, 'You can go home, then. Hermes is well again...but I'd like to see you again soon, Marcus, out of a crowd, hear what you've been doing, meet your family, and introduce you to mine and tell you what has happened to me, and how I happen to be doing this teaching and healing in Galilee.' He invited me to visit them in Caesarea Maritime as soon as I could, and I agreed to do it soon."

Two weeks of the month, Joshua and I were inseparable. Together, we encountered the turmoil and discontent of tax collectors, merchants, traders, farmers, fishermen, and their wives as well as the plight of the blind, lame, sick, lepers and hurting outcasts of one gender or another. I saw and heard stories of his amazing encounters with the most despised, helpless, and rejected among us. Just as he had tried to explain the power of love to his fellow rabbis in Jerusalem, we now demonstrated that power to all of those we met, including Romans, Samaritans, and foreigners of every kind, offering them all new possibilities.

One afternoon, to get away by ourselves, we hiked up the hill to sit in a meadow overlooking our beautiful lake with windblown fluffy clouds casting ever-changing shadows on the green hills beyond. Despite this peaceful moment as we relaxed on the soft grass, I still felt tense about looks and remarks from some of the leaders of the synagogue and their wives, and commented on the situation. Joshua smiled and put his arm around my shoulder. "Mim, don't focus on their symptoms of fear....We live in the realm of love. We can and we will overcome with love, every time we meet someone. Whoever we are, we're children of God. Love can overcome fear. Mercy and justice can flow over this land," he said, "and let it begin with me."

"And let it begin with *us*, Rabboni," I sighed as I rested my head on his shoulder. He assured me we would find people, one person at a time, who would join us.

"Hmm...no matter what happens," I mused, "if I understand your experience on the road to Jericho...but I'm not sure our synagogue leaders understand you yet."

"No," Joshua laughed. "I don't think so, especially if I ask healed lepers like Simon to show themselves to the priests, so they can re-enter the community. It's too unexpected, but don't worry, Mim. We just have to keep loving without fearing the consequences."

# CHAPTER EIGHTEEN

We began going into the countryside to teach where we could all be together, men, women, and children, not separated as we were in the synagogues where Joshua was more and more criticized for breaking laws and traditions, healing on the Sabbath, eating with outcasts, befriending tax collectors like Matthew who had actually begun to follow him, living below his class, honoring me as a full partner, and treating women with the same respect as men.

One time, going into the country to the grassy slopes overlooking the lake, quite a crowd followed us as we passed villages along the way. The last village's residents must have thought an invading army was coming and quickly hid their supplies, women, and children with only a few men remaining in sight to guard their closed up homes. Joshua greeted them and invited them to join us.

It was an idyllic day with a soft breeze and small clouds playing with the sun. On the grassy, wildflower-sprinkled hillside, the crowd settled down in small family groups and Joshua answered questions and talked about the unexpected, about the open, curious mind of a child, about the power of forgiveness and love, and taught that things are seldom what they seem...the quiet way and the patient way and the soft way do eventually overcome. As the sun moved lower in the sky, Philip interrupted to suggest it was time to start home, to wind things up and send people home before they became too hungry. Practical Philip!

Joshua said, "Well, then let's feed them now before they get into trouble." Thomas said, "You must be joking!" Peter chimed in, "There must be thousands of them." Followed by Philip, demanding, "How can we do that?" Our son nudged Andrew, standing between him and his father, showed him his lunch basket of barley bread and fish. He'd been excited and hadn't eaten his lunch. Andrew stepped back, put his arm around our son, and said, "Joseph, here, has five little loaves and two fish he's offering very generously, but I'm afraid it won't go very far among so many, master."

Looking at me with a smile, Joshua reached out and put his arm around Joseph. He drew him to his side and asked everyone to quiet down. Then he told our servants to go up the hill to help people get reseated and then come back down. When most were settled and curious to see what would happen next, Joshua took a loaf from Joseph's basket, lifted it up to heaven, and said, "Here we are, Lord, your children. Even the breath we take is a gift from you. Blessed are you Lord God, King of the Universe, who brings forth bread from the earth. We offer you and our neighbor what you have given us, so you may be glorified through us."

Joshua broke the loaf and began to pass it to those nearest him, Diana, nearby, offered her basket, so Joshua broke bread into small pieces, and as he passed it, another basket was offered so he broke yet another loaf, and another basket came forward, and more bread was broken; then the same with the two little fish...baskets, pieces, passed, added to, from person to person...a loaf here, a fish there...people were sharing the little they had, just as I had done with the wine in Cana, just as our son did with his lunch basket. A contented hum could be heard as baskets were passed with food, and everyone had a bite, and then another, enough to eat. Joshua asked our servants to go up the hill and collect the baskets at the far end of the crowd. They returned, amazed, with twelve full baskets. Joshua, glowed with delight, held up one basket, motioned toward the others. The crowd quieted. "God has provided again, more than enough for all of us to eat. Thank you for sharing! Thanks be to God!" and all of the people echoed, "Thanks be to God!"

Joshua held up his hand to quiet the crowd again, and said, "It's time to go home and take the good news of God's love and forgiveness and abundance to everyone you meet. Let's start by taking these twelve baskets of food as gifts to the people of the villages we passed through on our way here, people who were afraid we might steal their food. Let's show them that there is enough for everyone."

A cheer went up, and Thomas, Judas, James, Simon, Andrew, Peter, James, John, Bartholomew, Matthew, Philip, and Thad, with the twelve full baskets, led the procession back down the hillside to the nearby village to give gifts of leftover bread and fish to the amazed residents, and then continue on toward Capernaum passing out food in each village along the way. Our children were delightedly dancing around in the middle of it all with Diana and Philip's little boys and other friends all helping in their way.

As the crowd left, Joshua and I were glowing with happiness. He asked me to stay with him and go up the mountain to a cave he knew, to spend the night in peace and quiet. Alone, walking up the now deserted hillside, Joshua reminded me that this amazing miracle of unselfish sharing, that had happened that afternoon before our eyes, especially in such a very large crowd of strangers who'd become neighbors, was the very way God had blessed Job and restored his fortunes, giving him twice as much as he had before his disastrous testing. God had inspired Job's friends and relatives to make a feast for him and bring him gifts, share their abundance and bless him.

Joshua's teaching that day had been brilliant, but what an unforgettable experience to inspire so many to let go of selfishness and share with one another! We relished the quiet time to ourselves to absorb it all, to thank God in silence before our next challenge.

# CHAPTER NINETEEN

When we returned to Capernaum the next day, excitement was in the air. At the head of the synagogue's request, a delegation from Jerusalem had arrived and conferred with the synagogue's leaders. Thomas told us that a rabbi had come to the door and asked to meet Joshua to discuss some charges, to debate and clarify what was acceptable. Joshua sent Judas to ask them to come to our home the next morning.

After our mid-day meal, Joshua asked our servants to gather around the table. They were nervous. "I know you're concerned about the meeting tomorrow," he began, "but I want to set your minds at ease. We'll simply do what we do every day and make people welcome and comfortable and share what we have and ask God to bless us." Joshua paused and smiled. "Remember, just be thankful for what is given. We don't have to try to be powerful; with love and truth, we will be. We'll do nothing special and yet leave nothing undone."

Joshua, with an arm around Sarah and Joseph, who had gone to sit on either side of him, continued, "If we release our will and simply ask for God's will to be done, we can relax and live with the opportunity that comes, rather than live with anxiety and illusion. Help one another today and tomorrow will take care of itself."

The next morning, as I opened my eyes and stretched, Joshua, with his eyes twinkling, began a familiar psalm, "The Lord is my light and my salvation, the stronghold of my life, of whom should I be afraid?"

I smiled and responded, "When my adversaries attack me and slander me, they'll stumble and fall...."

"Though a throng were to encamp against me," Joshua smiled at the exaggeration, "still my heart would not fear. Even though war were to rise against me, still I'd be unafraid."

He took the hand I reached out to him, and we continued the psalm together, "Only one thing have I asked, that I may live in the house of the Lord all the days of my life, to behold the beauty of the Lord." That was enough to contemplate, but we continued until we chanted together, "I believe that I'll see the goodness of the Lord in the land of the living! Wait for the Lord, be strong, and take courage. Yes, wait for the Lord!" A morning kiss, and we were ready to meet the surprises as they unfolded. Who had come from Jerusalem? How would they question Joshua? Would they be open to his teaching?

As we were eating breakfast, Omah, who didn't want to miss anything, came with some of her famous fig, almond, and pine-nut cakes. Peter and the other fishermen arrived, and then the men from Jerusalem. Chosen by Joseph Caiaphas and Annas, they were a well-balanced group of six scribes and six rabbis known for their strict interpretation of the law; six of them Pharisees, six Sadducees. Hiding our disappointment that neither Nicodemus nor other open-minded followers of Hillel and Gamaliel were among them, we greeted each one warmly and invited them to the table.

Omah, whose father had been head of the synagogue before he died, greeted the current leader as he arrived with his wife and led them to seats at the table's far end. Elders and their wives followed, the women separated as was their custom, sitting on benches behind the men at the table. Soon the room filled with the curious of one persuasion or another, all wanting to be part of this auspicious visit from Jerusalem.

This was a great opportunity for local people to see how the Temple authorities would respond to Joshua, who taught with such authority, healing diseased minds and bodies, treating men and women as equals, socializing with the not so respectable fringes of society, even Romans and Samaritans, treating his servants as students and friends, and healing even on the Sabbath. Was this the new fashion in Jerusalem? Standing room only now, the room became packed right up to the door.

Thomas, at the door, caught Joshua's eye, and asked through hand gestures what he should do now with no more room, and more people outside. Joshua nodded, and in a loud, pleasant voice, said, "Welcome, friends! Peace!" The room quieted as quickly as the wind when a storm passed by at sea, the hush passing out the door to those still outside. It was clear from Joshua's tone with these first words that he was at ease and at home, the rest of us invited to join him. "We will speak loudly enough for everyone to hear." Then turning to the men at the table, "Welcome, friends. How may I help you?"

His colleague, but a conservative rabbi in the School of Hillel, Daniel, responded, "The synagogue leader, Arrah Bar-Hanani, sent a letter to the Council asking our opinion of your teaching and of your conduct in the synagogue and in the countryside. Coming from the Temple, you have a reputation for being highly skilled in understanding and interpreting scriptures, but it seems to be new teaching, and Bar-Hanani wants to know if it is approved teaching."

Joshua smiled, "I'm sure that you've explained to him how we discuss possible meanings and applications of each word, each law, for hours, wringing everything that we can from Moses, the prophets, the psalmists, and the sages who've gone before us."

"Indeed," Seth, a scribe, joined in. "But since you left our discussions in Jerusalem, it seems that you have...." He hesitated to choose his words carefully, "It seems that you have been acting outside of the law, teaching these people a new understanding, perhaps endangering the wrath of God, questioning their faith in our traditional teaching, and failing strictly to keep the laws."

"No," Joshua drew the word out slowly. "I have been encouraging people to live fully in the spirit of the law, Seth, to follow in actuality the advice of the prophets."

"That's not what we hear," replied Amos, another rabbi. "How can you break the laws of the Sabbath in front of everyone at the synagogue? Heal someone in the middle of your commentary on the reading of the prophet?"

"Ah, Amos," replied Joshua, "I'm glad you asked. Is it lawful to do good or to do harm on the Sabbath? If a child falls into a well, or a donkey falls into a ditch, would it not be lawful to pull them out?"

"Well, doesn't the law clearly say that we are to do no work on the Sabbath?" replied Amos, somewhat defensively, beginning to see where his question might lead him.

"What constitutes work? An action you do to further your own interests, or an action that you do to further God's interests?" Joshua asked.

Samuel jumped into the argument, each of our visiting scholars taking a turn. "The limits of the law are clear, the exceptions are clear: either you follow the rules or you don't. How can you be sure of God's interests? How can you introduce new exceptions on the basis of your understanding of what God's interests might be? How do you know that God isn't punishing you, or your donkey, or your child, in your hypothetical situations?"

"Samuel, I don't know where to begin," Joshua chuckled, rubbing his chin thoughtfully. "Our history, our prophets, in incident after incident, revelation after revelation, teach us that 'God has loved us with an everlasting love,' to quote Ezekiel. Do you remember that God has chosen time after time to bless us, to protect us, to use the weakest, the most unlikely, among us to save us from the consequences of our own pride and selfishness? Hasn't prophet after prophet told us that God loves us and simply asks us to love in return, love those who come into our lives, respond to the need of others?"

"Not necessarily on the Sabbath," responded Daniel. "Which law takes precedence when there is a conflict? How do we love and keep other laws and statutes?"

"Daniel, the Sabbath was made for us...to rest and be thankful, to realize the abundance God has given us in the first six days of every week, more than enough to enjoy and to share with others," Joshua responded. "If God then sends someone with need into our lives on the Sabbath, how can we withhold the blessings we enjoy?"

Amos started, "But—"

Joshua uncharacteristically interrupted, perhaps reading his mind, "But, Amos, don't be afraid. You're concerned about failing to keep every requirement of the law regardless of the spirit behind it, aren't you? Do you remember the passage from Micah that we discussed several years ago? Isn't it relevant?" At this point, my husband proceeded calmly to quote from memory a rather lengthy passage from the prophet:

"'With what shall I come before the Lord, and bow myself before God on high? Shall I come before him with burnt offerings, with calves a year old? Will the Lord be pleased with thousands of rams, or with ten thousand rivers of oil? Shall I give my firstborn for my transgression, the fruit of my body for the sin of my soul?' God has shown you, O man, what is good; and what does the Lord require of you but to do what is fair and just in every encounter with another, to love being kind and compassionate, and to walk humbly with your God."

With Micah's words, the discussion moved from whether or not it was legal to heal on the Sabbath, to what might be required for forgiveness, what it might mean to do justice, to love kindness, or to walk humbly with our God. Seth began this part of the discussion, including questions about the unacceptable people with whom Joshua was seen talking, dining, stopping to touch, to heal. Joshua posed questions to them about any restrictions they could find in the law concerning love of neighbor...whether walking humbly with God might mean responding openly to the need of whomever we met....As this part of the discussion developed, we heard a noise on the roof above us and dust began to fall.

Despite Joshua having reminded me to expect the unexpected, I admit I was surprised, perhaps shocked is a better word, and wondered what was going on. Who was destroying our roof and interrupting this important meeting? In the thick of their discussion, while concentrating on the fine points of their differences, Joshua and his colleagues were at first oblivious to the disruption, but as the sound became louder and as a hole in the roof opened to the sky above us, Joshua looked up; then he caught my eye with a lifted eyebrow and a bemused expression that silently asked me, "So what surprise is coming next? What's this about?"

I shrugged and looked up again to see that tiles were hastily being removed. I threw my shawl over my head to protect myself from the falling bits and pieces. I saw one unfamiliar face peer down into the room, then another, then more tiles were removed over the center of the table in front of us, and soon a kind of pallet was carefully being lowered on ropes through the hole in the ceiling; then I heard Simon and Philip's voices from above, asking what these men thought they were doing, and a couple of the men, blurting out anxiously in rapid succession, "He just fell off the roof of the house we're building. He can't move. He's barely breathing! He'll die unless Joshua can heal him quickly! We had to try!" While shouting at Simon and Philip, they continued to lower the pallet in front of us. Lying on it was the limp, pale body of a workman whose eyes were wide with fright. Pallet and body now gently settled on the table, four worried faces looked down on us from the corners of the hole in our roof.

One of them spoke, "Excuse us, our friend just had a terrible accident. Help us, please!"

Another one added, "We were afraid he'd die if we waited. We'll fix your roof again."

Joshua looked up and smiled at these men. His eyes glistened. He stood and said, "All right, I will." He looked at the frightened man lying in front of him and gently brushed the dust from the man's hair. He calmly and deliberately said, "Your sins are forgiven, Ben." He paused, and added with a smile, "and I forgive you, too." The man's eyes blinked. That was not exactly what he or his friends were hoping for or expecting.

The men sitting around our table were now more disturbed by what Joshua had just said than they were with the interruption and the near dead body lying in front of us with all the plaster dust. "Out of line!" "No one can forgive sins, except God!" "The nerve!" "What does he think he's doing!" "Annas has to straighten him out!" "That's absolute blasphemy!" Disgruntled mumbling came from every side. Joshua sighed. Silently standing by Ben's body, he looked questioningly around the table, into the eyes of each colleague for any sign of the mercy and kindness they had just been discussing.

Finding none, Joshua continued, "Let me ask you another question, then, my friends. Which is easier? To say to this man, 'I forgive you,' or to say to him, 'I heal you'?"

A stone cold silence fell around the table, an almost breathless silence in the room as local onlookers wondered what would happen next to their neighbor. Joshua, still reluctant, not in a hurry, looked around the table at angry faces again, looked for any inkling of compassion. Finding none, he quietly said, "So that you all know that we *do* have the power to forgive, Ben, I not only forgive you, I heal you. Get up and get going! Lift the pallet up to your friends, be more careful, and bring them with you when you come back after work this afternoon to repair the roof."

That was the end of the discussion with the delegation. The four friends let out whoops of relief and joy as Ben stood up on the table, good as new, but embarrassed to be standing on a table in the middle of such an important looking group of people. He lifted the pallet back up to his friends amid loud cheers from those standing in the room. He kneeled to thank Joshua, and then with a jump, grabbed onto a beam and pulled himself up through the hole in the roof to be grabbed and hugged by his friends.

People inside and outside the room were buzzing with amazement, relief, excitement, those closer telling those farther back what they'd seen. Many knew Ben, knew he was a daredevil, not afraid of heights or of taking chances if there were a risky task to be done on a roof. Stories were repeated from person to person. Hadn't they said he was tempting God with some of his antics? Maybe he needed to be forgiven before he could be healed? Talk didn't stop as everyone went home for a mid-day meal.

Joshua, still standing, tried to speak to each one of the delegation as they stood to leave. Resentment of Joshua, who had left their comfortable life of orderly, theoretical argument for this disorderly, spontaneous way of teaching and healing and responding to such interruptions, simmered. The tension was palpable. They couldn't argue with the healing they'd seen right before their eyes, but they didn't like it.

By the grace of God, we had come through this challenge by the synagogue and the establishment in Jerusalem with an unexpected twist, the arrival of someone who desperately needed help, unable to move, barely alive, barely able to breathe, a metaphor for our country's condition, I thought, desperately needing Joshua to forgive and breathe new life into it, enable it to function in good health. That incomprehensible grace, that unexpected twist, focused a searing light on our differences like a strike of lightning, heightening the contrast between Joshua and the rest of us. Never before seeing my husband in this light, I wondered with the others.

What would be the consequences of this encounter? We didn't have long to wait. Joshua had brushes with the crowds wanting to take him by force to make him king. It seemed his popularity and notoriety were spreading out of control as people still looked outside of themselves for a magical entrance into their imagined Kingdom of God and a perfect world. Joshua seemed to withdraw more and more into silence, to seek the solitude of early morning hikes into the hills, feeling his message was being lost.

Three of John's disciples arrived one day with news from prison. The cousins still had an intuitive connection and sent messages to each other in quotes that I doubted the messengers understood. Joshua felt grateful for his cousin's concern and returned our news and encouragement to him.

Feeling imprisoned by the celebrity status we had unintentionally acquired, wanting to continue to share our simple
message of God's love and forgiveness, we decided to send
our most devoted students and servants, men and women,
out to villages to tell the story of our good Samaritan and to
show the power of love while we stayed home, hoping our
students and servants could do what now seemed impossible
for us to do.

That week, we had a visit from Justus, swaggering up to
our door on a new spirited, Arabian horse, attracting a lot of
attention from our neighbors and passersby who wondered
who this was with such a fine animal. While I wouldn't say
Justus was completely vain, he did please himself with the best,
most prestigious animal and trappings he could afford from
proceeds of his caravan raids. Fit and always well-groomed
himself, Justus had a good heart and believed wholeheartedly
in the rightness of his cause and excused his little vanities for
the impression they would make on others, all for the good
of the cause, he thought. He'd come to Galilee to consult
with his father, Judas, his uncles, brothers, and cousins, who
were all involved in the Zealot cause here. Justus and Joshua
again had a long talk into the night, arguing about the waste
of Joshua's popularity with the crowds, as Justus saw it, and
the futility of a rebellion, as Joshua saw it, trying to make
peace by force. They again parted with great affection, but
still unable to persuade the other.

Our students and servants returned with glowing reports
of their experiences, and so we sent them and others out, two
by two, to tell their stories, forgive, and heal throughout the
region. We were content with this new phase of our journey,
although it was not without its challenges. Peter, for one, still

seemed to have difficulty understanding Joshua's way. One day we were sitting around our table, listening to stories of their experiences and Joshua's questions and teaching, when Peter complained about some of the men going with their wives, and then, almost out of the blue, said, "And Miriam, why is she always at your side? She seems to know more, be closer to you than we men are. It's not proper. You need to train us men to sit on your right and on your left." My mouth must have dropped open; I felt stung and wondered how Joshua would answer.

Joshua just brushed Peter's complaint aside with his usual patience and humor. With a light laugh, he answered, "Well, Peter, I suppose I will just have to make her male, then. But I want to hear more about how you and Andrew did in Gennesaret?" And the moment passed.

But two months after our visit from Justus, late one afternoon just before supper, Joel, John and Joshua's cousin from Jerusalem, arrived at our door, pale and exhausted. Thad, who was at the door and let him in, went to fetch water to bathe his feet and ask Susanna to bring some spiced wine for him and all of us to drink. I could see from his face and body language that he was torn with urgency and reluctance. Joshua sensed this, also. "It's all right, Joel. Just tell us what you need to say."

Joel closed his eyes tightly, as though it might not be so bad if he didn't see the consequences on others of his news, which despite the two full days of rushed travel, he had not come to terms with himself. Simple, first...just the conclusion, "John was beheaded."

My heart stopped beating for a moment. Joshua, Thad, Susanna, and I, the four of us in the big, suddenly very empty room, were stunned. We sat in silence for a while before Joshua found his voice, "Tell us more, Joel."

It was as though Joel couldn't go on, didn't know where to start. "He...Herod—"

Joshua interrupted, if you could call it that, to encourage Joel, "Just start at the beginning," which Joel did, after another deep breath.

"Herod had a big celebration of his birthday and invited everyone that is anyone in Judea and Galilee...all of his officers and ambassadors, our esteemed prefect, Pontius Pilate, and all of his Roman officers and magistrates from Jerusalem, Joppa, Caesarea Maritime, Sephoris, and Tiberius, and then Annas and Caiaphas, and a group of us priests and administrators who assist them, to a big feast at Machaerus. I think he wanted to impress us with the power and magnificence of his fortress...and we were impressed. The main event was a big, lavish banquet on the birthday itself, and he spared no expense to fill the tables with delicacies while musicians entertained us and we ate and drank, and I, for one, thought he might not be so bad after all. This was such a generous show of goodwill to all of the leading men of Galilee and Judea and quite an accomplishment to get all of us together. The climax of the banquet was an extraordinary dance performed by his and Herodias' daughter, Salome, who is very beautiful and seemed to float above the floor as she gracefully swayed and moved to the music, entrancing us all. Herod was so overcome with delight when she had finished that he called her to him, and loudly, perhaps under the influence of wine and the spectacle, thanked her profusely and offered her anything she would like up to half of his kingdom. She was demure and asked to consult her mother before deciding, and we all approved of this wise and gracious response on her part. But we were stunned a few minutes later when she bowed before Herod and asked for John's head on a large charger."

The shock to Herod and the others in the banquet hall couldn't have been greater than it was to us, even though we had heard the terrible news, "John was beheaded" first. Still, this story had turned so suddenly from a celebration of lavish beauty to unspeakable, callous cruelty. I was appalled, as I knew Herodias and her daughter, Salome, and had attended meals and banquets with them from time to time when we lived in Jerusalem.

"Poor Herod," my sympathetic husband murmured. "He was caught in his own trap... and John was caught with him."

"Yes," echoed Joel, "caught in the web, maybe not so happy with his brother's wife after all. His embarrassment is a high price to pay...powerless to work his way out of it with any dignity."

My mind was racing, I still hadn't found voice to express my horror and the presentiments of power and intrigue rotting our humanity at every level. Joshua had said, "Don't be afraid; perfect love casts out fear." But this seemed to be a very big challenge. What quirky turn of a power struggle could catch us or others we loved.

Thad hadn't spoken either. Suddenly, he started to cry, and jumped up and ran out of the door. "Poor Thad," I sighed, refocused from my own grief to his. "Oh, poor Thad!" and I began to weep, too.

The terrible news that John had been beheaded in a capricious event at court spread through the village and countryside. Thad, Joel, Joshua, and I went into deep mourning along with Andrew, Philip, and their wives, and then the others as they heard the news. A few of John's other disciples came to join us and tell us of burying his body. We told each other many stories of John, through tears and laughter. Joshua assured us that nothing, not even death, could separate us from the love of God, and with pain in his voice, quoted Job, "The Lord gives; the Lord takes away. Blessed be the name of the Lord."

With the loss of his cousin, Joshua decided we should go up to Jerusalem early for Passover; he wanted to contact Justus again, to try to avoid losing him in a foolish power struggle. It wouldn't be an easy trip. Whenever we went out, word would precede us and people would flock to see Joshua to ask for healing, a favor, his advice, or to make him king. Occasionally, some wanted to complain or argue with him, and now and then, some simply wanted to thank him again for something he'd done for them, or for a relative, or a friend.

# CHAPTER TWENTY

Forty days before Passover, we traveled once again with our family and servants toward Jerusalem, following the lush Jordan valley route toward Jericho, but the way seemed empty and barren now without the prospect of seeing John. His followers tried to carry on. We stopped briefly to visit them, and then made the long climb up toward Jerusalem with heavy hearts.

At the top of the ascent, we again arrived in Bethany at the hillside home of Martha and Simon and were surprised to find John Mark, who had just returned home from his long trip with Uncle Joseph. Our son was transformed into a young man of the world. On cushions in the shade of the fig tree in Martha's courtyard, we all gathered on rugs around one low, put-together table to hear all about his adventures while we enjoyed Martha's familiar, and yet very special, aromatic goat stew with fresh bread and my favorite nut and honey filled dessert. It was a love feast, with stories tumbling out in rapid succession, one after the other, again to both laughter and tears. Lamps were lit.

Music, dancing, and stories continued into the evening. We'd lost John, but John Mark, his namesake, was safe at home, cause enough for thanksgiving and celebration.

Eventually, Joshua suggested we retire to the terrace outside our room. After making the rounds, kissing everyone goodnight, we climbed the steps into the glorious starlit darkness, each carrying a small lamp from the table. We settled comfortably onto a cushioned bench, and gazed up at the stars shining brilliantly as lights below began to dim.

"Glory to God in the Highest," Joshua exclaimed. I nodded and joined him, "And Peace to all on earth!" We were deeply content to be reunited with John Mark and our family in Bethany.

Silent for a while, we enjoyed the quiet of the terrace and the warmth of being together, in spite of the fresh evening chill. With Joshua's arm around my shoulder, we took pleasure in quietly observing the star spangled sky. I wondered whether our servants really understood us. They were still swayed by the gossip of the crowds and the swagger of Temple representatives.

My thoughts drifted to an earlier conversation with Philip, who had said that Joshua and Peter had had another sharp exchange on the road that morning. Peter was talking with James and John and Andrew about the last big crowd. Joshua had overheard and asked Peter what was so exciting. Peter replied, "People say—" Joshua shook his head. "No, Peter, who do *you* say I am?" Peter responded, "You're the promised Messiah from God, you—" Joshua stopped him. "I suspect that may be true, but don't tell anyone. Do you know what that means? It means my way will be rejected, and I will suffer and die." Peter started to argue, but Joshua stopped him, "You just don't understand, Peter." Philip had said that a dead silence had fallen on all of them as it did on me when he told me.

Joshua gave my shoulder a little squeeze and said, "Mim, my love, I've been thinking about what's next. We read Isaiah's prophecies before we started on this path. If I understand them, the only way others can know this peace, this paradise we enjoy, is through our sacrifice, although I keep looking and asking God for another way."

"It seems we've sacrificed so much already—"

He interrupted me with a kiss and changed the subject. "Now that we're back, I'll have to go to Bethlehem again, to check on the flocks with Jude and be sure they are ready to drive the lambs into Jerusalem for the Passover sacrifices, but every time I go, I still feel the pain of my tribe's loss of their baby boys because Herod the Great wanted to kill me after hearing about my birth from the Wise Men almost forty years ago." He paused, swallowed. "Maybe I'm more sensitive than usual after Herod Antipas beheaded John, but I still feel a loss like that is more difficult to heal than a broken bone or a blind eye," he acknowledged with a sad smile. "I'll have to try to talk with them again about forgiveness and peace, and I wonder how I can."

"Oh, my love," I responded. "Herod the Great's cruelty seems so difficult to forgive, even after all of this time, killing every baby boy in the area to be sure he killed you, but—"

Joshua gently interrupted me again as I faltered at the idea of the babies killed. "I've been haunted with those stories all of my life, but I need to help them forgive."

Tears filled my eyes as I thought of the pain of those mothers and fathers after our joy embracing John Mark again today. I admitted, "I'm not sure you can."

"I'm not sure, either," Joshua sighed. "Hatred of Herod the Great and his family runs so deep in everyone...everyone lost someone. It doesn't help that Herod the Great later insanely killed his own two sons in the palace."

Greek tragedies and other stories of people killing their own children horrified me. "What tormented, twisted thinking led him to do that?" I blurted out. "After killing your own children, how could you live with yourself?" I asked. "What a devastating hell people create for themselves!"

Joshua put his arm around me. "I'm sure it is, Mim." After a few minutes of silence, wondering what more could be said, he stood and began pacing. "Men in Bethlehem resent me for not leading them in a fight against Herod Antipas and Rome. I hear something every time I'm there." He paused, "I haven't sought revenge. That's what they expect...tradition, revenge...a strange honor even if it means we all die in the attempt. They want revenge, no matter what," he sighed, "and the worst of it is I suspect that revenge will now be offered by Justus and his Zealots and not by me."

"Can't you show them how futile more killing is...? We've seen so much misery," I said as I looked up at the stars again. "Why do we need to be revenged? Why can't we see it is a never-ending cycle...be brave, stop it, and forgive?"

"It's more difficult when you've suffered an outrageous loss, Mim. For them, all Romans are the enemy because they support Herod and Herod's...."

I nodded. "But our friend Pilate is the prefect, after all, and he says they're doing good, protecting people, keeping order."

"Well, I suppose if we really lived in the Kingdom of God, we wouldn't need protection for safe travel and free trade, would we? Isn't it ironic that while they proclaim "Roman Peace," the emperors are still busy killing their wives, their children, and one another just as Herod did? Their Roman Peace isn't my idea of peace."

I stood up, too. "I don't think there'll be real peace on earth until—"

Joshua interrupted and took my hands. "Mim, men have hoarded and competed and been violent since the beginning of time. Why? What sense does it make? What is ever really gained from violating others or seeking revenge? It's a vicious circle that never accomplishes anything very lasting or satisfying. What can I do to bring peace? That's all I've ever wanted."

I had no answer. I wanted peace, too. He took a deep breath, "None of the men in Bethlehem have traveled through as much of the empire as John Mark or I have; none of them have seen the vastness of Roman power. Our rebels would be tortured and crucified or enslaved like rebels in other provinces. I just can't lead men into a futile battle. I want to prevent suffering, not heal broken bodies and spirits afterwards."

"I understand, but I don't think people know what to do. Their crops are destroyed in raids and reprisals, and they struggle to survive even though they don't want to be involved.  What can they do? What can we do?" I asked, thinking I sounded too much like Justus.

"Every system is made up of individuals choosing," Joshua replied with quiet determination. "Peaceful change *can come* one person at a time, one choice at a time. A tax collector can abuse his power or be compassionate, as can a soldier or a priest or a merchant or a husband or a wife.  Each of us has to choose...choice after choice."

I sighed and nodded my agreement. "I suppose you're right," I acknowledged.

Pensive again, he said, "This trip will be critical...have dangerous consequences," and then added, "but I'm tired of thinking about all of this; aren't you? I'd just like to go to bed with you." We laughed and kissed. He could always bring a smile to my face no matter how tense and serious our discussion. After a very long day, the challenges we were facing seemed enormous, and I was happy to let them go. We were both ready to sink into the comfort of our bed and dream.

# CHAPTER TWENTY-ONE

The next morning, we went down to the aroma of warm bread fresh from the oven and more news from Martha. The children went to visit their old tutor. John Mark went back to Jerusalem to see his friend Mathias. Alphaeus, who'd heard that we'd stopped with Martha on our way home, came with Judas to greet us. Afterwards, Joshua and I climbed back up to our terrace to resume our previous evening's conversation.

We had just reached the terrace when I asked the question I woke with, "What danger? Will you meet Justus? Do you think the Romans know about his rebellion yet?"

"Possibly," Joshua replied. "There's always the possibility of betrayal, and yes, I'll see Justus sometime soon. The danger is that he may try to persuade the men in Bethlehem to fight to make me king, unless I can persuade them to give up what I'm certain is doomed to failure."

I soaked in the warmth of the morning sun, but I felt dismayed at the prospect of fighting and a bit guilty that I was here talking about it with Joshua while my sister was bustling about down below with her servants, even though we were her guests. "What will we do if the Zealots try to make you king? What will the priests do?" I couldn't hide a nervous chuckle. The impossibility of it all seemed strangely funny to me.

Joshua smiled, too. "I don't want to imagine," he said. "Nothing about their plan can work. Fighters can't bring in the King of Peace. It just doesn't work. Rome won't go away unless God draws them away."

"Like Pharaoh," I said, then returned to the subject of the approaching Passover. "When will you go?"

"That depends on what I hear from Simon. I asked him to go into Jerusalem to find Justus, find out when and where I can meet him, and find out when and if he plans to go to Bethlehem."

"You men talk and decide to fight or not, but we all bear the consequences," I sighed.

"Yes, my love, we all bear the consequences, full partners in love and war."

That afternoon, Justus' brother Simon arrived back in Bethany. We three went down to a quiet corner of the court-yard to sit in the fig tree's shade. Lazarus and Martha's husband, walked in and I went on to the kitchen to find Martha and ask her to join us. We brought out her special spiced wine and sweets, settled onto the cushions, and poured the pleasant elixir as Simon continued his report with barely sup-pressed excitement, "Justus says they are planning the upris-ing for Passover when the roads and Jerusalem will be full of pilgrims. They'll have Zealots in each of the hill country towns, on the pilgrim routes, and in the larger towns like Jericho and Capernaum, ready to fight as the word is passed that fighting has begun in Jerusalem.

"There'll be Zealots in villages near the fortresses ready to intercept messengers, and to attack soldiers who leave. They won't fight pitched battles, but strategically, as they have on the roads where surprise and knives are as effective as swords. He says attacks throughout the country will show Zealot strength and win support from the people. When Jerusalem is free, Justus believes that the priests baptized by John can reform the Temple and unite Pharisees, Sadducees, and Essenes."

Simon paused to sip the spiced wine as Joshua raised his eyebrows in wide-eyed amazement at the last part of the agenda, before breaking out in a broad grin. "Now that would be a real miracle! My dear friend certainly hasn't lost his idealism or love of fantasy."

We were all overwhelmed. Simon leaned over and picked up one of Martha's stuffed dates, ignored Joshua's comment, and continued. "And then he plans to restore the throne of David, have you anointed king. The crowds will love it! He wants to tell your tribesmen in Bethlehem, and get them to be your official bodyguards."

There was stunned silence. Simon continued, hazarding still more enthusiasm. "He knows there are priests who won't be happy with this part of his plan. It's no secret that some of your ideas irritate them, but you're the right one, the only one Justus trusts to be king. You and Miriam have the bloodline rights, you know, she from Saul and you from David. No one can argue there could be a better combination...descendants of the first two anointed kings."

While Joshua and Justus had argued about this privately in Galilee, Justus still had such elaborate plans for our lives, sucking us into the abyss of his power struggle. Joshua looked drawn, though Simon, warming to his story, didn't notice. "Just think, Joshua; you can rule a peaceful kingdom where Temple worship is pure, where the poor are cared for, the sick are healed, the blind can see, where no one cheats or steals because everyone has enough, where mercy and justice will flow like a river to all the world. Jerusalem can be the capital of the world, not Rome. Others will hear and bring tribute as they did to Solomon, come to you for wise judgment."

We were still silent, wondering how to respond. Simon continued in a more matter-of-fact, confidential tone about the coup. "Jerusalem will be the focus of the attack, of course, for all that it symbolizes and because it's the center of power, with the largest garrison of soldiers. Jerusalem will definitely be the most difficult to attack and take over. That's why Justus is planning this for Passover when we can outnumber the soldiers at least ten to one. The men from Bethlehem can come in armed when they bring the sheep for the sacrifices, join the battle, and protect you once other Zealots, blending with the pilgrims, have taken the lead."

Joshua put down his wine cup. Simon's enthusiasm—Simon who'd followed us for three or four years apparently without understanding, I thought—presented a daunting challenge to Joshua. To persuade Justus—and now Simon as well as his brothers, followers, and tribesmen—that this dream would only turn into a tragic nightmare for all involved, seemed to be overwhelming to me, and I suspected to Joshua also from his facial expression.

"The tragedy," I said quietly, "is that everyone thinks he is doing good, pleasing God."

Joshua nodded and silently mouthed, "I love you."

Simon didn't notice. He held his cup out toward Martha, who poured him more spiced wine. "Justus is organizing the attacks on Jerusalem and here in the south while our father is coordinating attacks in Galilee. With a few of his aides, Justus plans to go to Bethlehem in three days to recruit new Zealots. You can meet him there and help with the planning. More men than usual can easily herd sheep into Jerusalem for the Passover sacrifices. They'll be unnoticed in the confusion of traditional activity. The Romans won't interfere or watch too closely."

Joshua stood up. "Thank you, Simon. Your brother is planning more than I imagined. That's a lot for me to think about, and from the looks on their faces, the others don't know what to think of it all either!" We all laughed. "I need a walk. Mim, will you?"

"Yes, I'd love to. Do you need help preparing supper, Martha?"

"No, you go on," she said as she stood to gather up the things we'd brought from the kitchen.

Simon, suddenly a young Zealot it seemed, still excited with his news, offered to help Martha while my brother and brother-in-law, remained seated, silently trying to digest what they had just heard.

As soon as we were alone on the path up the mountain, Joshua broke his silence. "My trip to Bethlehem will be even more complicated than I thought. I'm so tired of this.

They've been raiding caravans since before I was attacked. I offer an alternative to fighting and revenge, but they don't want it and people suffer and die."

"I understand how those who've lost family join the fight, mistaking revenge for justice," I said, asking one question right after the other, "but how many wounded have you healed? How can you break the cycle? How can you persuade them before it's too late?"

"I think I'll have to show them, Mim. I can only live the way myself, and tell the best stories of my life! Justus' fantasy invitation to an ideal, righteous revolution followed by everyone living happily ever after in a perfect kingdom with a perfect Temple is very appealing. It's everyone's dream, our built in longing for paradise. Who can resist fighting for it?"

"It seems as though good intentions are the enemy of...of entering real paradise now," I replied.

"People forget our stories. God's paradise can't be entered by violence or achievement. Mighty angels guard it, barring anyone who tries to enter by force. Paradise can't be reached except by trust and love."

"But all of our histories are about one battle after another, one group after another, trying to conquer and control," I said. "I think those stories about battles make people feel fearful and hopeless or determined to fight to win battle after battle at any cost. They forget the stories of paradise and peace."

"They're definitely not about peace on earth. You're right; every victory is just the starting place for another battle. Even their gods struggle with jealousy, trickery, and revenge."

While talking, we walked up through an olive grove to a knoll overlooking the mountains and valleys surrounding Jerusalem. We stopped to gaze at this expanse of life in all of its vibrant variation spreading before our eyes. Joshua put an arm around my shoulder; my arm slipped around his waist. After a few minutes, he turned me around to face him.

Holding both my hands, holding my eyes in his searching gaze, he asked, "Do you realize what's coming, Mim? We're being drawn out of our paradise into a battle others are choosing. Whatever comes, we have to focus on our love for each other and for God. However we're tempted to judge good and evil, we must trust God's love, give thanks as difficult as it may be, keep loving and forgiving; and leave the rest to God."

With a knot in my stomach, not yet seeing all that he did, I replied, "I'll try. I know nothing can separate us from God's love or our love for each other."

Joshua drew me into a strong yet gentle embrace, a kiss that lasted an eternity. When we finally drew apart, my head on his chest, listening to his steady heartbeat, he said barely above a whisper, "I wish I could do it all by myself, spare you the pain, but I need you. You're my love and my joy."

"And you're mine," I whispered in return, content to be in his arms wherever he was.

As we started back down the path toward Martha's, we were silent. After a while, Joshua asked what I thought I could do now before Passover when his life seemed so uncertain. He didn't want anything to interfere with my preparations for our largest Passover feast ever.

That reminded me of the Zealots again...and my same question about why we all celebrated Passover and yet Zealots didn't trust God to free us again.

Joshua shrugged and smiled. "Well, that was an embarrassing departure of slaves with so much wealth, wasn't it? Except for the death of Pharaoh's son, I imagine there's no mention of it in Egyptian history. If it weren't for God's command to remember it every year, we would probably forget it too. They say that history repeats itself, but it seems it's the history of fighting, not the history of trusting God. People don't seem to think that could happen again."

# CHAPTER TWENTY-TWO

The next morning, I awoke from a dream, feeling a vague apprehension, and rolled over to see Joshua watching me. His warm smile felt like sunshine as he put an arm around me, kissed me, and began, "Great things you've done, O Lord my God!"

Reflecting his delight, I continued, "How great your wonders and your plans for us!" A good psalm to start the day as we declared together, "There is none who can be compared with you."

We kissed again, sealing our love, and our willingness to continue discovering together where God would lead us.

That morning at Martha and Simon's urging, we decided to stay with them for a few more days before going on to Jerusalem. We'd been gone so long there were so many stories to tell each other, but now Justus and Zealot plans demanded our attention.

Joshua sent an urgent message to his brother James, who knew so many in Bethlehem and would be a wise companion. Joshua asked him to come to Bethany and then to go on with him to Bethlehem so they could talk on the way. But first, he wanted time alone on the mountain, and asked me to come later with food. Late that afternoon, I found him on the knoll where we'd talked the afternoon before. I gave him the news of Bethany and asked about his day. "Wonderful, Mim...peace and quiet...aware of God's presence in all of this beauty."

"It's unbelievably beautiful," I agreed as I turned to gaze at the hills and valleys dotted with pastures, groves, vineyards, roads, paths, animals, and people coming and going.

"It may have been more beautiful in morning light," Joshua admitted, "but sharing it with you is better." He slipped his arm around me as we enjoyed the constantly moving mosaic of muted color, the Temple gleaming in the sun on Mount Moriah, the heart of Jerusalem, where God offered to meet humans, and yet humans refused to meet God, going their own ways full of pride and greed, demanding of God rather than listening to God, killing the prophets. Dark shadows were in our golden city, I thought.

We continued quietly to look out over the valley, Herod's hill fort looming on our left, then little Bethlehem in the distance. "Will it be peace or will it be war?" Joshua asked. "How can I be a man of peace when they want to make me the prince of another war?" This Zealot plan was so contrary to the peaceful life of teaching and healing that we had been living. After another silence, for I couldn't answer, he said, softly, "I forgive them. Will you?"

I felt a chill. Whatever it meant, all I could weakly say was, "Yes, with God's help," and then added, "But first I need to get past my anger at the way John was treated and now Justus' plans for us." I put my head on his shoulder. "How can we make a difference? How can we change anything no matter what our sacrifice?" I wondered aloud, betraying my frustration with a too sharp edge in my voice, asking my same questions.

Joshua looked down, brushed my hair back from my face. "John, Justus, and I discussed those questions over and over again, you know," he smiled indulgently at my struggle and repetitive questions. "Each of us had a different answer, a different way of trying to help people out of the misery that surrounds us...." His voice drifted pensively.

"We've tried," I murmured, thinking about my promise to forgive with God's help, "for as long as I've known you, but I'm struggling. John killed, Justus bent on being killed in a rebellion....What about us? What do you see?"

He gently squeezed my shoulder. "This morning, Mim, I just felt thankful to be here asking those questions. I thought...." His voice drifted again; he sighed, "And then I gave up thinking, and was simply glad to be alive in all of this beauty. Eventually, I heard footsteps, and here you are with wine and delicious food, if it's as good as it smells."

I got up with a laugh and opened my basket of food and spread it between us on the rock and offered him some still warm bread. We ate with relish the delicious treats Martha and I had packed. "On the way up," I said, "I wondered if you'd taken this main path again or branched off somewhere. Remember? 'The great way is easy, but people choose to go off on side paths.'"

Joshua laughed, "Oh yes, when things seem out of bal-ance—and they certainly do with people going off in all directions to solve our problems—it's best to stay centered in the way."

"How could a saying, maybe a thousand years old, be so relevant?" I asked.

"I don't know," he answered, "but speculators still seem to thrive and farmers lose their land. Authorities still ignore it and spend money on armies instead of caring for people. It's still relevant...things haven't changed much. Some are still blatantly extravagant while others can hardly find food or shelter...one side path after another to pain and suffering," he sighed. "If people finally just care for the weak and share what they have with each other...what a great day of thanksgiving that would be!"

Joshua helped me pack up the basket with the uneaten food, and suggested we take a path over to the mountain's other side.

We stopped at a place where we could look east over a bleak wilderness toward the Jordan valley, the salt sea, the mountain Moses climbed to see the Promised Land, and the fortress where Herod beheaded John. Joshua stood at my back with his arms around me and observed that we couldn't actually see the fortress, but he believed it was still there, transient and illusory. "I showed Justus what power leads to in the old ruins," he reminisced, "yet here we are how many months later? Will he ever see the futility?"

"I don't know," I sympathized. "I guess he just can't see the consequences."

"That's my frustration. The gods of war never reward their followers with paradise. They think I'm naive saying don't fight, but can't they see they'll harvest what they sow?"

"Isolation and fear," I surmised. "I remember you told me that in order to stop living in selfishness and fear, we have to move past ignorance and desire, and past the false choice of kill or be killed, and even past our own comfort and anger with those who disagree with us and threaten us. I think of it often. Can't Justus hear that, too?"

"I suppose so." Joshua rubbed his chin on the back of my head. "But that's not what he wants to hear. Yesterday, even Simon was swayed by his brother's vision."

I was as astonished as Joshua at Simon's enthusiasm for the bloody coup. "Where is my friend, Deborah? Where are the women in all of this fighting?" I asked.

"Probably as involved as the men are," he said pensively as he rested his head close to my right ear. "You know I'm criticized for treating you and the others as seriously as men; I'm told I've no respect for tradition, but aren't women's ambitions and jealousies and manipulations and fears just as destructive as men's are?"

Without an answer, we were quiet until he gave me a squeeze and asked in a soft voice, "Dear God, aren't these the same problems over and over again, the same truths revealed to wise men and women around the world, throughout the ages? Why do we still refuse to love, and insist on fighting and trying to possess?" and then after a big sigh, he asked, "Will my followers fight over my teachings, too?" I had a sad suspicion. Did we have the courage to go on with our vows in the face of what we observed from history?

We turned around and slowly walked back to the rock. Eventually, Joshua broke the silence again. "Just thinking about John," he mused. "His followers are still baptizing, but they're already fighting among themselves, disagreeing with each other about his message, busy creating rituals in his name." Joshua shook his head just thinking about it. "Do you remember his answer for the men who wanted everything to fit into their rules?" he asked.

"Didn't he send them to ask you if you were the Messiah, or if they should look for another?" I chuckled. "You were so patient...knew he just wanted to hear from you."

"Yes, I'm sure he was tired of explaining he wasn't the Messiah and didn't fit the prophecies, but in his funny way, he was needling me again, as he always did."

"They were so intent, counting the baptized; they seemed to think it was a competition about baptisms and numbers and really didn't hear either of you."

"Well, I sent them back with our private code, our reference to Isaiah's prophesy, but no numbers. I just told them that the blind see, the deaf hear, and the lame walk."

I laughed again. "And John must have wished they could see and hear and walk, too."

We got back to our rock in time to enjoy a spectacular sunset, and Joshua asked me to spend the night on the mountain with him. "I'm still in love with you, you know," he said, tousling my hair a bit before kissing me. "Some say we're even beginning to look alike!" We laughed!

"Mmm...well...in that case...since I'm still completely in love with you, too," I responded, "Martha won't mind; she'll understand when we don't appear."

Picking up the basket, we strolled arm in arm to our cave, lit an oil lamp, rolled out the cushions we stored there, and settled into them.

Joshua took me into his arms, and whispered, "Mim, no matter what happens in the next few days, remember that in the beginning God is the one from whom all things come and to whom all things return." I felt calm and secure in his arms as he continued, "If we close our minds, by judging good and evil, and let our minds fill with desires, we'll always be upset, but if we open our minds and keep from judging or wanting what's not ours, we'll always find peace."

His words reverberated in the cave and in my heart, and I was sure I had found peace, fathomless peace, in that moment, in his arms. I promised myself I would remember as Joshua extinguished the lamp, and continued, "Through love we can see into darkness and learn how to forgive. Love is our light and forgiveness is our strength. Love will light our way to peace with God and with everyone we meet."

"I'll remember, my love," I promised, aloud this time, but ever so softly.

"This is called practicing eternity," he whispered before tenderly kissing me to sleep.

# CHAPTER TWENTY-THREE

I awoke with the light's first rays coming through the cave's mouth. Joshua was already awake. The beautiful words he had spoken before I fell asleep were still wafting about my head. Forgiveness is our strength...love is our light. He'd said he was the light of the world, and I thought I could glimpse it in his eyes. I smiled, put my head on his chest, and promised myself again that I would remember.

I felt him take a deep breath. "I woke up thinking how much I'd like to have another conversation with John," he said, barely above a whisper, "even if it were in Herod's prison. What would he think of what Justus and I are doing?"

"What are you going to do?" I asked, suddenly returned to decisions facing us.

"Have some breakfast, even if it's only what's left from last night," he laughed, jumping up. "May I serve you breakfast in bed?" he teased, "and then I'd like to talk...about the Torah...I've been thinking about the Torah, too...."

"Thank you," I replied, "but it's unfair to propose we have a serious conversation so early in the morning. Have you noticed, perhaps, that it takes me a while really to wake up?"

"Indeed I have, my dear, on several occasions," he replied in the same teasing tone.

"So I propose that after I've brought you something to eat, I go on outside to revel in the beauty of this incredible sunrise. I'll wait for you out there."

He delivered the food basket to my bed, took some bread, cheese, and figs, leaned over to kiss me, and went out into a salmon-colored sky. How could I resist joining him? After nibbling some bread and cheese, I stood to roll up the cushions and tuck them away. He ducked his head in again and quickly came to help me. "It's too beautiful to miss. I want to share it with you!" he further tantalized me.

When we stepped out of the cave, I saw he was not exaggerating. The predawn sky was exquisitely colored. "Bravo, God!" I said, hurrying up the path with him in time for sunrise. We sat silently, hand-in-hand, smiling with pleasure at being alive in the crisp morning air, at watching the magnificent show. As the sun began to slide up over the distant hills, we were unable to look directly into the sun, looked at each other, grinned, and kissed until sure the sun was well up over the horizon, safe to look at the sky again.

"Mim," he asked, "will you keep your notes and take time to write down what we've talked about, what you remember of our life together?"

"Yes, of course," I responded, wondering at his urgent tone. "I've been trying to keep a record of your stories and of our adventures keeping our vows. You're still my most honored, beloved teacher, you know. I promise I'll write everything I've learned."

"Including our conversation last evening?"

I smiled, "Yes, Rabboni, my love, including our conversation last evening, and the one we're about to have this morning. But why so urgent?" My answer seemed to satisfy him, but my question hung in the air as we sat in silence again.

After a while, he cleared his throat. "We both know the prophecies for the Messiah...the rejection, the pain, the suffering. I don't know when or how, but I think I'm headed toward fulfilling those prophecies. I keep looking for another way for people to understand and willingly, even joyfully, enter God's Realm without the need for an anointed leader to be sacrificed, but that hasn't happened. They've argued... and here I go again! Prophets see the Messiah as one who's chosen to suffer, as well as one chosen to rule as Justus and Peter fantasize. It seems so simple. Why is it so difficult?"

"I don't know," I said.

"Thanks for being patient with my struggle. I've been asking God if I actually were to be the Messiah, would my sacrifice really bring peace to the world? Would it change anything? Would people finally understand and stop fearing and killing each other?"

"I'm not sure," I responded sadly. "I'm not sure people would understand a once-and-for-all sacrifice, no more killing of one's self or anyone else in the name of any god."

"I'm not sure either. We're looking at the City of Peace... the city that killed the prophets...the city where I've questioned Gamaliel and others, studied with Hillel as a boy. I'm not the only one who knows the writings of the great prophets and rabbis."

"But it seems you're the only one who actually lives what they've taught."

Joshua took my hand, again. "Samuel said, 'Here I am, send me,' and my mother said, 'Let it be for me according to your word.' That's what I'm praying, now, also."

"So few have said, 'Your will be done' to God...and really meant it," I responded.

Joshua put his arm around me. "I love you so much, Mim...and I love our children, and our family and servants, and even my fellow rabbis who debate and question...and my friend," he shook his head, "my hardheaded friend, Justus, and his Zealots."

"And I love you so very much," I said, feeling a pang at his summary. "You have so much to live for," I added with my unspoken plea to be careful of where love might lead.

"We all do, Mim, but life without love is..." he hesitated, "living death...a lonely hell in an ever-disappointing world....I've been thinking about Isaiah's view of the Messiah. Do you remember where he writes, 'The Lord God has given me the tongue of a teacher, that I may know how to sustain the weary with a word.'"

I smiled and nodded, continuing, "Morning by morning he wakens me to listen and to learn. The Lord God has opened my ear, and I was not rebellious, I did not turn back."

Joshua gently squeezed my shoulder with his arm, offering me comfort and protection in spite of the images he called up as he continued, deep sadness in his voice, "I gave my back to those who struck me, and my cheeks to those who pulled out my beard. I didn't hide my face from insult and spitting. The Lord God helps me...Who will contend with me?"

As he paused again, I continued, feeling very loyal but not very brave at these images, "Who are my adversaries? Let them confront me. It's the Lord God who helps me. Who will declare me guilty?" I asked with Isaiah.

"Mim, my love," Joshua answered, "I think that's what I'm going to be facing as we go through this Passover. Isaiah foresaw the weeks ahead of us, as I think I'm beginning to, also, but remember, he said our adversaries will all wear out like a garment, the moths will eat them up. So let's try to remember we can love them and forgive them."

"I'll try when the time comes," I sighed, as my stomach began to tighten; my unspoken plea for caution, for tempered, perhaps half-hearted love seemed feeble and unworthy.

"I know you will, but I've been thinking about something even more difficult...sacrifices. In 'The Teaching of the Priests,' do you remember the sacrifices?" he asked.

I thought for a minute; it seemed a complete change of subject. "Well, yes, the sheep...the perfect males for forgiveness of sin....Oh, there were so many," I gave up. "Everything seems to require cleansing and a sacrifice," I sighed. "I'm not sure of them all."

"And the sheep...the perfect females for communion with God," he patiently prompted me.

"Yes, and then once a year, for atonement with God, to enter the holiest part of the Tabernacle...'The Tent of Meeting,' the high priest sacrificed a young bull for himself, and

then two male goats for the people...one was sacrificed on
the altar, and the other was sent into the wilderness." I felt
pleased now to remember those details.

"You remember well, my dear...and do you also remember
that when Peter complained that you, a woman, were always
at my side, my beloved disciple, that I laughed and told him
that I'd just have to make you male, then?"

I laughed and said, "Yes, I do remember it now that you
mention it. Peter still doesn't understand us...man and
woman and God together in the Garden...a woman, not a
possession, but a companion and completion. It did seem a
funny thing for you to say, but I didn't think to ask you about
it later."

"Mim," he hesitated and took a deep breath, "sacrifice is
as old as history, offering substitutes for ourselves to try to get
rid of guilt. I may be wrong, but I've begun to think that the
two goats brought to the Tent of Meeting's entrance to be sacrificed for the people's sins might be a foreshadowing of who
we are. If I am the Messiah, I think I'll be flayed and killed to
atone for the sin that separates people from God and one another. But after I'm sacrificed, no longer able to defend you,
all of their guilt, their hatred and fear and selfishness, will be
piled on you, and they'll send you out into the wilderness as
they did the second goat designated with the scarlet thread...
banished completely to the place beyond...and that thought
is more painful than the first."

I was stunned. Studying the Prophets, I had reluctantly
understood that if Joshua were the anointed one, he would
suffer, and if he suffered, I would suffer, too. But I hadn't
thought of the sacrifices for atonement...that two were sacri-

ficed in very different ways. My mind could hardly encompass it...to be sent away, not even for my offenses, but for the offenses of those who would sacrifice Joshua. It felt bewildering, overwhelming.

"Have no fear," I thought. " Perfect love casts out fear... but how?"

After giving me a little time, Joshua said quietly, "I'll always be with you, Mim; I know you need time. I'll continue to ask for some other way." But the glorious sunrise had vanished into a dark cloud hanging over us.

"I know...I need to understand," I began hesitantly, "and trust God...but I've taken those goats for granted, never thought of them foreshadowing—"

"Let's keep reading," he said as he got up, pulled me to my feet, and held me tenderly in his arms, adding, "I'll keep looking for another way...but it's time to go back down the mountain now...time for me to go to Bethlehem."

His brother James and several servants, both from Galilee and from Judea, were ready and waiting when we returned. Joshua explained his plan for the trip to them...stay with their brother Jude in the old family home, talk to as many as they could individually before Justus arrived, and then go to the meeting with the Zealots.

Joshua took a minute to say goodbye to me, trying another approach. "One or two of the shepherds in the fields that night I was born are still alive. Maybe I can remind them of Gabriel's message, 'Fear not! Unto you is born a Savior,' remember? 'Peace on earth! Goodwill to everyone in whom God delights!' Maybe they'll remember and help me persuade the others to save the world from more killing and war. What do you think?"

Unsure, I could only respond with a fervent, "I hope so," as I threw my arms around him.

He sighed, kissed me, and whispered, "Thank you. See you in a couple of days."

# CHAPTER TWENTY-FOUR

As the men went out the gate, I realized I could do nothing more at the moment. Different from our other separations in Galilee when groups had gone out with Joshua to teach and heal, this was, well, maybe it was just that, after all. Maybe that was all one could really give the world. Maybe giving Justus eyes to see and ears to hear, to avoid the certain disaster into which he was pulling us, maybe that was healing.

I went into the kitchen and found Joseph and Sarah with Martha, just finished making their favorite honey-sesame treat. Enthusiastically, they told me about cooking with Martha, visiting with their friends and their tutor, and with Uncle Lazarus and Aunt Hannah. Martha had an errand and left us as Joseph and Martha asked about my trip up the mountain, and where the men had gone, and why? And then, apparently from something that happened while visiting their friends, came the question from Sarah, "Why are people so fearful and jealous, Mother?

"That's a good question," I responded. "Let's take some of these delicious treats into the courtyard with some cool water...and I'll tell you a story." Once settled on cushions under the fig tree, I continued. "There are stories about fear and jealousy in every culture, but an old one in ours is about Abraham and his family in the book of beginnings. Abraham had two sons, Isaac by his wife Sarah, and Ishmael by Sarah's servant, Hagar, a custom some followed in those days. Each boy was fearful that he might be loved less by his father than the other. They fought and teased—"

"We know, Mother," interjected Joseph. "We all do; everyone I know does..." he said with a meaningful look at his sister.

"Ah, yes, well they were jealous and fearful and competed for their father's attention and love, perhaps like their mothers," I continued. "In a land with a limited supply of water, maybe they thought there was a limited supply of love as well. Maybe Abraham's love wasn't enough so they had to compete for it."

"But is love limited?" Sarah asked. "If I love you, can't I love Father and John Mark and Joseph too?"

"What do you think?" I asked.

Joseph said, "I think so. It feels like I love you and father and—"

Sarah continued, "And it feels like you and father love each other, and us, and John Mark, and Aunt Martha and Uncle Lazarus, and Thad...and...."

Joseph took up the list with a quick summary, "And all of the people you help."

"I don't think love is limited, either," I said. "We're born to love. God is love and we're all God's children, so if love is without limit, there's no scarcity, no need for competition."

"Oh, God loves us like Father?" asked Sarah.

"Yes," I replied, "and He waits for our love in return. Your father went to Bethlehem...in a way to discuss how to love God with his brothers and cousins and Justus."

"I know, Uncle Justus," my son responded, grouping his father's spirited friend with his uncles. "Don't they agree? Doesn't Uncle Justus love God?"

"Oh, yes, I'm sure he loves God, but your father disagrees with his friend about how to love God and...."

"But they're still friends?" my son interrupted a bit anxiously.

"Oh, yes," I replied. "Just like you and your sister are, even though I remember hearing you argue from time to time." And we all laughed.

"Did Abraham really love both Ishmael and Isaac?" Sarah asked, returning to the story.

"Yes, but sometimes it did seem strange," I admitted. "Ishmael, the oldest, was the first one whom his father took to Mount Moriah to offer as a sacrifice to God, to show how much he loved God...that there was nothing in the world he wouldn't give God, even his first son whom he loved very much."

"That's extreme!" declared Joseph, shocked at the thought. "Father wouldn't—"

"No, absolutely not! It was a bad idea about how to love God. God didn't want Ishmael to be sacrificed and sent a ram rushing up the mountain to get caught in the thicket near the altar. Abraham untied Ishmael and took him off the altar and together they caught and killed the ram, placed it on the altar, and sacrificed it."

"Ugh," opined Sarah. "That's awful. It doesn't sound like love to me. Can you imagine how you'd feel if father tied you up and put you on top of a bunch of sticks on a big rock altar?" she asked Joseph.

"Not really, but I wouldn't be very sure of his love. I'd be nervous...no, I'd be really scared. I probably wouldn't ever trust him again. I'd probably stay out of his sight as much as I could and be very jealous of you, thinking he loved you more," my son replied.

"That's probably what happened. But it wasn't long before Abraham did it again, to be sure he wasn't holding anything back from God. To prove his love for God, Abraham decided to take Isaac, who'd probably heard about Ishmael's trip and was teased by him before they left that there might not be a ram this time."

"Ooh, that would be even worse," said Sarah twisting up her face. "You'd be scared from the beginning because you'd know what was going to happen...maybe."

"You're right," Joseph agreed emphatically. "The suspense must have been terrible. Isaac must have had lots of questions about whether to keep going with his father, or just sneak out at night and run away," he added, clearly wondering what he would do.

"Well, God provided a ram again," I said. "Each time, God provided for Abraham a ram to take his son's place," I said, trying to be reassuring. "God loves us and showed Abraham and all of us that human sacrifice is not what God wants, just love and mercy and—"

"That's good, I mean that God loves us, but if Father did that to me, no matter what he said about how much he loved me or why he tried to sacrifice me, I just wouldn't get it. I don't think I could trust him or his love again," Joseph blurted out.

"Well, that may have happened to Isaac and Ishmael," I said. "They didn't stop feeling insecure, teasing and competing with each other. In fact, it got worse. They got their mothers involved and they couldn't live together in peace. Hagar and Ishmael had to leave their home and go out into the wilderness to find a new one, even though Abraham didn't want to send them away."

"What happened? Isn't the wilderness dangerous?" asked Sarah. "If Abraham really loved Hagar and Ishmael...his love sure seems strange to me...."

"Oh, he did, Sarah," I responded. "He gave them food and clothing and water, but it didn't last long in the heat as they wandered through the sparse hills. Hagar loved Ishmael and gave him more than his share of the water. Finally, finding shade for him near a big rock, a safe place to sleep, she went off to cry to God, who'd saved Ishmael on the altar, to save him now or he would die. God did love them, and just like with the ram, He sent someone to help them, to give them water, food, and a safe, new home. I think Hagar learned that no matter how desperate or alone you feel, God is with you, and sends someone to help you."

"Just like Simon helped Father on the road to Jericho," Joseph asked.

"Yes, just like Simon, our good Samaritan," I agreed.

Lazarus came in just then and asked the children whether they would like to go with him to Bethphage. Delighted at the prospect of an adventure with Uncle Lazarus, they were off, leaving me to take tea bowls back to the kitchen and go to my room to get out my writing materials, and ponder the children's questions and the story of God's love for both of Abraham's sons, but quickly, my thoughts turned to Joshua who should be arriving in Bethlehem soon.

As Joshua had prepared to go, he had told me he was convinced that nothing in this world—not life, death, pain, struggle, loss, absolutely nothing—could separate us from the love of God. "I'm willing to die for that, Mim," he'd said. That might be what he'll tell the men this evening, I thought, but he'll add that he's not willing to fight, or kill for that. There's a big difference. I hoped they could see it.

My story for the children reminded me that God doesn't ask us for human sacrifice, but asks us to love others with mercy and justice, which is just what we ask of God. Would others see this? I wondered.

Could Joshua help Justus and the other men understand our history, as he did? I suspected that Joshua would be explaining to them, as he had to me, that what the world needs, and always has needed, is love, not war. Love gave him the power to forgive, to heal, to feed, to calm whoever came to him. Judging, fighting, robbing, and killing have never led to a good outcome. That's just the way it is, and always has been.

My thoughts tumbled around and around, repeated what we had been saying and living, as I tried to write until eventually I was interrupted by a call to dinner. Martha was so generous, and hospitable. She had mellowed through the years and understood that neither Joshua nor I fit into the traditional pattern of husband and wife, and that he support-ed me in my writing. "You're his beloved disciple, Miriam, as well as his wife," she'd said.

That was a big, and much appreciated, affirmation from my sister. She was happy pursuing her wifely duties of man-aging the household, though she too had help, and was spending more time now, herself, reading poetry and the Torah and histories. I think my choices had influenced her.

After dinner, Thad took the children off to see a new lamb, which had just been born that afternoon, and I told Martha, Simon, Lazarus, and Hannah a little more about Joshua's mission to Bethlehem, and the dangers to all of us if the Zeal-ots tried to carry out their plot.

My brother spoke up protectively, "Miriam, Simon and I were dumbfounded to hear Justus' brother go on and on about his brother's plot, and then that grandiose vision that somehow the whole world will bow down and bring tribute to Joshua and you...really more grandiose than Solomon's kingdom. I'm worried about you and Joshua, about your safety if Justus tries to pull you into this. Maybe you and your children should just go away for a while until this whole thing blows over, or collapses on itself. Couldn't Joshua's Uncle Joseph arrange something for you, or maybe make a trip to Cypress to visit his sister Anna and her family?"

"I don't know, Miriam," Simon added, "but it seems pretty risky to stay here. Joshua is such a fine teacher and has such a gift for healing....I owe my life to him after he healed me of leprosy, but it seems such a shame to let Justus' big ideas draw you into what's certain to be a disaster. What can we do to help? Do you think I can talk Joshua into taking you all on a trip? I think Lazarus has a good idea."

Martha and Hannah chimed in their agreement with their husbands before I could respond. In fact, Martha added the final straw, "Just look what happened to John when he tried to make things better and persuade people to repent." Sisters have a way of cutting to the quick.

"Everything you are saying makes perfect sense," I replied, bravely trying to cover the growing despair I felt. "Joshua is intent on saving Justus from this folly, too. I hope Joshua can persuade him to change his mind, give up the rebellion, and work for peaceful solutions, but I'm worried, too. I don't think either Justus or Joshua will quit."

Later in my room, softly lit by my favorite little oil lamp that Joshua had brought me from his travels in Gaul before we were married, I felt uneasy. I'd been avoiding thinking of the sacrifices for atonement. I thought again of the story of the Garden of Eden, Adam and Eve, choosing their own way, choosing to know good and evil, and then immediately judging each other, God, and all around them...yet God still loved them and sacrificed two animals to clothe them with skins to protect them as they left the garden.

That reminded me of the two goats offered for atonement and I shuddered.

Then I recalled Joshua telling me he'd seen people in so many places make sacrifices to so many gods represented by so many figures of human and animal forms, beautiful, exaggerated, grotesque. Everywhere, people thought they could avoid what they feared by sacrifice to various gods on altars of every size, shape, and material.

Every altar had its priests and attendants and a whole group of people supporting it, interpreting what was required to be offered to the god in order to have good health, good crops, good fortune, safe travels, safety from invasion, safety from attacks by neighboring tribes, enough water, enough food, fertility...more family, more herds, more, more, more, safe arrival in this life, safe arrival in the next. The list went on and on. Unbelievable! With all the cacophony of beliefs, why would anyone believe us?

Could people ever hear the still, small voice of the true God within them and understand that nothing separates us from God's love? Could people really ever see that we were not afraid to have the sufferings of the world, their sufferings, piled on us? Could they know at last that nothing can separate them from God's love whatever happens, and at last, believe that God is Love, gives them life, and loves them no matter what?

Joshua returned, weary, two days later. From the moment I saw him, I knew that Justus and his Zealots could not understand how Joshua thought he could bring about any change without a fight. "Priests and kings and governors don't just give up power on their own, ever!" Justus had almost shouted in the meeting. "It's a great ideal, but you have to be determined to take power away, and then fight for it," he'd said with great assurance.

"Justus just couldn't hear my examples of how force has never worked very long for anyone," Joshua said. "He really didn't want to hear how many Roman legions are available to put down any rebellion, but most of all, he didn't want the other men to hear it. 'What they don't know won't hurt them,' he growled at me angrily in a low voice."

"Oh, how sad," I said. "How unfair...."

"Justus' frustration level rose every time I questioned him," Joshua continued. "Gestas looked like he was ready to silence me in front of everyone, putting James and Jude on edge, making Justus even more nervous, caught up in the expectations of his own men. The idea of fighting feeds on itself, Mim. I couldn't stop them or squelch the excitement of fighting to take control, no matter how illusory their fantasy.

"My only chance was to get Justus alone, which I finally did, but he's truly possessed now and has completely lost sight of our goals,  just focused on fighting Rome and Herod. He told me I was unrealistic, spoiling his chances, 'our chances,' he said. I asked whether he would call this off if I could persuade his father of its futility. He laughed. If I could persuade his father, he'd listen...but he's not worried. He's sure he's following his father's wishes...said he wasn't called 'Son of the Fathers' for nothing."

"How can fathers sacrifice their sons? I wondered, thinking of Abraham again. "Where is Simon? He's a Zealot, but—"

"He is. You saw how excited he was. He trusts me, but he's loyal to his father and brother. It's important for me to persuade his father for his sake, too. That's my only chance to stop this madness, and I don't have any time to lose."

"How can I help? I'd go with you, if—"

"I know...but actually, I suspect you can help more by visiting Elizabeth and Claudia and your other friends in Jerusalem, learning what you can about what's been going on in the inner circles of the Temple and the fortress while we've been in Galilee."

"Like what?" I asked.

"Oh, like what the current relationship is between Annas and Herod after he beheaded John...like what they're planning? What they're worried about?"

"Gladly! We've been gone so long, getting back will be a pleasure, hearing what's new with children, grandchildren, and aging parents." Joshua began to laugh and shake his head. "But don't worry, my dear," I added. "In the midst of all that, I know I'll hear all the gossip about what's going on with their husbands, too. Elizabeth and Rachel will know about Annas, and I'll see Aunt Judith, though I don't always trust her."

"That's the question, Mim: Whom can we trust? The more information we have, the more likely we'll find a peaceful way through this without the need for sacrifices." Joshua sighed. "I've tried to talk Justus out of this every way I can. I don't want anyone to get killed...."

"What a catastrophe! Why can't he see it? Will he if his father agrees with you?"

"He's given his word...." Joshua seemed tentative.

Something sent a chill through me. Could Joshua see into the future? I wasn't sure he liked what he saw. I blurted, "Oh, I really want to be with you...whatever it means...."

"You will be, Mim; you're always with me in spirit. I'll take Judas and the others from here, a trading caravan. Maybe I can even find a way to eliminate the rivalry between the Galileans and those from here, while—"

"Ironic isn't it? You'll have your hands full with our own servants and students," I interrupted, "while talking peace with the Zealots...."

Joshua shook his head again. "Can you believe Peter and James and John are still arguing about rank and who's going to have what exalted position? They're not joining the Zealots, but they're still caught up in earthly kingdoms no matter how many times I try to explain it to them."

I heaved a sigh. "They don't seem to understand any more than Justus does."

"No, but some of them do, Mim. I'll do my best. I'll try to convince old Judas, appeal to his friendship with my father, and show him how much rests on him. I hope he'll choose peace for all of us."

After these words, we were quiet, lost in what must be accomplished on the road to whatever Joshua saw in the future.

# CHAPTER TWENTY-FIVE

The next morning, after pack animals were loaded with oil, Joshua was on his way back to Galilee with the men by the Jordan Valley route, down the road to Jericho again with whatever risks lay ahead from being attacked by robbers to being swarmed by people wanting to be healed or to make him king. As I packed my things and prepared to go to Jerusalem that afternoon, I kept praying, "Thy will be done," and kept hoping it would mean peace for everyone.

After the children and I arrived in Jerusalem and resettled ourselves with Rhoda, Nathan, and the household there, I went to the scroll room and picked through our scrolls of Psalms, to find a prayer written for Solomon, which I remembered and wanted to pray for Joshua. I found it and carried it out into our bedroom, to the bench under the window. "Give the gift of wisdom to Joshua, O God, the gifts of insight and just thinking...Please help him stand up for the abused, and let the Zealot elders see the harm war will bring to their children and everyone around them," I added. "Let righteousness flourish and peace overflow the land...and may we all fall on our knees before you our rescuer."

"Oh God," I continued to pray, "help Joshua restore the wretched of the earth. Let him live! Bless him from morning to night. May he always be remembered as the one who brings peace and be famous forever. May everyone enter his circle of blessing without religious or political distinctions." I finished, "I bless You, Unnameable True God. You're the only one who works such wonders. Earth is filled with your glory!"

This old prayer still seemed relevant. I would try to do my part, at least in the Temple and fortress. I would try to avoid Herodias and Salome, though they were in Jerusalem occasionally. The thought of their cruel request for John's head was still wrenching, and though I lived with a man who forgave everyone, I wasn't sure I could if I were face-to-face with one of them. I didn't feel ready for such a test.

My reunion with Elizabeth was wonderful. We spent the afternoon by the fountain in her courtyard, enjoying the shade and fragrance of her large potted citron trees. The sound of falling water was soothing and covered the sound of our chatter, protecting us from passing servants' ears. We hardly stopped to catch our breath as we laughed, exchanged stories, simply continued our last conversation. But, of course, we had many more stories to share about Mathias' studies, John Mark's travels, my life in the country, which Elizabeth could hardly imagine, and her life in Jerusalem with all the gossip and intrigue. I heard about Joseph Caiaphas and her father, and then her continuing problems with her mother, who always reminded her of her duty. She lived a privileged life, but it wasn't free.

I invited Pilate's wife, Claudia, and their son, Pilo, along with Marcus' wife, Amelia, and their son, Hermes, to come to our home the next afternoon. We mothers chatted while sipping our special honey herbed wine and nibbling sweets on our terrace. Sarah and Joseph enjoyed playing with the children. Joshua had healed Hermes, the son of his old friend, Marcus, a centurion now on duty at the fortress, when everyone thought he was dying, and then healed pale, little Pilo, born crippled and taken everywhere by Claudia and Pilate for a cure. After Claudia heard about Hermes, Marcus had been brought to the fortress for duty, and Amelia, Hermes, and she came to our home with little Pilo one day when we were in Jerusalem. Joshua had compassionately held the little boy in his arms, whispered something in his ear, and Pilo had smiled, nodded, thrown down his crutch, jumped down from Joshua's lap, and run to play hide and seek with Hermes, Sarah, and Joseph. What a day that had been!

We had all been close friends ever since, sharing that wonder. Pilate was most deeply grateful that his son finally could learn to ride a horse and follow in the family equestrian tradition. My husband and he especially enjoyed their new friendship since Joshua was modest about his gifts, always interested in and sympathetic to the other. Joshua was one of the few open-minded, well-traveled, and broadly educated men with whom Pilate could freely discuss ideas.

While the children scooted in and out for treats between their games, we delightedly shared stories of our latest activities as well as what was happening now in Jerusalem, the goings and comings of legions, current power struggles in Rome, problems of supplies with so many continuing caravan raids, how one could manage a household not knowing what one could depend upon, for instance, the indispensable silphium from Cyrene. With rumors of more trouble on the roads, they were glad that I was home. They and their husbands had their hands full between their homes in Jerusalem and Caesarea Maritime. As Joshua had suspected, I heard that Pilate had asked Syria for reinforcements for the Passover feast, for which Marcus was thankful. Nothing was said about any potential Zealot rebellion. I hoped Joshua could stop it in time to keep peace.

Rachel came the next afternoon. I'd received a message from Joshua that morning sent with a caravan from Capernaum. "I'm in trouble, I cry to Yahweh, desperate for an answer." That was all, but I knew the rest of the psalm and the rest of his message.

"Deliver me from the liars. They smile so sweetly but lie through their teeth." I knew the conversation with Judah hadn't gone well. He had listened, smiled, and said he knew nothing of a rebellion. Joshua must be mistaken. Justus was away on some family business. He was so sorry to hear the story of John's beheading which Justus had told him about with great sorrow. Certainly, Herod was an enemy of all decent people. All decent men needed to be on guard, ready to defend themselves and their families against such tyranny. Joshua, no doubt, had asked the psalmist's questions. "Do you know what's next? Can you see what's coming?" If you persist in lying and pretending only to be arming men to defend themselves, then armed, a simple misunderstanding can ignite an argument and draw everyone into the hell of conflict. Or worse, in the name of defense, an otherwise decent man may strike the first blow.

I suspected that Judah had demurred, still smiling, saying that Justus would be consulting with the Temple priests, who were no doubt disturbed at the treatment of John, one of their own, after all. Joshua would ask about the poor people punished after every raid that the Zealots carried out, about the danger to Justus, about the swift death to anyone suspected of insurrection, about additional legions to be brought in from a neighboring province, about fires that would be set, scorched earth and famine.

"Pointed arrows and burning coals will be your reward."

The conversation would have continued for some time, Joshua seeking a way to dissuade his friend's father from sending his sons and nephews and their sons into battle, to their deaths; the old man denying, through smiling lips, that he could do anything, had any part of it. At his age, what could he do to stop quarrels? Joshua, would have left, sad and yet compassionate. The old man risked losing everyone he held most dear. Joshua would have concluded with the psalmist, "I'm all for peace, but the minute I tell them so, they go to war!"

So that was his message. There seemed to be no way to stop a war with more misery and suffering for everyone. The choice was clear, but men chose the way of war, killing and dying, rather than the way of peace, loving and living. Sadness overwhelmed me.

When Rachel arrived, I was so glad to see her. Of all of our friends, Nicodemus and she were still the closest and our conversations the deepest. A favorite niece of Aunt Judith, she was Elizabeth's strong and confident cousin, very well-connected in the web of families ruling the Temple, even a descendant of Hillel on her father's side.

Rhoda had barely brought us spiced wine and left when Rachel, looking worried, asked in her blunt, straightforward way, why Joshua had gone back to Galilee before the feast, so soon after returning to Jerusalem. She didn't wait for an answer but said she was worried as she'd heard rumors of trouble on the roads before Passover, and she launched into a story that had been troubling her ever since she had heard it.

"It seems that Zachariah, when he passed Joshua on the Jericho road," she confided, "was not returning to Jerusalem from baptism by John after all, or at least not directly."

"Oh?" I asked a little surprised.

"No, he used John as an excuse to go to Jericho to meet with a Galilean, Justus... some are calling him Bar-Abbas... anyway, the chief of the Zealots. Wasn't he a boyhood friend of Joshua?" she asked. I nodded and she continued, "Well, Nahum was returning directly from baptism, but not Zachariah who, it seems, is an emissary between Annas and this Justus Bar-Abbas person. Apparently, there is protection and mutual benefit between the Temple and the caravan raiders. It's rumored that part, some say 10 percent, of the spoils from raids comes into the Temple treasury, which allows for certain amenities in the households of Judith and several of my other relatives. I have bits of the story from several of them."

Rachel, satisfied with this information's significance, read the concern on my face. "This, of course, is not to come to any Roman ears," she said in a lowered, confidential voice. "But it may explain why the Temple is of no help to the

Romans in finding those responsible for caravan raids, and why Zachariah didn't stop to help."

"I feel as though everyone around us has been smiling and pretending," I replied.

"I know," sighed Rachel. "That's why we're friends...and why I'm worried."

"How can we ever start to make things better? After John was imprisoned, neither Annas nor Caiaphas made any public protest...his imprisonment spoke for itself just as you say the raids speak for themselves."

Rachel's face darkened. "Yes, I think so...Aunt Judith confirmed that, not directly, but...."

"I don't know where we're headed, Rachel. I think it will take a miracle to bring about the justice and mercy and peace we keep talking about." I couldn't hide my misery.

"There are so many levels of intrigue," Rachel responded. "I doubt that anyone can cut through them. There are so many special interests to be protected. Nicodemus just wants to study the Torah and Prophets, stay out of the daily haggling and posturing going on around him. But it's difficult, even with the best of intentions!"

"The best of intentions," I sighed, thinking of Joshua, but I didn't want to say more until I knew more. Rhoda brought sesame nut cakes and our talk turned to our children, preparation for Passover, and topics over which we had a bit more influence. Rachel brought me up to date on new merchants in the city, the women she'd talked with who shared our interests, and cautions about whom and what to avoid now.

We promised to spend another afternoon together in a few days.

Daily, I was reminded of just how intricate the web of social, political, and religious connections was in Jerusalem. I rewove myself into that web, carefully renewing relationships with the wives of administrators and magistrates and merchants as well as rabbis and priests after my long absence, connecting even beyond my circle of close friends.

I found women's concerns in Jerusalem were similar to those in Galilee. Though wealth rearranged misery, it didn't preclude it. Fears, jealousies, and illnesses were as ubiquitous as were concerns for children, grandchildren, and husbands. I was relieved to hear nothing of the Zealots. Vague rumors arose about various rebels and troublemakers from time to time, but only in connection with frustration at continued caravan raids that impacted needed supplies, and with satisfaction that an occasional robber was caught and crucified... brought to justice.

# CHAPTER TWENTY-SIX

Returning home from another visit with Elizabeth several afternoons later, I received an urgent message from Martha. Lazarus was suddenly very ill so she wanted me to come immediately. While Rhoda helped me pack a bag, Sarah and Joseph came home with Thad. John Mark came in with Mathias about the same time that another message arrived, this one from Joshua saying he'd stopped in Jericho with Abigail and Zachaeus for a few days to prepare our servants for Passover. I asked Thad and John Mark to come with me to Bethany and then go on to Jericho early the next morning to get Joshua. Nathan went to get our donkeys. Mathias asked to go too, and dashed home to get Elizabeth's approval while John Mark went to help Nathan and Tobias with the donkeys.

When we arrived, I could see anxiety on Martha's face, hear it in her voice. Lazarus was worse than when she'd sent the message. Sarah, Joseph, and my messengers went to the kitchen to get something to eat and then settle into their usual rooms for a good night's sleep so they would be ready to go early in the morning.

Martha and I went immediately to Lazarus' room where we found Hannah at her husband's side. We kept vigil with her, taking turns bathing Lazarus' head, arms, and chest in cool water with herbs, urging him to drink as often as he appeared awake. I held my brother's hand, prayed to our Heavenly Father for mercy and healing, massaged his feet, did whatever I could, with little affect. He had smiled faintly when he saw me, but he couldn't hold his eyes open. Neither Martha nor I felt like sleeping. In whispers, we insisted that Hannah, who hadn't slept well the night before, nap from time to time. We had never seen Lazarus so sick. Tension and exhaustion took their toll.

At the first cock crow before dawn, I slipped out of the room with Martha still awake, and went to awaken Thad, John Mark, and Mathias. They also had heard the cock and were already dressed and packing bedrolls. Thad went to the kitchen. John Mark and Mathias kissed me and were off to get three donkeys ready to go as soon as the bread was baked and packed along with other food they'd made ready the night before.

Thad remembered our visit with Abigail and Zachaeus and said they'd have no trouble finding their way. They were quickly off with my urgent message to Joshua. When I returned to his room, Lazarus was delirious, his fever raging. I hoped Joshua could return home before sundown. "Please God, give them a safe journey and a speedy return," I prayed on my way to the kitchen to get warm bread and honey for Martha and Hannah, and fresh, cool water for Lazarus.

Exhausted, Martha, Hannah, and I took turns dozing through the day, waiting for Joshua. The boys, they were boys

again in my anxiety, traveled the very road where Joshua
had been attacked. I dreaded the memory, the approaching
conflict, the layers of intrigue in Jerusalem, the sacrifices
required to save others if Joshua couldn't find another way.
Now Lazarus was sick to death; it all felt like too much. I
needed Joshua.

My anxiety increased as the sun set. I was startled by the
sound of any animal passing the door. When no one arrived,
fantasy took over and I wondered whether my messengers
were in need of being saved along the deserted road. Then I
wondered whether they had found Joshua, if they had given
the message urgently, explained how serious it was. Martha,
Hannah, and I spent another night taking turns caring for
Lazarus, who was fading under the relentless fever, and wondering quietly in whispers what could have happened to our
messengers and to Joshua.

Finally early the next afternoon, Lazarus, with all three of
us awake and at his side, took his last difficult breath, and
died. We were stunned. Hannah, Martha, and I couldn't
speak, couldn't hold back the flood of tears as we mechan-
ically began to prepare his body for burial. In shock, we
bathed his body in our tears as well as in the special waters
and ointments that every household has on hand, to be followed by the spices and wrapping cloths. A servant ran to a
neighbor with the news, and soon the village gathered in the
courtyard, quietly at first, and then they began to wail.

John Mark and Mathias, looking worried and bewildered,
came in just as we finished wrapping Lazarus' body with
spices. Confused, they couldn't believe what was happening. John Mark said, "Father told me not to be frightened;

Lazarus is only sleeping. He'll be back in several days when he's finished teaching."

"How could he be so wrong?" I asked, astonished. "I've never known your father to be so wrong!" I cried, feeling I was sinking into an unknown abyss.

John Mark immediately stepped forward and put his arms around me, to comfort me, and said softly, "I don't know, Mother. He said something about the glory of God. I think there's something we don't understand...."

I was comforted by my son's presence and simple faith in his father. Mathias and he were safely back, and Joshua had received my message, but my tears wouldn't stop.

John Mark and Mathias had arrived in time to help Simon and Alphaeus carry Lazarus' body to the tombs at the edge of the village. We were a sad procession, the four carrying the body followed by Hannah, with Martha and me, my children, the members of our households, our lifelong friends in the village, all weeping, to place the body of our beloved Lazarus in a new tomb hewn into the rock, to roll the stone over the entrance. We stayed and wept until almost sundown, which began the Sabbath rest.

Mathias and John Mark stayed the night, and then rode to Jerusalem the next evening to tell the news. Elizabeth and Joseph Caiaphas, Rachel and Nicodemus, and many other friends hurried out to Bethany the next day to console Hannah, Martha, Simon, and me. But how could I be consoled? My beloved brother was dead; my husband, who had healed so many, had not come to our rescue. I grieved a double loss: the death of my brother and the abandonment of my husband, though I could not publicly admit the latter.

Through tears and a broken heart, I remembered Job again: "The Lord has given, the Lord has taken away. Blessed be the name of the Lord." And I cried and cried.

Late the following morning, we were still surrounded by others who'd come from Jerusalem, friends, family, and neighbors talking about Lazarus, a respected leader, a wonderful husband and father and brother, how he enjoyed a good joke, how he willingly helped friends and neighbors, how he managed the olive orchards, how he was a good and beloved master. I laughed and cried; the sweet and the bitter all mixed together. But I couldn't understand what had happened to my husband who'd said that nothing, not even death, separated us from the love of God. But God, where is your love? I've seen you heal others through Joshua. Why not our beloved Lazarus?

Later, I learned that, unnoticed, Thad had peeked into the room, and not seeing Martha, gone to the kitchen where he found her supervising, helping prepare the mid-day meal for everyone. After embracing her, he quietly told her Joshua had sent him ahead to ask her to meet him on the edge of town, near the tombs.

As bereaved and disappointed as she felt, my sister realized she was being asked to be the go-between, to begin our reconnection with Joshua. She went quickly to meet him, to express privately our disappointment. She later told me Joshua was on the verge of tears himself and told her he not only had the power to forgive and heal, but to give life as well. He asked her to trust him and to ask me to come to the tombs to see him alone first, not in a room full of people.

When Martha whispered Joshua's request in my ear, without hesitation, I got up and quickly left the room and began to run. Tears started flowing again, and by the time I reached him, I couldn't stop the accusation bubbling heavily in my heart, "If you'd only been here, I know he wouldn't have died," as I fell sobbing into his arms. He held me and cried with me. Enveloped in his arms, I knew I wasn't abandoned even though I still didn't know what happened or why. "I know you loved him, too," I confessed when I found my voice. As tears subsided, we became aware we were no longer alone. The whole room full of mourners, Martha and Hannah included, had followed me.

Joshua gently asked me, "Where have you laid his body?"

I couldn't find my voice again, but simply took his hand and led him toward the tomb, followed by the others who by this time were murmuring and commenting, not giving us the privacy he'd wanted. "There, the new one," I said barely above a whisper.

Seeing Alphaeus and his son James in the crowd, Joshua asked them to roll back the stone. They looked dubious, but were used to taking his orders. Martha, now following close behind with Simon, spoke up, "It's been three days...the smell...you don't...."

Joshua turned and said, "Martha, didn't I tell you that you would see the glory of God?" then to Alphaeus and James, and now John Mark who had bravely gone up to join them, "Go ahead." And they did.

As they put their shoulders to the stone, Joshua prayed aloud, "Blessed are you, Lord God, King of the Universe, who brings forth life. Thank you for listening to me. I know you always do, but please let everyone here know it and believe that you have sent me and that I'm here to do your will."

The stone was safely rolled to one side, the three had turned to see what Joshua would ask them to do next, but he simply called out loudly, as though he were in the next room, "Lazarus, Lazarus! Come out! Come here, please!"

All eyes now turned to the opening in the rock; all talking stopped; all ears strained to hear struggling sounds coming from inside the tomb. A bit of white, wrapped, grave cloth emerged into view. Joshua addressed the three nearby, "Help him. Unwrap him." Astonished, they jumped to help. Thad went up with the tunic Joshua had asked him to bring from the house after he had given Martha the message.

From wailing, to murmuring, to silence, to astonished jubilation, the crowd went wild. Everyone in the village was drawn to see what was happening and joined us in the excitement. I was transfixed with amazement in spite of all of the previous wonders I'd seen my husband perform. We three women, who had kept the vigil, who knew Lazarus was dead, who had wrapped his body, were overcome with joy to see Lazarus alive again, moving, being cared for by three men. Joshua was quiet and waited patiently with his arm around me for the unwrapping and dressing of Lazarus. Out of the corner of my eye, I saw some priests and rabbis who didn't look at all pleased. We would have to deal with them later, I thought, as they began to drift toward the back of the crowd, collect their wives, and head back to Jerusalem with no more mourning required.

They didn't stay to see Lazarus, in full healthy color, walk down the short path from the tomb to where we stood wait-

ing for him, didn't see him embrace Joshua and then turn to
Hannah and hold her gently for another long while as they
sobbed together. Martha and I waited our turns, and after we
embraced him through tears of relief, Lazarus and Hannah
led us all in joyous procession back to Martha and Simon's
for the most wonderful mid-day feast I have ever enjoyed.

Everyone in Bethany, having heard the news, came to
celebrate, brought food to share, drums and instruments to
make music. We sang praises to God, who loves and saves
us, with more enthusiasm than at any festival I could remember, along with toasts, storytelling, and teasing of Joshua and
Lazarus. In amazement and wonder, our eyes shone brightly
with tears from time to time at such an unexpected event, our
mourning so suddenly turned into celebration.

From the depths of despair and abandonment, to the
heights of awe and bewilderment, nothing fit my expectations. I felt this was a life-changing day for me. It seemed
Joshua was taking me to a whole new level of trust.

# CHAPTER TWENTY-SEVEN

As the afternoon began to turn into evening, we were in for another surprise. Joshua's cousin Joel, his former student and now a priest, who'd come to us with the news of John's arrest and beheading, came into the festive gathering with a long face and anxious eyes, searched us out, and urgently asked to speak privately. I felt a chill of apprehension as I followed Joshua and Joel out of the celebration and climbed the stairs to our upper terrace. Joel seemed unsure whether I should be included, but Joshua dismissed his concern.

"It seems I'm again the bearer of bad news," he began apologetically. "But I heard you were back in Bethany from Caiaphas' brother-in-law, Jonathan Bar-Annas, who'd just returned to Jerusalem from here. He was fuming. He felt he'd been tricked into coming out to mourn with you, Miriam... Martha, and Hannah, of course, too. Then according to him, Joshua arrived and did 'a trick'...or maybe Lazarus was never dead and you three women tricked him. He didn't know, but he was very upset."

"How dreadful!" I exclaimed, "How could he...?" Lazarus' resurrection seemed impossible even to me, but I was hurt that our very real pain and our honor were questioned.

"Sorry, but that's not what I came to tell you. It was just to say how I knew you were here. Justus, Gestas, and Demas were trapped and captured yesterday by the Romans. Pilate tried them this morning and convicted them of insurrection...called them robbers and thieves, and sentenced them to be crucified the morning before Passover when everyone will be in the city sacrificing their lambs."

I blanched, shocked at the news, but Joshua remained calm, and asked, "How did the Romans know? How were they discovered?"

"As I said with John, it's difficult to tell what's accidental and what has been planned behind closed doors," Joel replied. "The rumor is that a Roman informer overheard a priest and one of John's disciples talking about big changes that were coming soon because one of John's good friends would save the people of God again, finally set up a righteous kingdom. The earnest disciple was encouraged with more wine and some skepticism to interest the priest in joining the rebellion. He revealed more and more details and eventually the whereabouts of the leaders."

"I'm sorry, but not surprised," Joshua said. "Will the Temple do anything to save Justus?"

"I don't think so, even if they wanted to," Joel replied. "You see, they likely set up the tip; had the priest, your cousin Zachariah again, appear a little knowledgeable and sympathetic to John's naive disciple to find out everything he could in an inn known to be frequented by several Roman informers. If they did this because they were in trouble, challenged by Rome because of the rumors that they've been supporting Justus and receiving tribute from him, they're in a compromised position with Pilate. One way or the other, they're not in a position to save Justus."

We were silent for a few long minutes. In the background, the sound of the celebration continued. At last Joshua said, "Yes, I see. Annas and Caiaphas are in quite a delicate position, caught between cooperating with a very popular uprising and maintaining a workable but very unpopular relationship with Herod and Rome...who appointed them after all...but I don't think they can be seen to be sympathetic, or cooperating with either side...and I don't think Justus is the only one who needs saving."

"Well, I don't know what you can do about it," Joel responded. "But I thought you would want to know. You're a friend of all of them, I think." And then he added, "If anyone can save them from this mess, it's you...but I don't know how even you could work this kind of miracle. I wish I could help."

"Thanks, Joel; maybe you can," Joshua said thoughtfully. "Let me think this over and I'll be in touch with you. Your contacts around the Temple may be a big help. Keep your ears open, and please keep me informed of anything that may be in the wind. If we each do what we can, I'm sure there will be a way to save our friends." I invited Joel to stay the night and took him downstairs to get him something to eat and drink, find a place for him to sleep, and then get two cups of wine for Joshua and me before climbing the stairs again.

When I returned, Joshua smiled, stood, and carefully took both cups from my hands and put them down on the table at his side. He took me in his arms and we held one another until we melted into one being...our hearts beat as one, our lungs breathed as one...eternity. Finally, we drew apart, looked into one another's eyes searchingly, and found our answer. We had tried to avoid this, but no matter what was ahead, our answer was simply, "Yes." For everything that had been, we were thankful. For everything to come, no matter how difficult it might be, we would say, "Yes."

The evening air was fresh, perfumed with rosemary and sage. We each took a cup and sipped the spiced wine in silence. Joshua had already had time to think. Finally, he broke the silence. "We have nine days until the crucifixions....I didn't know our sacrifices would unfold this way....I'm surprised at what God seems to have prepared for us. I thought John was preparing the way, but now it seems Justus is, too."

"I'm confused. I thought you were trying to avoid this, or something even worse, losing Justus and many others in a bloody fight. But now you think God is preparing this?"

"I didn't expect this, but yes, Mim, it seems John, Justus, and I have been intertwined since we were born. I'd like to spend another day on the mountain tomorrow. Will you meet me in the afternoon near our cave with something to eat? I'd like to spend the night there with you and have some time to talk quietly through our plans for the next nine days. I think I see our path, but I want to be sure there isn't some other way."

# CHAPTER TWENTY-EIGHT

By the time I reached Joshua on the mountainside the next afternoon, I was especially grateful for our quiet reunion. Away from Martha and Simon's home, now buzzing like a hive of bees, I could gather my thoughts. Everyone was shocked at the news of the betrayal, arrests, and planned crucifixions, especially Simon. Thomas and Philip had each taken me aside to tell me about all of the talk of the Messiah, the prophets' predictions of pain, misery, and death. They were worried that Joshua was depressed after talking with Judas Bar-Hezekiah, were troubled by others' talk about making Joshua the Messiah without understanding or considering all of the consequences, and now were concerned about the arrest of his best friend.

Others from Galilee, especially Peter, Andrew, James, and John, who were still enthralled with the idea of Joshua being the Messiah, just didn't seem to understand. Joshua had gone over and over again the prophecies that the Messiah would suffer and die, so if he were to be the Messiah as they insisted, it would not be all glory and passing out rich, powerful positions. It would rather be sending them as messengers of the Kingdom of God, after he had suffered and died for it.

Philip shook his head, and with every ounce of patience he could muster, said, "Miriam, they listen, but they don't hear. They still don't understand the kingdom Joshua is talking about...it isn't about a political system, but another world of our relationships with others...a world of the spirit." I was glad Philip understood.

On the mountain, I heard much the same summary of the trip from Joshua. And then, reassured that I was still with him, he questioned me about his insight into the sacrifice for atonement. He wondered, after considering it, whether I were still willing to do my part if he were killed, to accept the sins of the people heaped on me, as he knew they would be, and then be led into the wilderness. I told him I was still willing, but I couldn't imagine yet what that would mean, couldn't imagine life without him, or how he might be sacrificed first on an altar.

Joshua seemed to be holding back tears as he answered by putting his arm around me. We sat side-by-side on our favorite rock, he squeezed my arm gently and gave me a little kiss above my ear. Something seemed surreal, unbelievable to me, that we could actually go through what Joshua envisioned might be necessary...somehow the sacrifice of ourselves. Even though we understood God didn't want human sacrifice, people continued to require sacrifices in God's name. Could we free people once for all?

Joshua interrupted my musings, cleared his throat, and began to tell me what he believed our way would be through the next week. "We'll give them what they want, Mim," he said with both humor and sadness in his voice. "Tomorrow, I'll begin to arrange with the men for the prophesied triumphal entry into Jerusalem on the day after Sabbath...they can find an ass with her colt for me. Before the evening sacrifice with all of the pilgrims coming up from Jericho, I'll make the expected grand entrance of the promised king. But as heir apparent, I'd like the pleasure beforehand of a quiet day of rest on the Sabbath with you and the children in Jerusalem."

"The quiet day with you and the children sounds wonderful, but I'm not so sure about the triumphal entry. I don't feel comfortable in crowds...don't trust what might happen."

"After a quiet day together, I'd like to bring Sarah and Joseph back here to Bethany with me early Sunday morning, if Martha will take care of them. They're quite intrigued with Lazarus, so it shouldn't be a hardship, and I'd rather they didn't witness what I think is likely to happen in Jerusalem."

"We won't be showing the way of love?"

"Well, we may be," Joshua laughed. "In fact, we will be, but in a way few will understand. I'd rather explain it to them later."

"They seem to understand more of your way than the crowds do."

Joshua laughed again and asked, "Don't I remember saying that one must accept the Kingdom of God like a little child?"

"Oh yes," I agreed, my mood lifted for the moment with motherly satisfaction and pleasure at the way our children were growing in understanding.

Our conversation turned to the visits I'd had with Claudia, Elizabeth, Rachel, and others, the rumors, confirming Joel's stories last evening. Joshua smiled and nodded, saying, "I didn't realize how those boyhood discussions with John and Justus would turn out. I didn't expect this any more than I expected what happened on the Jericho road, which is what seems to have led us here." He shook his head and laughed sadly.

"We don't see very well into the future," I ventured, not yet seeing the humor.

"No, but we all keep busy making plans, Mim, trying to fix the future our way," he said, "only to find out that the un-imagined happens, becomes the surprise. To live in heaven, or paradise, or the Kingdom of God, which people think boring, is just the opposite, I think…it's living in constant surprise, in the delight of a good joke or an unexpected dis-covery."

"But how…?" I started to ask.

"We just have to see the humor for ourselves as life un-folds," he said with dancing eyes.

"I guess I need help," I responded. "Lazarus' illness and dying wasn't funny, but the shock of seeing his bound hand and foot trying to come out of the tomb was, I admit. If we hadn't been crying so hard, it actually would have been funny. He was bound so tightly he could hardly move. We had no idea he'd ever need to move again."

"Well, everything isn't humorous, Mim. Moses and Hero-dotus…many have written of unspeakable cruelty of humans toward those they've overpowered. But I was thinking about John, Justus, and myself again, all wanting to bring peace, justice, and wellbeing to our world. It strikes me as sadly humorous that my impractical, peaceful way would eventually require me to forgive them for their failed attempts. We couldn't imagine it."

"Say more; I don't understand."

"My challenge now is to forgive Annas and Caiaphas for their corruption. John tried to reform them and failed...I even joined him, criticizing them myself for making a sham of worship." Smiling again, he continued, "But now I must forgive them, and John for trying to reform them; help them in order to save Justus. Who would have thought that possible? Or that it would help me forgive Justus for the mess he's made with his rebellion? Or the timing, that together we would be part of the Unnameable God's new Passover...setting people free from slavery to religious rituals and sacrifices...free to laugh, to love, to forgive, to truly worship in spirit anywhere, anytime. I wondered how we could do that."

"Oh, that's almost too much, my head is spinning....You're way ahead of me."

"Sorry. There may be another way, but this one seems pretty clear to me now. The irony is that after the gift is given, we don't know who'll receive it or understand it."

I unpacked the basket of food. "That's true of all gifts, but you're seeing more than I do. What can I do to help?" I asked, offering some olives, bread, and his favorite cheese.

Biting into his favorite cheese wrapped in still warm bread, with an appreciative "Mmm," he added, "This is a great start!" and we both laughed. After a few moments of savoring the flavors of our food, Joshua continued, "Let's plan an early celebration of Passover this year with our servants and our extended family. While the servants and pilgrims help me make the triumphal ritual entry, you could avoid the crowds by going to Emmaus where mother is visiting Uncle Cleopas and Aunt Mary to invite them all to come to Jerusalem and celebrate Passover with us early on Thursday....I'd like that."

"If we have donkeys I think I can. Maybe Thad and Salome could go with me?"

"A good idea, and John Mark can go with you, too, and branch off to Bethlehem to find Jude, to be sure he and the men in Bethlehem know what's happened to Justus, Demas, and Gestas. On your way back home, you can join them and the other shepherds driving our sheep into Jerusalem. The timing should be perfect. You and I can meet each other in the sheep market."

"And choose the ram and ewe for our own sacrifices," I finished.

Joshua laughed again. "Talk about a plan!" he said. "Yes, I want to keep our tradition, but only after I have everyone's attention."

"Oh, I think you'll have it...and then?" I asked, beginning to see his humor.

"And then, after we make our sacrifices, I think that will be enough for one day if we can work our way through the crowds to return home. Our men will be helpful with that and managing my ride into Jerusalem, as prophesied."

"But pretenders do that almost every year!" I protested as I began to tease.

"True, but I plan to gather a large crowd of pilgrims from Galilee the following day to show how we taught in the hills and villages of Galilee, the realm of God right here, right now, men, women, and children, together in the Temple courts. You can help to gather as many women and children as you can to join us in the large court just past the merchants where we met Zachariah."

It was my turn to laugh. "Well, that should get the attention of Zachariah and your rabbi friends and the scribes and priests, if your triumphal entry doesn't."

Joshua nodded, "Yes, I think I'll be able to teach about our loving, inclusive God...and stimulate some lively dialogue."

"I'm sure you'll get lots of questions."

Joshua nodded and laughed again, his eyes twinkling at the prospect. "I'm looking forward to it. I may be able to persuade some, yet," he said. "We'll see, but I look forward to returning to the Temple to teach again...everyone...our servants, the pilgrims, as well as my rabbi and student friends at the Temple...everyone together."

I was delighted at the prospect of finally fulfilling our vows...praising God in the presence of *all* of the people in the Temple in Jerusalem, teaching the way of love, the way of our good Samaritan. "That sounds wonderful...but don't forget Wednesday is our dinner with Simon and Martha in Bethany," I hastened to remind him.

"No, I haven't forgotten. I'll have stirred up enough questions by Tuesday that our friends at the Temple will need a little break. I want to be with our family in Bethany."

"We're all looking forward to it. If it hadn't been for you... but I don't even want to think about it. How shall we manage Passover Thursday? How many?"

"Let's see...Mother, Uncle Cleopas and Aunt Mary, Sarah and Joseph, John Mark and maybe Mathias, Thad, our servants who've been back and forth with us...probably about twelve of them with their families, you and me, and Elijah—we can never forget that the prophet Elijah might return to earth to join any of us in our Seder."

"Of course not," I said. "We always have a place prepared for him, without saying. But what about Uncle Joseph and his family?"

"Uncle Joseph and James will come with their families, and maybe Jude will stay in the city with our sheep, maybe his family can come from Bethlehem. Perhaps Lazarus and Hannah? They could bring Sarah and Joseph and then take them back to Bethany with their cousins. I don't think Martha and Simon will come; do you? But we can ask. Can we manage them all in the upper room?"

"Maybe seventy? I think so...we can put tables together, spill out onto the terrace if necessary...the children will like that. Can you find some extra help, perhaps from pilgrims... students from Galilee? Rhoda and Judith depend on Diana now, so if she's at the table with us, they'll need extra help... and so will Nathan, Daniel, and Tobias...."

"Of course. We can all help and we'll still need some extra help and extra lambs for roasting," he said. "I know several students who'll be happy to help. It's always wonderful to gather everyone we can for Passover...to celebrate what we've been trying to teach."

When we finished eating and repacked my basket, Joshua took me by the hand and drew me close, whispering in my ear, "Do you have any idea how much I've missed you these past few weeks?" to which I replied, "Half as much as I've missed you?"

# CHAPTER TWENTY-NINE

Early the next morning, we walked hand-in-hand back down the rocky but well-worn path to Bethany. Martha agreed to care for Sarah and Joseph. Joshua talked with her Simon, Alphaeus, and then Thomas and Judas about procuring his donkey for Sunday while I had a quiet talk with my brother and Hannah before returning to Jerusalem. I would never again take for granted seeing Lazarus alive, being able to talk with him. They sensed that Joshua and I were about to risk our lives and offered to help me any time, whatever my need. I was grateful.

Once again in the comfort and privacy of our golden, old Jerusalem home, our Sabbath was one I shall never forget. All of our servants were sent for a rest. I lit the candles. Joshua broke and blessed the bread, poured and blessed the wine. Getting up from the table, he put his hands on my head and blessed me, compared me to Wisdom with familiar words from Solomon, "Happy is the man who finds wisdom and understanding in his wife. Better than silver or gold, she is more precious than jewels, and nothing I could desire can compare with her. Long life is in her right hand; in her left, wealth and honor. Her ways are ways of pleasantness, and all

of her paths are paths of peace. She is the tree of life to those
who live with her; those who hold her fast are called happy."
Intense energy flowed from his hands. Tears filled my eyes;
my accumulated concerns melted away. In short, I felt loved,
appreciated, and blessed.

Next he laid his hands on John Mark's head and blessed
him. "My son, may God give you wisdom and discretion.
Don't let them escape. They'll be inner life for you and you
will walk on your way securely, your foot won't stumble. If
you sit down, you won't be afraid; when you lie down, your
sleep will be sweet. Don't be afraid of sudden panic, or of
the ruin of the wicked when it comes; for the Lord will be
your confidence and will keep your foot from being caught.
Don't withhold good from anyone to whom it's due when it's
in your power to do it." John Mark's eyes glistened with his
blessing.

Next, Joseph sat up a little straighter in anticipation of
his turn. Joshua laid his hands on his head, "My son, may
God bless you with memory. If you remember my words
and treasure my commandments, then you will understand
righteousness and justice and every good path, for wisdom
will come into your heart, and knowledge will be pleasant to
you. Discretion will watch over you, and understanding will
guard you." I could see that Joseph was memorizing these
words, treasuring his blessing.

"Thank you, Papa," he murmured softly.

Joshua nodded, then placed his hands on Sarah's head.
"Now, Sarah, last, but not in any way least. Do not forget
my teaching, but let your heart keep my commandments for
they will give you length of days, and years of life, and abun-

dant welfare. Be always loyal and faithful so you will find favor and good understanding in the eyes of God and others. Trust in the Lord with all of your heart, acknowledge God, and God will make your paths straight." Then with a wink to me, he added, "Charm is deceitful, and beauty is vain, but a woman who fears the Lord is to be praised. Give her the fruit of her hands, and let her works praise her in the gates." Our daughter beamed.

We enjoyed our meal together, the evening, the morning, the entire day of rest. Family stories, questions about when we were growing up, questions about John Mark's travels, questions about his father's travels with Uncle Joseph, questions about what it meant to be loving in one circumstance or another filled the day. Joshua gently prepared the children for some of the week's events, explaining as clearly and simply as he could the complications of "Uncle Justus," for so they thought of him, being arrested and condemned to crucifixion, and how he hoped to rescue his best friend. He said he wanted John Mark to go tell Jude and the shepherds in Bethlehem, and he wanted Sarah and Justus to go to Bethany with him, to stay there to keep Martha, Simon, Hannah, and Lazarus safe and occupied for a few days. Each of us had our part to do.

With a very early start, the next day went as planned. Cleopas, his wife Mary, and Joshua's mother were all happy to see me, Thad, and Salome, my traveling companions. They were curious as to why we were celebrating Passover a day early, but as his mother said, "Life is never quite what you expect with Joshua!" At any rate, they were happy to come to Jerusalem a day early, and to celebrate with one part of the family on Thursday, perhaps another part of the family the next night.

Returning, I met the shepherds driving the sheep, raised in the shadow of the Migdal Edor, the tower that had marked Rachel's grave near Bethlehem, as prescribed for the Temple sacrifices. It was quite a magnificent sight. I spotted our eldest son helping his uncle and cousins, quite happy and at ease with the whole process. He'd inherited that from his father. Looking across the valley to the Mount of Olives, I saw the procession of pilgrims heading toward Jerusalem, and I knew Joshua was with them, the crowd so similar to these flocks of bleating sheep. I could hear their songs, their chanting this far away! Animals and pilgrims were sweeping us along. There was little any of us could do but move toward what was awaiting us.

At the sheep gate into the city, I dismounted and gave my donkey to Thad to take home. As I moved on foot through the gate with the animals and then on into the market, the stench was almost overwhelming. Urine, feces, wool, sweat all mixed in the glaring sunlight. Joshua and I met, as he'd foreseen, in the middle of it all..

With his shepherd's eye, Joshua picked out of our flocks the perfect ewe for me, the perfect ram for himself. He embraced John Mark, Jude, a nephew or two, and then with the ewe and ram under control with one hand while protecting me with his other arm, we walked toward the Temple, pushed along by the crowds. Thomas, Simon, Philip, and the others followed, trying desperately to protect us from being entangled in the mass of humanity as we headed to the Temple to make our sacrifices.

Like steering a boat in a fast-moving stream, Joshua maneuvered us around people gathered around a merchant here, a moneychanger there, up steps and through gates and dark, narrow passages until we finally reached the part of the Temple where the priests were receiving the sacrifices. Guiding us past several priests with their attendants and the collection of people waiting to make an offering, we came to the place where Joseph Caiaphas, himself, was receiving offerings that afternoon before the evening sacrifice. Those ahead of us made their offerings, faded away, and then there we were, face-to-face with our longtime friend, whose assistant today was none other than Nahum, the priest who had first passed Joshua on the Jericho Road.

"What a pleasure to see you again, Joseph...find you receiving sacrifices yourself today. Miriam and I've come to make our offerings for sin and communion," Joshua said.

Joseph Caiaphas returned the smile. "And I'm pleased to see you two, again...setting a good example for the hordes that I hear are following you these days. I'm told you've not been so careful about all aspects of the law, but that's what this sacrifice is about."

"Indeed," replied Joshua, "sins known and unknown, things done," a nod to Nahum, "and things left undone." Smiling he added, "May God forgive us as we forgive each other."

"Ah, that seems to be the problem or question, Joshua," Caiaphas replied. "You seem quick to forgive, but on whose authority? And even without being asked?"

"Well, it's a lesson I learned in the dirt of the Jericho Road. It changed my life, Joseph. Maybe one has to be that close to death to see clearly, but I hope not. I hope others can learn from my experience as well and hold nothing back from life, even forgiveness."

"We must talk further. Elizabeth and I welcome your return to Jerusalem, but now...."

"Yes, of course," Joshua replied. "You have many more offerings to receive. Peace to both of you," Joshua again acknowledged Nahum, "and greet Elizabeth and Mathias with our love. We must talk again before the week is out." And with a minimum of ritual, we left our ewe and ram to the care of Joseph Caiaphas and our respective assistants.

As we walked out across the crowded Temple courts toward our home, we made very slow progress. Joshua was recognized by so many from Galilee who just wanted to touch, or talk, or ask for healing for themselves or a friend or relative. My husband was gracious and responded as often as he could, while moving slowly toward the quiet haven of our home. Word quickly passed from person to person, and people who had been part of the procession began crowding around, hailing him as Messiah, king.

Once we managed to get outside the Temple, we looked at each other and realized our home would be stormed by a crowd if we continued. Turning quickly into a little side passage, and then immediately into one of our favorite shops to gain some quiet, he said, "Stay here until I lead them all away. The men and I will go back to the country or Bethany tonight. It will settle down as they'll all need to eat and find shelter. You can go on home in peace and some anonymity, but remember to bring as many women and children as you can tomorrow morning to meet us in the court just beyond the merchants and moneychangers."

My eyes began to tear, again, as I trembled. "Thank you; I will. Go in peace, my love...."

"Your love is vital to my peace, Mim," he responded, brushing away my tears, "as is knowing that God is loving us both every minute wherever we are. Go in God's peace, Mim." He kissed me and was gone before we could be discovered by the crowd.

The next morning, I arrived in the Temple court along with a large group of women and children, servants, neighbors, Omah, Adah, Diana, and many women we knew from Galilee whom we gathered as we passed through the crowded streets. We joined the crowd and the confrontation that Joshua had expected. The crowd following him and our servants swelled with pilgrims, students and the rabbis, scribes and priests who were not on duty at the moment. I recognized many, including Nicodemus and Zachariah.

Some in the crowd were persuaded and supportive, some antagonistic, looking for an opportunity to trap him. The biggest question discussed was the one of authority. What was Joshua's relationship to God? How could he say and do what he was saying and doing? Why was he polluting the Temple, gathering who knows who, foreigners, outcasts, rabble in whatever state of cleanliness, women, and children...teaching them all. The Temple had strict rules about how to honor God.

Joshua was clearly enjoying himself, I thought, parrying, asking questions in return, often showing how silly some of their questions and criticisms really were. Of course, this

response irritated the questioners, especially when Joshua
seemed to be so knowledgeable and quick to respond while
at ease and in peaceful command...really entertaining the listeners. He was a great master teacher and let many learn
from their own mistakes.

I saw frustration rising in the men I knew who were part
of the Temple establishment. This display wasn't what they'd
planned for pilgrims coming to the feast. A distraction, a
challenge to their authority, it made them look foolish in everyone's eyes. I overheard several planning to call a council
that afternoon, to turn things around. "Imagine, he even
uses a Greek form of his name now that he's left us!" "This
can't be allowed to go on." How would Joshua ever get to
talk to Caiaphas again, I wondered.

Around mid-day, Joshua sent Thad with a message that the
men and he would go back out of the city again for the night.
If I wanted to see what was next, I should be back here early
in the morning...but in any case, he would slip away and
meet me in Bethany on Wednesday.

As I left, I was somewhat reassured by Nicodemus and several other rabbis who passed me. They were clearly enjoying
themselves, and seeing me, Nicodemus said, "What a brilliant performance, Miriam...you must be very proud of him.
He has a way of raising difficult questions to a new level!"
Others nodded approval and greeted me. I went home and
wrote down as much as I could remember of what I'd heard.

Thad had stressed "early" the next morning. I didn't want
to miss anything, and so at the first cock crow, I stretched,
said a prayer, and got out of bed to dress in suitably dull street
clothing. I went to the kitchen where I found Diana. She

went with me to the Temple, before we would go on to the market to buy food for the feast on Thursday. People were just waking, some merchants were beginning to set up stalls, others were beginning to open their shops in the refreshingly cool morning air.

As we approached the Temple court, I heard a commotion. There were Joshua, students, and trusted servants overturning the still empty tables, sending away the merchants and moneychangers who were just arriving, not allowing them to set up their places of business. This action was not going without protest on this busiest sales day of the entire year. They had paid dearly for the use of the tables today. What were they to do with their birds, their souvenirs, their Temple money to be exchanged? A lot of swearing followed, and calling for Temple guards, calling for whoever was up and had any authority to stop this nonsense. Joshua had simply taken command, ordered them, "Out, Out, Out! God's house is holy! It's not a market! Do your business elsewhere! I've told you so before. You've had notice. Time is up!"

Our unarmed servants simply stood guard on the overturned tables at intervals down the length of the market corridor. They were reinforced by pilgrims and students who were early risers, who had seen Joshua and the men come into the city and had followed along. As the minutes passed, the crowd of the curious grew, some looking for a confrontation, some simply wanting to hear more from this great teacher who seemed so different, seemed naturally to have such authority.

I stopped with Diana at a safe distance away to observe all of this, but Joshua saw me out of the corner of his eye, smiled, and gave a little nod in my direction, as if to say he were glad I'd come to see.

It was Zachariah who finally arrived with several scribes and priests whom I recognized as antagonistic questioners from the day before, and after them, a few Temple guards. They demanded to know what was going on. The crowd gathered around.

Joshua smiled and said, "I'm glad you asked. You were concerned about defiling the Temple yesterday so I thought I would help you out today. Don't you know the passage in Isaiah, 'Thus says the Lord: 'Keep justice and do righteousness, for soon my salvation will come, and my deliverance will be revealed....Foreigners who join themselves to me to love my name and to be my servants, everyone who keeps the Sabbath and holds fast my covenant I will bring to my holy mountain and make them joyful in my house of prayer. My house will be known as a house of prayer. I will gather the outcasts of Israel and I will gather others as well.' By whose authority do you allow men to do business in the Lord's house of prayer?"

Before they could answer, astonished at Joshua's assurance and command of Scriptures, Joshua asked another question, clearly enjoying himself, but very serious. "Have you not studied Jeremiah either, where he reports that the word of the Lord came to him, 'Stand in the gate of the Lord's house and proclaim there this word, and say, "Hear the word of the Lord, all you men of Judah who enter these gates to worship the Lord. Thus says the Lord of Hosts, the God of Israel: Amend your ways and your doings, and I will let you dwell in this place. Do not trust in these deceptive words: 'This is the

Temple of the Lord, the Temple of the Lord, the Temple of the Lord.' For if you truly amend your ways and your doings, if you truly deal justly with one another, if you do not oppress the foreigner, the fatherless, or the widow, or shed innocent blood in this place, and if you do not go after other gods to your own hurt, then I will let you dwell in this place, in the land that I gave of old to your fathers forever.'"

The crowd grew by the minute, but was hushed to hear this teacher quoting the words of the Lord. They had not heard anything like it. It was as though God himself were speaking. They didn't want to miss a word...quite a contrast to the din of the past few days. Sensing the rapt attention, Joshua continued to speak the words of the Lord recorded in Jeremiah, "Behold you trust in deceptive words to no avail. Will you steal, murder, commit adultery, swear falsely, burn incense to the gods of fertility, and go after other gods that you have not known, and then come and stand before me in this house, which is called by my name, and say, 'We are delivered!'...only to go on doing all these abominations? Has this house, which is called by my name, become a den of thieves and robbers in your eyes? Behold I myself have seen It, says the Lord."

At this point, there was stunned silence. Everyone knew the truth of what was said. After a moment, Joshua continued in a slightly more confidential tone, one of a wise father giving his child a lesson, some advice. "Our God is living spirit, and those who worship must worship in spirit and in truth wherever they are. Each one of our bodies is a Temple for the living, indwelling God. Be careful not to defile your Temple, your body, with unclean desires of your heart...greed, wanting and taking that which is not yours to take, seeking control over others, using and abusing others. It's not what is seen on the outside, but what God sees on the inside that defiles. We worship either the true, life-giving God or a false god with every breath we take."

"But I've failed time and again. I've come to the Temple to seek forgiveness. I know I need it, to be clean again..." whined someone close to the front of the crowd.

Joshua smiled and said, "Yes, we've failed from the beginning of our lives. Remember the story of Adam and Eve. God had skins ready to cover them, had already made the sacrifice himself, was ready to forgive. Forgiveness is not for sale; it can't be bought or earned. It is a gift to each of us."

The mumbling within the group from the Temple grew louder during this answer, and the objections were even more intense after Joshua said, "Forgiveness is not for sale." That was too close to Temple practice. Someone from the back said, "But Rabboni, Moses gave us instructions from God to worship where God chooses."

"Yes," responded Joshua, "as a son of God, you remember in the Ten Commandments, the warning against worship of any stones, images, people, places, or things. Our God is without image, nothing to be contained or controlled. Where you worship doesn't matter. What you love, what you give your life to is your true worship. God chooses your heart, your mind, your very being. Don't dare approach the True God with anything less!"

Many were in awe of Joshua, others were not. Their questions became more antagonistic as they hoped to catch him in a blasphemy and be rid of his probe into their lives and practices. They wanted to regain control, to get back to business.

Understanding their aim, Joshua, with good humor, again and again showed the triviality of their self-imposed rules and regulations, avoiding the basic truth of life. After a while, he thanked the listeners, signaled his men, and left the Temple.

# CHAPTER THIRTY

That afternoon, I went over plans for the Passover meal with Rhoda, Judith, Susanna, and Diana. Confident we were prepared, I left them and went to our room to rest and reflect. John Mark found me there, bringing news that his father was still surrounded by a crowd of questioners. Joshua sent me a message, "The cave," which John Mark found mysterious.

"It's all right," I laughed. "Your father just wants some quiet time. I understand. Let's go to Bethany before sundown. Do you want to ask Mathias?"

We arrived a day early for our celebration. Martha and I exchanged news and I asked for her help, a basket of food, some wine, and her silence. She understood and led me to the kitchen to pack an ample basket for two. I promised to help with the dinner the next morning, slipped out of the house, and climbed a little used path up the mountain.

Trudging up the path alone as the sun began to set, I hoped I'd understood Joshua and that he could get away. As I climbed out of the orchards onto the path leading to the big rock, I heard a whistle, looked around, and there coming over the far side of the hill was a familiar figure. I was reassured and hurried to meet him. Our eyes danced as we met with a warm embrace, relieved simply to be alone together, to share a simple supper and a brilliant sunset, before continuing on to the further shelter and silence of our cave.

The next morning, we woke early with the first light before dawn. Savoring the last moments of our quiet refuge while we nibbled at the leftovers, Joshua told me that the men and he would go to Jerusalem again for a short while, to check with Cousin Joel and Nicodemus to see what they'd heard. Seeing a flash of concern cross my face, he added, "But don't worry; I'll be at Simon and Martha's for dinner well before sundown." And then as an afterthought, he said, "But I'll have to bring a few of the men with me. They won't let me out of sight, unless I slip off to the mountain like I did last night."

"Three or four?" I asked. "Thomas, Judas, Alphaeus, James, and Matthew are already invited with their wives, as well as Thad, of course."

"Three or four," he said with a smile, brushing a wisp of hair back off my forehead, and running his fingers lightly through my hair. "Oh, Mim, I hope God has another way to save these headstrong people from the consequences of their choices. I don't see another way, and I'm willing to die to save them, but I don't want you to suffer. His eyes, shining brightly, welled with tears. "If I do, if I must, can you...will you love me if I die?"

My eyes filled, too. "I'll always love you, but I don't want you to die...." We held one another so tightly no earthly power could separate us.

Finally, Joshua began, "Our Father," and I joined, "Your will be done in our lives today."

That evening, he came with his four Galilean fishermen whom he was still teaching, into the great room of Simon and Martha's home, which now had tables laden with their best linens, goblets, and dinnerware. It was quite a contrast to the full day of Temple intrigue and prison gossip they had experienced in the dusty streets, Temple courtyards, and small nooks and crannies in the market where men gathered to exchange rumors. Our Bethany families and servants, along with John Mark and Mathias, Sarah and Joseph and I, all dressed in our best robes for this special celebration of his healing Simon of leprosy, were eagerly waiting for him. The new arrivals washed their feet and took places at the table. Joshua was seated between Simon and me at the table's head, Martha on the other side of Simon, Lazarus beside me, then Hannah, our children, and so on. Our family seating was perhaps unusual.

Before sitting, I stepped to a nearby alcove, retrieved the precious alabaster jar from the place I'd hidden it, and carried it to my place. Joshua had followed me with his eyes from the moment he came into the room, and now saw what I carried. Our eyes glistened. I trembled. He helped me open the jar. The earthy fragrance of myrrh filled the room. I anointed his head with the precious oil, and then unable to hold back the tears, I slipped down to his feet. He bent down, took some remaining oil from the jar, and tenderly caressed my head, anointing me as well. My hair had completely tumbled from my best scarlet red shawl. My tears wet his feet and I began to wipe them dry with my hair and shawl. No one but Joshua understood this token of our sacrifice to come. I wore my best dress, my simple wedding dress, and his favorite deep red shawl, brought from Jerusalem with the precious alabaster jar.

Though unexpected, our family sensed something significant. That was not the case with Peter and the other three from Galilee who began to murmur and complain about this unexpected interruption and extravagance. Peter was particularly disgruntled, and asked Judas, "Where does she get the money? That's a year's wages spilled out for what? Can't you do a better job of controlling her spending?"

Martha told me later that sensitive Judas had looked uncomfortable and shrugged. So Peter turned to address John and Andrew sitting on either side of him. "How are we ever going to have a righteous kingdom with this kind of thing? We've been with poor people all day and they need all the help we can give them."

Joshua gently took the beautiful jar from the floor beside me and placed it on the table between us. He tenderly lifted me up, seated me, sat down again, and took my hand. He looked around the table and said, "What Miriam has just done is wonderfully significant. She has anointed me with our family treasure which was given me by the Wise Men. The time has come." Addressing the four across the table, almost with despair, he added, "You men can do something for the poor whenever you want. Miriam has shown her love and understanding. Simon, Lazarus, John Mark, Peter, all of you, I solemnly charge you to tell what Miriam has just done whenever you tell my story."

A moment of awkward silence followed as the criticizers realized that again, they really didn't know what was happening. Joshua turned to Simon, our host. "Enough about me, my patient and gracious brother-in-law! Let's get on with this celebration of your health and wellbeing. Simon, you're a wonderful part of my life. I've looked forward to this celebration," he paused, and laughed, "for about a year now!"

Tensions dissolved. "I see you've already provided us with wine, so I propose a toast. May Simon, who gives the best parties I have ever attended, live many years in good health, loving and caring for Martha, and this good company. May God always be honored and blessed in your home, and bless you and your household, my friend, with abundant love, overflowing to all whom you meet!" We all responded with a hearty "so be it," raised our goblets, and drank. Food was served, lamps were lit, musicians played, we sang and danced into the night with stories and laughter.

We spent the night in our room in Bethany, content with our mutual anointing, our willingness to go through the next door together, wherever it might lead. Joshua left early in the morning with Thomas, Judas, and the Galileans. John Mark, Mathias, Thad, and I hurried back to Jerusalem to prepare for the Passover. Joshua sent several students from Galilee to help with preparation and serving so this could be a special meal not only for our family but also for those who had followed us back and forth between Jerusalem and Galilee the past few years.

Late that afternoon, I welcomed our extended family as they arrived. Our home was filled with savory aromas of roasted lambs and all of the accompaniments. Uncle Joseph arrived early to visit with Mother Mary. John Mark went to the Temple with Mathias to find Joshua still engaged in conversations with rabbis, students, and earnest pilgrims. Eventually, they were all able to slip away and make their way home. Joshua greeted those still in the entrance, and then he took me by the arm and excused us.

We went to our room for a few minutes alone together. He changed out of his robe, washed his hands and face, and put on the beautiful robe he wore at our wedding, woven without a seam, which he kept to wear at special occasions. I gave him his favorite brown shawl he'd wrapped the children with while telling them stories, and freshened myself. I wore my simple, white wedding dress, again with my favorite red shawl, which he'd given me. We kissed, breathed a deep, silent prayer, and went back to the others and climbed the stairs.

Joshua had new things to teach us, and first, a surprise. As we gathered in our large upper room and found our places at the table, he took the towel and wash basin from Tobias who was prepared for the cleansing ritual, washing our feet. He asked Tobias to follow with a jug of fresh water, and Daniel with a basin and towel for our hands, as he began with his mother, and moved quickly around the table, washing and drying our feet with the towel himself, a common and menial household task. Surprised, his mother and Uncle Joseph accepted his gesture, as did the others until he came to Peter. Unable to accept this reversal, Peter blustered, "You shouldn't wash my feet; I should wash yours! It's not proper!" Peter looked to others for support in his argument.

Joshua smiled and sighed, "No, Peter, you don't understand yet what I'm doing. If I don't wash your feet, you still won't learn what I'm doing, how I'm living."

Embarrassed, Peter said, " Master, not only my feet, then...
my head and hands as well."

Joshua laughed, "No, Peter, just your feet for now." Joshua
continued around the table, finally to me. As he sat, I slipped
to my knees, took the basin from Tobias, washed and dried
my husband's feet. Our eyes met, glistening with our understanding.

I stood, lit, and blessed the lamps, praised God for bringing light into the world, and then, I praised God for bringing
the light of my husband's life and understanding into our
world, casting out pretense, darkness, and fear. A few eyebrows raised at my addition.

Joshua took one of the large rounds of unleavened bread
and raised it, blessing God, King of the Universe, for bringing forth the fruit of the earth. He tore a piece and gave it to
his mother along with the bread from which she tore a piece
for Uncle Joseph, and so on, a bite for everyone to share with
a neighbor. As the remaining piece of bread came to me, I
turned with it to Joshua. We tore the bread in two and ate
together.

After the chatter quieted, Joshua poured wine into our
beautiful, large goblet, which he'd brought back from his trip
to Gaul with Uncle Joseph, one of the treasures we used on
special feast days. Pale green glass, it had a simple and ele-
gant shape and design, a grapevine woven about it from the
base to the bowl. Joshua lifted the goblet and said, "Blessed
are you, Lord God, King of the Universe, who brings forth
wine to make our hearts glad. There is enough for all." He
passed the goblet to his mother, who took a sip, passed it to

Uncle Joseph, and so on around the table until it came to me, still enough for a sip for me and one for Joshua.

Not hurrying on to the familiar story of the Passover, Joshua asked everyone at the table to be patient while he compared his body to the bread, his blood to the wine...both gifts of our Lord God, King of the Universe, "I am as much a part of you, and you are as much a part of each other as the bread and wine are now part of us. We are one body by bread and wine, connected as children by flesh and blood. We are each one a child of God whose command is to love one another, not enslave one another with ideas or chains. Because God first loves us, we love those whom God sends to us." He paused for a moment. "And now, Sarah, what is your question?"

"Why is this night different from all other nights, Papa?" she asked with curiosity.

We answered with food and song. Slaves to a magnificent king who made lives very bitter with hard labor, we were rescued by the living God who had pity on us and sent Moses to lead us into freedom, into the wilderness and into the Promised Land of abundance, asking only that we never bow down to anything or anyone, that we love and respect others. How often we had failed even those simple necessities for our own and our collective peace and freedom.

We remembered slavery with bitter herbs and salt water tears, then the lamb sacrificed, lintels marked with blood, our firstborn passed over, not killed. We remembered that life is in the blood sacrificed for our freedom. God, the giver of life, offered a substitute for us. Through God's wonders and sacrifice, we escaped.

Since that night of escape, we have struggled either to return fearfully to the known of slavery to money, priests, lesser gods, rulers and their systems, or to trust fearlessly the unknown of a relationship with an unseen spirit, the Living Creative God of Love.

"Now, Sarah, I have a question for you," Joshua said as we drew toward the evening's end. "How will this night make a difference in our lives?" No one was prepared for this inquiry. Familiar questions pointed to past blessings. Joshua helped her, "Remember the lamb was sacrificed for us and bread and wine are part of us now, like body and blood. We are loved, have shared in the sacrifice, and are free to go with love into the unknown without fear." Then he spoke to our servants, "You've called me 'Master' and teacher. From this night forward, I call you friends and ask you to love and forgive and heal others...care for others as I have. Let our lives and our songs give blessing and insight to those who can't see for themselves." Joshua smiled. "Be compassionate from the depths of your hearts and live in my love and peace always."

Looking around the table, Joshua nodded to Judas, who quietly excused himself and went with Rhoda to open the door for Elijah, and then quietly slipped out. After a few moments, Joshua said, "Elijah didn't join us tonight, but perhaps next year. Let's all bless the Lord our God with one more cup of wine, and another song before my friends and I go to attend to some further business tonight."

# CHAPTER THIRTY-ONE

Tired, we left the room with songs running through our heads as well as questions. I hugged Sarah and Joseph, who left for Bethany on donkeys with Lazarus and Hannah, and then settled Mother Mary in her room, checked to see the clean up was almost done, and finally, went to our room. Wondering, I stayed awake in the light of my favorite little oil lamp, considering Joshua's last question and praying more Psalms. John Mark and Thad burst through the door a few hours later. "Father's been taken to Annas' house by Malchus and some guards...taken into custody, Mother!" John Mark panted, out of breath from running.

Startled, I asked, "What happened?" and then, "Let's go; you can tell me on the way." I threw on my scarlet red shawl again and they followed me out the door, talking as fast as they could, filling in the unexpected, inexplicable details by fits and starts during the few minutes' walk to the large old home of Annas and Judith, hidden from the street by high walls, adjoining their neighbors, almost creating the effect of a fortress. Before we reached the familiar, large, carved cedar door, which was lit at this late hour by torches held by a couple of servants, I asked John Mark and Thad to leave me quickly and go on to Bethany to tell Martha and Lazarus. Walking on either side of me, they'd been excitedly telling me what had happened with Judas, Malchus' ear, and the arresting party as fast as they could, before I sent them off.

In the quiet of a Sabbath afternoon eight days later, John Mark would tell me that after our Passover celebration, he'd left Mathias near his home and then jogged to catch up, and walked on to our olive press garden that night with his father and the other men by the light of torches here and there in the city, and then by the light of the full moon as they went out into the country. Just behind his father as they walked along, John Mark heard his father humming to himself, except when answering a question from Peter who still didn't seem to understand. Walking into our work yard, his father stopped near the olive press to wait for those following.

"When we were all together, Father said, 'I've been thinking about what difference this night will make in our lives... Passover...John is dead. Justus is in prison. Power is abused but people stay complaining in a system that enslaves them. Freedom and love seem too risky. How can God free them? Free us? Let's pray for God's will and the strength and courage to take the risk, whatever comes.' There was some yawning and shuffling of feet. We were all sorry for Thad and Simon and Justus and Father, but it seemed impossible to do anything for Justus now, the night before the crucifixion. What could we do? Sensing our dwindling attention, Father just started singing a psalm, 'Let's give thanks again.'"

My eyes glistened. I'd sung it alone that night in our room. John Mark continued, "I stood by Father, and got my usual squeeze on my shoulders as we sang 'for all generations.' Father asked Peter, James, and John to go with him to the other side of the press since they were the ones who still needed the most help with prayers. I followed him, too, after I'd said what I could to Thad and Simon. The others were tired but anxious and quickly finished talking while they settled onto familiar dirt and found a rock or wall to lean against. They weren't as interested in Moses and the Passover as Father was and just wanted to go back to Galilee as soon as possible and continue with his teaching and healing."

"No one felt at ease, though, with the tensions in...'the city of Peace'...which is such an ironic name. 'Too many speaking for God and fighting to the death in it,' Thomas summed it up. Peter, James, and John settled down against the big stones of the press. I went up into the garden to sit on my favorite low branch of the old olive tree beside the big rock where Father was sitting. We've had good talks there, but I didn't want to disturb him with my questions. I knew some priests and rabbis were angry with him, disagreed with interpretations of the law, but I didn't understand why all of the anger."

I raised my eyebrows with a bit of a smile. "It seems all of the rules interpreting the ten have certainly become complicated, don't you think?"

"That's what Father said. People are constantly having to buy offerings because they're always breaking some rule according to the priests. But Hillel, Gamaliel, and his students seem to point to the same summary of the Law as Father: 'Love the Lord your God with your every thought and breath, with your very being, and love your neighbor as you love yourself.' Why was Father in so much trouble?"

I sighed, "Your father asked, 'What if my neighbor is my enemy, or needs me on the Sabbath, or needs me to forgive him?' And then he lived his answers...."

John Mark nodded thoughtfully. "I was thinking about the rituals and sacrifices I've seen to one god or another while I was with Uncle Joseph and comparing them with our Passover. Father got up and began walking slowly around the rock, the silence broken only by chirping insects and an occasional cough or snort, and then he knelt, and said, 'Father God, you can get me out of this, can't you? Please take this cup away from me if there is another way, but I'm here to do your will.' He got up again and began walking and singing, 'Before gods I praise you. I bow toward your holy Temple, and acclaim your name for your kindness and your steadfast truth....'

"I knew the psalm and sang softly with him, 'On the day I called you answered me, you gave me inner strength. All the rulers of the earth will acknowledge you, Lord, for they have heard your word. They will sing of your way, for great is your glory. Though high, You see the lowly, and watch the haughty. Though I walk in the middle of trouble, You give me life in spite of my enemies' angry attacks.'

"I thought, that must be why we're here. Things must have been bad at the Temple yesterday and Father didn't want to stay in Jerusalem, didn't want to involve you." He paused. "Then we finished, 'Stretch out your hand, and rescue me. Finish what you started in me, O Lord. Your love is forever. Don't let go of me now.'"

"Yes," I whispered and smiled through tears. "Your father and I often prayed this."

"Father sat down again on the rock. I shifted my position and thought about what he prayed and took a deep breath and remembered, 'Be still, and know that I am God.'"

"Father began to speak as though God were sitting beside him on the rock. 'Lord, you search me and know me, when I sit and when I get up,'" at which point Father did get up and began slowly pacing again. 'You know my motives, my moving and my resting. You are aware of everything I do. I speak no word that you aren't already aware of it.'"

John Mark loved the psalm and asked whether I could imagine how many places he'd repeated it on his trip? Ephesus, Athens, Rome, Massilia, Nîmes. With the lines that imagine potters, he continued, "'You shape me. Your hand is upon me, guiding me. Your knowledge is beyond my comprehension. Where can I go from your Spirit or flee from you? If I ascend to the heavens, you're there. If I descend to hell, you're there.'

"I wondered why everyone doesn't understand that God is everywhere, shaping us, loving us. There would be nothing to fear. But there was no time for speculation as Father continued and I joined him in a whisper." I smiled at our son's honesty and joined him as he continued to tell his story. "If I fly with the dawn or dwell at the ends of the sea, your hand still leads me, and your right hand holds me."

John Mark stopped again to make another comment. "This always makes me think of walking with Grandfather Joseph when I was little. As he reached down and took me by the hand, I always felt so happy and secure. Smiling, Father continued, 'If I were to say that darkness will cover me, and light will turn to night around me, darkness doesn't darken for you, night is as bright as day. Dark and light are the same to you who created my inmost parts, shaped me in my mother's womb. I praise you for you set me apart. Your acts are wonderful and I know it in the core of my being.'

"Father sat down, seemed content, and continued, 'My body was not hidden from you as I was formed in a secret place, molded in the depths. Your eyes saw my unformed shape and all was written in your book. My days were fashioned, not one of them missing.' How can we worry or be afraid, I wondered. Life is a daily discovery."

I was learning as much about my son as I was about my husband and felt thankful as we continued together. "How beautiful, how rare your thoughts, O God, how countless. Should I count them, they would be more than the grains of sand."

"I was suddenly almost startled. Father was on his feet and began to pace around the rock as he continued in a tone of voice I'd heard only when he was deeply frustrated by injustice and lies and corruption that exploit people in the name of God. 'God, will you turn bloodthirsty men away from me?' he asked. 'Those who say your name only to scheme, who swear falsely and detest you, Lord? They offend me and I draw away from your enemies.'"

"Father kept walking, but was silent again. I imagined he was thinking of men who baited him as he was trying to teach, would swear to anything for a price, and looked at Temple worship as a privilege and an opportunity to make money. He sat down again and ran his hands through his hair and then held his hands up to plead in tears, 'Search me, my God, and know my heart, probe my thoughts, and see if

I have given in to any unjust thoughts. Lead me in your way of peace.' After a while, he dropped his hands, wiped his eyes, and sighed, 'Not my will, but yours, Father.'"

We sat in silence, my son and I, as he had with his father that night. "Father was a man of peace, Mother; he wasn't an agitator, and he began another psalm. 'Rescue me, Lord, from plots and violent men.' He stood and began pacing and circling the rock again. 'Preserve me from those who plot evil in their hearts and stir up conflict every day. They speak with forked tongues like serpents. Poison is under their lips. Guard me, Lord, from the proud men who plot and scheme to trip up my steps.'"

"Who do you think he had in mind?" I asked.

"I wondered, too, and thought of Mathias' father. Coming home early from Torah study one day, Mathias and I overheard his father make a deal with some men to give false testimony about someone at the Temple. Later, Mathias argued fiercely with him. I don't know, but Father continued, 'Contemptuous, they plan to trap me and spread out enticements to entangle me along my path. You are my God, listen to my plea.' I was praying the psalm with Father, but couldn't get my mind off Caiaphas!

"'Lord, God, my rescuing strength, shelter me on the day of their attack. Don't grant, O Lord, the desires of the vicious, don't fulfill their schemes, don't let them succeed. May the harm done by their own lips cover their heads with shame who seek to entrap me.' With all of those men at the Temple asking compromising questions and misquoting, Father must have been tired of all of their shallow verbal game playing while so many people were desperate for a better life," John Mark surmised.

"Father simply stood still, thinking while I wondered who could accuse Father of anything bad? He gave his life to teach, to heal, to help people. I thought he was struggling with the next words because he had said, 'Love your enemy,' but maybe all the psalm was asking was that evil actions be returned to the sender. He began to walk again, 'Lord, let them be covered with embarrassment as they slip themselves into the holes which they have dug for others. Don't let slander stay unexposed and unchallenged. Let violent men fall into their own traps.' He seemed exhausted and sat down again. I was less confident than he of the rest of the psalm, 'I know that the Lord will give what is right to the lowly, and justice to the needy. Yes, the just will give thanks to you and the upright will live in your presence.'

"Oh God, I really did hope so! Father seemed content for a few minutes, but the silence was broken by a loud snort, coming from the olive press where Peter, James, and John were asleep. I didn't realize they hadn't been praying along with us."

# CHAPTER THIRTY-TWO

"Father looked over at me," John Mark continued, "raised his eyebrows, and acknowledged what had happened. He went down to the snorers and nudged them, called their names, and asked how they'd fallen asleep so soon after such brave talk. I'll never forget his disappointment. He asked Peter if he couldn't stay awake for just one hour. 'Your spirit is always so willing, Peter. Pray you don't give in to temptation. Pray with me tonight.'"

Poor Peter. Joshua knew what they were facing, how delicate the path. It was another insight into Peter's bluster and failure, a foreshadowing of what has happened since.

John Mark continued, "Father climbed the steps back up to our rock, threw himself face down, and with a choked voice, prayed again, 'Father, I know all things are possible for you. Let this pass. Guide me. I'm here to do your will.' After a few minutes of silence, he got up and began to walk again, until on the far side of the rock, he stopped, turned, and faced the Temple. He lifted his arms and hands and began another David prayer.

"'O Lord, please hurry, listen to me when I call. May my prayer be as incense, my raised hands as the evening offering.'

He dropped his hands and wiped tears from his eyes again. 'O Lord, watch my mouth and guard my lips. Don't let me speak a hurtful word or plot injustice with vicious men, or feast on their delicacies.'

"Father walked on around and sat down to face me again. We continued, 'Let a just man strike me or a faithful man rebuke me; it would be a kindness. I'd rather that than let an unjust man's oil adorn my head, for my prayer is still against injustice. Let unjust leaders slip and fall on the rock of justice if they must, but let them hear my words which are sweet and true....'

"Father began to walk again, 'For my eyes turn to you, O Lord. I take refuge in you. Don't leave me unprotected; guard me from the trap they have laid for me, from the enticements of the unjust. May the vicious fall into their own nets while I go on safely.'

"Ominous in the fervent way he said it, I felt he knew something I didn't, but I thought, Bravo David! Bravo Father! Bravo God! He apparently didn't share my enthusiasm and no sound came from the direction of Peter, James, and John.

"Father heaved a sigh, and again walked down to his sleeping companions, leaned over, and gently shook each one on the shoulder. You can imagine that they were embarrassed to have fallen asleep again so quickly. The three struggled to their feet amidst mumbles of 'Sorry,' 'I thought I was awake,' 'Was it psalm...?' Father just grasped each man in turn by his shoulders, and warned him, "You need to pray as much as I do. Pray, that you'll have strength for what's coming.'

"Father again climbed to the rock, fell to his knees, and repeated his same prayer, 'Abba, with you everything is possible. Please, let this pass. But here I am, ready to do what you sent me into the world to do. I love you with all of my heart. Your will be done.'

"In the stillness that followed, I wondered what answer, what psalm might be next. I remembered being a child on his lap, hearing his heart beat as I lay my head against his chest, feeling him breathe. As if reading my mind, he prayed, 'Thank you, Father, for this breath, for this life. And thank you for my son, with me now as I am with you.'"

I smiled at John Mark's remembrance, at his father's thoughtfulness as my son said, "I really didn't know what he was facing, Mother, but I felt his struggle and understood that he was very reluctant to enter into whatever was coming next.

"After a while, he got up and I thought almost shouted what I soon realized was another psalm of David. 'I plea with the Lord. I plead for mercy and tell Him about my trouble.' I joined him and understood that whatever he was struggling with would affect me, too. I wondered what would cause my usually calm father to be in such a state. Apparently, Peter, James, and John didn't hear as still nothing came from their direction. I hoped God heard!

"'My spirit faints within me, but you know my path and know they've laid a trap for me on it. I look on the right and see that there is no one who recognizes me. Escape is gone, no one will inquire for me. I shout to you, O Lord. You are my shelter, all I have in the land of the living. Hear me, Lord, for I have sunk very low. Save me from my pursuers, for they are too strong for me. Bring me safely out of the prison to honor you. For honest and just people will draw around me when you complete me.'

"Prison made me think of Justus Bar-Abbas. He said he was thinking of him. Maybe these prayers were for him. But then I thought, 'Oh, my God, help! This psalm, this night! Father never sounded so serious: plots, traps, prison, no one to help, no escape, pursuers too strong for him? Bring him out of prison? Complete him? Was it Justus or was it Father? I panicked. Herod beheaded John in prison. What did he mean? What did Father know that he hadn't told us at dinner? He said something about not eating bread or drinking wine until in the Kingdom of Heaven. What did he mean?

"While I felt panic, Father sat down again, and seemed content with the prospect of completion. But after a while, he kneeled and began again. 'Lord, hear my prayer, listen to my plea. In your loving generosity, don't judge me, for no one on earth has been acquitted. Your enemies pursue me to throw stones, throw my life to the ground, to make me dwell in darkness like those long dead.'

"Father paused and sighed, 'And my spirit faints within me. I recall the days of old and all that you have done. I speak of your deeds. I thirst for you and stretch out my hands. Hurry, answer me, Lord, my spirit faints. Don't hide your face from me. Let me know your loving kindness in the morning, for I trust you. Let me know the way I should go, for I offer myself to you. Save me from my enemies, Lord, vindicate me. Teach me how to live, to please You, for you're my God. Let your holy spirit guide me on level ground. For the honor of your just name, give me life and release me from my distress. In your love, silence my enemies and free me from my bitter foes, for I am your servant.'

"'Let it be so; let it be so!' I murmured, but I had barely finished my prayer when I heard some commotion, men's voices in the distance coming from the direction of Jerusalem. The city had been quiet except for the muffled noise of pilgrims preparing to celebrate Passover, so I wondered who was making so much noise at that hour.

"Father heard the voices, too, and motioned for me to come to him. He held me tightly for a while, and then kissed me on both cheeks and thanked me for staying awake and praying with him. He asked me to remember the Psalms that we prayed and tell you."

"Thank you. They mean a lot to me," I said. "What happened next?"

"He told me he was leaving on a dangerous mission, and that he wanted me always to remember that knowing myself is wisdom, but knowing God loves me and always gives me enough to give to others would enable me to stay centered and defeat the fear of death. If I understood, as he did, that everything comes from God, happens through God, and ends up in God, then I would embrace God with my whole heart and live every day with fearless, generous love. He sent me back to my tree with his stole to absorb everything he'd said and prayed.

"Father went down to wake up the three sleepers. Poking them gently, he asked, 'Are you still sleeping? Well, that's all the sleep for now. Come on.' Then he walked around to the other side of the press, followed by the three sheepish, somewhat disheveled fishermen. Calling out to those on the other side of the press, he said, 'Time to wake up! Here comes Judas. He's bringing Caiaphas' guard. This is what we've been waiting for....'

"Men were now entering the work yard with their torches and staffs, a spear or two, a few other weapons. I left his stole on the tree branch and crept behind the press to watch and see what this was all about. Clearly, Father was expecting them, but the others didn't seem to know any more than I did. Judas came forward, greeted Father with the usual exchange of kisses. As they kissed on either cheek, I heard Father's usual, 'Shalom'; Judas' usual, 'Master.'

"Malchus came forward behind Judas and said to a couple of the men following him, 'This is the one; take him.' Two rough-looking men I didn't know came up, but not before Peter, wide awake now, not liking the looks of things, pulled out his sword, sliced off Malchus' ear with a shout, joined by a shout from Malchus, caught by surprise.

"As pandemonium broke out, Father, in his superbly commanding voice, the voice you told me stilled the waves of Galilee in a terrible storm and commanded so many evil spirits to be silent or stop tormenting people, said, 'Stop! Shalom!'

"Everyone froze in mid-motion, not a sound but the flickering of torches. Father stooped, picked up the ear from the ground, returned it to Malchus' head, and stopped the flow of blood. Then he turned to Peter and shook his head, 'You still don't understand! Put your sword away!'

"Father turned back to Malchus and said, 'My friend, why have you come out as though you were going to do battle? I only live a few doors away and saw you in the crowd every day this week. I told Judas where you could find me tonight. Do what you have to do decently. There are no charges against the others.' He held out his hands, virtually commanding Malchus' assistants to bind his hands, which they had just seen replace a severed ear and heal it. What kind of rope could hold them if they weren't offered willingly?"

"I know," I agreed. "Your father knew what he was doing; he chose the path."

"Everyone else was on edge, didn't understand what was going on, couldn't believe that Father was letting himself be arrested. His 'friends' began to back into the shadows and disappear into the garden, fearing they would be arrested, too. They didn't trust the Temple guards or Judas, now. It seemed like a nightmare. Not what they were expecting; they didn't know what to do but save themselves by getting away.

"The guards began to recover from their confusion. They didn't expect a healing before their eyes, the prisoner taking charge. Was it a trap? Would the disappearing men re-emerge from the shadows with weapons and others to overwhelm them? I left the shadows to stand by Father and to...to...I didn't know what, but I knew Malchus, and...Father saw me, gave me a negative nod, and then the familiar, 'Go, tell your mother!'

"Two nearby guards grabbed me by my robe. I slipped out of it and ran into the dark of the garden. Whether it was because of Father, their inertia, or their unwillingness to risk the dark, I don't know, but they didn't follow.

"I stopped behind a tree trunk, found Thad, before coming to tell you. We heard Father say, 'All right, Malchus; let's go to Annas' house first.' With that, Father still in control, the arresting party marched out of the yard, Father and Malchus in the lead, followed by two torchbearers, the others, and last of all Judas, whom I think didn't want to stay in the garden with the rest of us because of how it looked."

I reached out to put my arms around my son, to comfort him. "None of us knew what would come next, John Mark. Your father took a great risk, and I believe he did what he set out to do with great courage. Thank you for sharing all of these prayers with me. They help me understand."

# CHAPTER THIRTY-THREE

Arriving at the great door soon after Joshua, I found more torches lit, sleepy servants and guards still gathering nearby, probably wondering who would come next...an unusual night. As Jeremiah, the chief steward, led me to the reception room, I passed Malchus and stopped a moment to ask about his ear. With a funny look and then a grin, he turned to show me. 'Good as ever,' he said, wondering, I'm sure, how I knew.

As Jeremiah led me to a seat in a corner of the room where Annas had just entered to meet Joshua, he sent a woman to tell Judith, who soon appeared. A little sleepy and bewildered, she came to greet me. She didn't seem to know whether to be concerned over some tragic emergency or to be irritated at the intrusion at this totally unacceptable hour. She settled beside me to listen to the men.

Sensitive to opportunity, Joshua was shepherding us, I thought. Though Malchus was Caiaphas' servant, Joshua led the guards to Annas with an order given loudly enough for John Mark to hear. No one here expected us tonight. I remembered Joshua answering questions about when this would happen or when that would happen by telling stories to illustrate that the Unnameable arrives unexpectedly, urging people to live so they'd not be embarrassed at an inevitable surprise. If the Unnameable God is True Reality, one never knows. Excuses are irrelevant no matter how elaborate. No fig leaf covers us.

After an apology for the hour, Joshua and Annas began this conversation where another ended several years before with Joshua briefly summarizing the country in crisis, but now an impending disaster, an emergency that impelled him to come to Annas for help at this late hour. Annas, irritated, asked Joshua what impending disaster.

"Bear with me. First, I need to remind you of some background. My cousin John, Justus, and I were inseparable, as you know. Raised under you in the Temple, we were all concerned about corruption surrounding us at every level with one conflict after another. People bled from taxes levied by Herod, Rome, and the Temple. Perhaps my order should be reversed. The tithe and Temple sacrifices are always first." Annas, with irritated impatience, nodded agreement and accepted the dubious courtesy.

"We had three different ways to improve conditions. John's was reform...and many of his followers believe you made a deal with Herod to muzzle him in prison. I personally don't believe you foresaw the unexpected event that led to his beheading."

Annas closed his eyes, and with a slight bow of his head, acknowledged another courtesy, though he knew the rumors. When I'd visited Judith earlier, she told me they'd been deeply shocked. John's father and mother had been such close friends.

Joshua continued, "My friend, Justus, advocated armed rebellion. There are rumors you've been involved with him, accepting tithes from raids, giving him aid and support."

More irritated, Annas began to deny it, but Joshua pressed on. "For now, for the sake of argument, let's just suppose that the rumors may be true, but one of your priests let information about the rebellion and the whereabouts of Justus get to the Romans."

Annas sensing much more trouble than he wanted in the middle of the night, objected, "Wait a minute—"

Joshua smiled, and interrupted, "Just for the sake of argument, now, Annas. Similar to John's beheading, I'm not accusing you of wanting the exact outcome, in this case, crucifixions on Passover, a desecration of the feast. That was likely Pilate's idea, a rather strong message, don't you think, that he'd heard the rumors of your involvement."

Annas shifted uneasily in his chair while Judith, with a smile that was a little too forced, pretended this was preposterous. Actually, I thought she seemed a little frightened at the suppositions, likely too true to be ignored.

"You must know," Joshua continued, "that any number in your entourage have been following me and baiting me, trying to engage in the debates you and I have had for years. They've not fared well since they're not well-grounded in our Scriptures. Some, who actually can't read well, still proclaim their belief in tradition and authority without understanding it. Angry and frustrated, they've dedicated themselves to my arrest by whatever witnesses and means they can find."

Annas started to object, "You can't be—" but Joshua continued, "Caiaphas was only too willing to send his guard with my servant Judas tonight when I sent the message that I was available. They came with swords and rope to 'capture' me, if you can imagine."

Annas sputtered, "You asked them to—"

Joshua interrupted, "Please be patient just to the end of my assessment of our crisis. Justus and John both have many armed followers ready to strike, leaderless, but dangerous, if Pilate tries to make a martyr of Justus this morning on Passover. They blame you and Joseph Caiaphas and the Temple for collaborating with Rome and Herod. Be honest. If you and Caiaphas try to get rid of me with a rigged trial, liars and misquotes, leading to death by stoning, as rumored, it would be an outrage to the pilgrims from Galilee, and to everyone in the city who knows me as a man of peace. Teaching has been my way of—"

"Consider what you've taught," Annas angrily replied, dodging the issue of the plot.

Joshua persisted, "A rigged trial now would put you in the embarrassing position of trying to hold me prisoner until after the feast, or committing a stoning during the feast, both against the Law and the temper of the crowds of pilgrims from Galilee. If you survived the Zealot attack on the crucifixion party and the chaos that would follow, Justus Bar-Abbas and I both would be made martyrs, which would be doubly dangerous and would draw even more men into the conflict."

Joshua had methodically brought Annas to realize that he must do what he could to avoid the unintended consequences of his previous decisions, which Joshua had described too accurately. Tacitly acknowledging the suppositions, he asked, "What's your solution?"

"I propose that we go to Joseph Caiaphas, where I can explain the details of how the three of us can cooperate to bring about a peaceful solution." Our eyes met as I began to realize what he would propose to them. He added, "Miriam will come with us."

We stepped out into the night's quiet chill, two torchbearers, Joshua and Annas, followed by Malchus and Jeremiah, the little band of guards looking tired and bedraggled, and then Judith and I followed them, with four more guards carrying torches to light our way. As we approached the carved oak gate of Caiaphas, I caught sight of Peter lurking in the shadows. I motioned him to follow and asked the gatekeeper, as we passed, to let him enter the courtyard, too. Servants, warming themselves around fires near the gate, had waited all night, expecting someone. Malchus announced our arrival, and the guards stepped aside so Judith and I could follow our husbands past the large potted citron trees and on up the steps into the reception hall.

Joseph Caiaphas had waited impatiently since he'd met with Judas, paid him something for his trouble, and sent Malchus with guards to get Joshua. He wondered whether he'd been made a fool, been double-crossed, since they hadn't returned, wondered how he'd gotten into this. He'd looked forward to silencing some of his critics without taking responsibility. Surprised to see Annas, his mother-in-law, and me with Joshua, he sent a message to Elizabeth that her father, mother, and best friend had just arrived. This situation was not at all what he had planned or expected.

After a moment of awkwardness, Annas asked Caiaphas to clear the room of servants, guards, and priests lounging about, waiting for Joshua to arrive. As soon as the room cleared, Joshua said, "Joseph, I apologize for making you wait. When Miriam and I offered our sacrifices, I said I wanted to talk with you, but with the crowds and confrontations around the Temple, there seemed no better time or way. I couldn't have escaped my followers, and I doubt you could have escaped yours."

Joseph adjusted quickly, saying, "That's true; it's been a very busy week for me," and couldn't resist adding, "in no small part due to you and your activities. I've heard complaints about you and arguments between people from nearly every party and faction."

"Well, perhaps I've been able to raise issues that are significant. It's painful, like lancing a boil before it can be healed....I'm looking for true peace, Joseph."

"That's always been your position, but you're irritating people by questioning instead of following the laws that we approve. That's not peace."

Joshua replied, "I understand that's your way, Joseph. We're here tonight because of a crisis, a result of your way of keeping peace, enforced peace, without justice and mercy, manipulating others to your will or get rid of them. Let's get to the heart of this and find a solution."

Just then, Elizabeth, looking worried, hurried into the room, came to sit beside me, and was shocked to hear Joshua describe the collaboration and double dealing with John, Herod, Justus Bar-Abbas, Pilate, and the evidence that, while still smiling, Joseph was conspiring with strict interpreters of the law to condemn him by whatever means, to stone him to death. Elizabeth and I watched her husband's face for an inkling of innocence, but found none.

Joshua continued, "This morning the city is ready to explode. Both John's disciples and well-armed Zealots believe you collaborated with Herod and Pilate, and have plotted their revenge. Men from the entire nation, already bitter and angry at heavy taxes and gouging at the Temple, are now outraged at your double dealing and betrayals. All of them have been insulted by Pilate with the announced crucifixions. Most of them blame you and Annas, and they are ready to strike this morning when the Romans try to crucify their leaders. They'll lash out in every direction. You're both in danger."

Judith and Elizabeth were frightened, wondering how their world could be so insecure. I was on the verge of tears because I knew this situation was what Joshua had been struggling to prevent for the last two months, or two years, or perhaps his entire life. I also knew his solution. It still seemed unbelievable to me.

Some probing followed. How much did Joshua really know? How true was his information? Finally, Annas said, "You promised to offer us a solution. I don't see any way that we can intercede with Pilate. As you observed, anything we say or do now will damn us one way or the other." Caiaphas started to object, to deny his involvement, but was cut off by his father-in-law. "It's too late for that, Joseph. We don't have much time until the crucifixion party will leave the fortress this morning. So, Joshua?"

"I tried to talk Justus out of the rebellion, but began to prepare for what I saw coming while praying for another way to bring peace. Even tonight, I went to my olive garden still praying for another solution, while I sent Judas here to arrange our meeting, which looked to all of our followers like a betrayal, playing into your rumored plot to have me arrested, falsely accused, and stoned."

Caiaphas was clearly uncomfortable seen plotting to condemn and kill his friend, the husband of his wife's best friend, the father of his older son's best friend, the man for whom his younger son was named. "This is not what I planned," he sputtered. "I'm an impartial judge, probably unable to save my friend in the face of the evidence against him, but...." Pausing, he added ruefully, "I feel as though Judas was a trap, Joshua, like the Trojan Horse!"

Joshua smiled, "Well, truth will out. It's uncomfortable facing the unintended consequences of our intentional acts, my friend...."

Annas had grown more nervous and impatient. "So what is your solution, or the solution that you've been preparing for while trying to avoid it?"

Joshua took a deep breath, and said quietly, "It's better for one man to die for the nation, than for the nation to be destroyed. My solution is for you to substitute me for Justus Bar-Abbas this morning, to diffuse the anger of the armed men who are gathering even now in small groups throughout the city and around the fortress. You can surprise them. With Justus Bar-Abbas free with our help, they won't strike, but will wait for his orders. I will die for him, and for you, as well....You see, I believe I was born to bring peace on earth, peace with God. It's the only way I can do it today. When you study the Torah again, perhaps you'll find foreshadowing of what I'm giving you."

Caiaphas shook his head in disbelief, "I don't understand, Joshua. What's in it for you?"

Annas, annoyed at Joseph, said to Joshua, "I think I understand that you've arranged this evening, this conversation, to set the stage for saving your friend Justus from a tortuous death, and saving us from the outbreak of armed chaos in Jerusalem today?"

"Yes, I believe that I can do it with your help. I'm willing to offer my life, and trust that the Unnameable God will accept my sacrifice," Joshua replied.

"What is our part?" Annas asked, darting a glance at his son-in-law to keep quiet.

Joshua laughed, "Well, it really shouldn't be too hard for either of you. Joseph Caiaphas will call some of his followers hanging around outside to an emergency council meeting. There's not enough time to call a proper, full council, but I'd rather that men who would argue and object not be involved or blamed for this, anyway. When I came in, I think I saw Zachariah and some of the others who are always ready to do what you ask, Joseph. They've been hecklers in the crowd this week and are already here.

"Then, Annas," Joshua continued, "your part will be to attend the emergency council meeting, but once Joseph has managed to convict me, you'll declare that it's not possible to stone me before Passover, but that you can persuade Pilate to crucify me this morning, at which point, you two will march me over to the fortress, and between the three of us, we will persuade Pilate and the crowd to substitute me for Justus."

"How is that different—" Joseph Caiaphas started to ask.

"It's different, Joseph. You couldn't get two witnesses to agree, couldn't get Gamaliel or Nicodemus or enough of the council to convict me or come to a meeting to make it legal this morning. You couldn't stone me without making yourselves ritually unclean for the feast. I will only tell the truth, Joseph. There's nothing to convict me of any wrongdoing worthy of death. You both know that I have only quoted our Scriptures. No, Joseph, you will have to put on quite a scene, an exaggerated show of outrage, confuse your friends in the council into thinking that something I said makes me guilty of death, even though you know it doesn't."

"But what about Pilate?" persisted Annas.

"My friend Pilate already knows that ordering these crucifixions for the day of the feast, while expressing his contempt, was rash and has put him and his men at great risk. He can fight and win small skirmishes, but not an entire population rising against him. Legions from Rome, under a new commander, would come, but it would be the end of Pilate's career, if he and his family survive." I was amazed at my husband's analysis.

"But what kind of charge could we bring? He is contemptuous of our religious practices. What would he believe? Knowing you, why would he crucify you?" Joseph asked.

"I've thought of that," replied Joshua. "Annas can, of course, explain my conviction of an infraction of our religious rules, which also forbid you to execute judgment and stone me so close to the feast. That won't impress him, but it will get us into the conversation. He's under pressure because Herod is leaving for Rome soon and Pilate doesn't want to be the subject of court gossip about rebellions, or some 'King of the Jews,' which is what the Zealots and pilgrims are calling me. Herod, in his confused state, fears I'm John come back to life, fears he was tricked and the bloody head he saw so briefly was not John's, but the head of a substitute. He fears that I/John am out to dethrone him."

Seeing our glazed looks, Joshua laughed, "That's just to explain that Pilate can be persuaded, find an excuse to substitute me for Justus Bar-Abbas. Your part is to lead the crowd in bringing this about; make them feel that it's their decision, that you're with them and there's no longer a reason to fight Rome. Everyone is saved except me."

How could he smile, I wondered, but he did, eyes twinkling with some unknown wisdom.

"This isn't a game, Joshua," Annas rebuked him. "It's life and death for all of us."

"You're right, Annas," Joshua said, sobering immediately. "I'm facing more pain than we can imagine, and I've been to the depths of depression as I've seen this unfold, wondering how we make such a tangled mess of our lives. But there's no time to lose if we're to do this. We must begin immediately. Will you accept my solution, my gift?"

Annas looked to Caiaphas, and then back to Joshua. "We will, with God's help, deeply in your debt, deeply grateful if this works. What can we do for you?"

"Care for Miriam and my children. Protect them from those who'll want to punish them as well," Joshua answered. "As for your gratitude, we'll see. After the first Passover, our ancestors weren't grateful, as I remember. Freedom wasn't what they imagined. I don't give this Passover gift with many expectations."

The council members were summoned. Witnesses were called who couldn't keep their stories straight. Several arguments broke out. Caiaphas struggled to keep order. Before too long, Joshua nodded to Caiaphas, who asked him a direct question. Hearing Joshua's quiet answer, Caiaphas shrieked, tore off his shawl, and wailed, "Blasphemy! From his own lips! We don't need more witnesses!"

Joshua suppressed a smile and played his part; Annas played his part; Judith, Elizabeth, and I played ours as we sat quietly in a corner. A few young men, reminding me of Peter, given more to bravado than careful thought, as if on cue, put on quite a show of being offended for the honor of God and their high priest, childish games which disgusted Caiaphas, who brought them under control as soon as he could.

A cock crowed for a second time, and Annas, aware of the short time remaining to reach the fortress before the crucifixion party would depart, took Joshua by the arm, nodded to Joseph Caiaphas to take the other, and they quickly moved out into the courtyard to call for the guards. Elizabeth was still dazed by what was happening, but she held onto my arm tightly as I got up from the bench in the corner where we sat. I helped Judith get up, and she joined me on my other arm as we three followed our husbands out into the still dark chill of the early morning.

# CHAPTER THIRTY-FOUR

As the sky began to lighten, the guards were hurriedly organized. New torches were lit in the pre-dawn shadows. A
formidable procession marched out of the gate, first torchbearers on either side of two armed men, then Joshua flanked
by Annas and Caiaphas, followed by more torchbearers and
guards, and then we three women followed by two more
armed men flanked by torchbearers. Some of the council
members and so called witnesses straggled along behind as
did Judas, I noticed.

My heart sank deeper with each step on the cold, rough
pavement. We were walking toward my husband's sacrifice of
himself for the sins of all of these loveless men, as well as for
his headstrong friend, Justus. "Justus," I wanted to scream,
"why did you do this? Why did you betray the wisdom and
love that Joshua has given you since the day he met you?"
"Joseph Caiaphas, Uncle Annas," I wanted to scream, "why
can't you stop this? Why did you betray the office of high
priest to gain, I don't know what. What did you hope to
gain?" "Joshua," I wanted to scream, "let's leave now. They
don't understand or appreciate you! No matter what you give
them, they'll want more, and want it their way. Can't we just

love the Unnameable God and each other?" But I knew he would have asked, "And the near one, even the stranger and the enemy?" with a patient smile. "But can they," I would respond, "will they love you and the Unnameable? Will our sacrifices really make a difference? Will these people ever really love as you do?"

Of course, nothing passed my lips, and we were soon at the fortress' entrance. At this early hour, an unusual number of angry-looking men were milling about outside the gate, clustered in small groups around the walls. Joshua, flanked by Caiaphas and Annas, walked to the large, impressive entrance gate to the inner court, and was admitted immediately. I realized the guards were protecting us as much as detaining Joshua. The guards and torchbearers took positions on either side of the gate as we three distressed and troubled women reached it and were quickly admitted. Would the men have parted for me, had I been alone, I wondered. Flanked by the two high priests' wives, I was protected by them, and at the same time, my mind flashed to Joshua's description of the two goats presented by the priests for the atonement sacrifice. I had the eerie feeling I was the next victim being presented for sacrifice by their wives.

Once through the heavy gate, I was surprised by a friendly face. Our good friend, Marcus, was the centurion just inside the entry; he looked as surprised to see Joshua and me as I was to see him. "Special duty," was all he said, acknowledging my companions. I guessed he was overseeing his men guarding the entry and other strategic locations in the fortress during the feast. "What brings you at this early hour?" he asked. "Claudia will want to know you're here. I've already seen her this morning. She didn't sleep well last night," he confided, ordering one man to lead us toward the reception area, another to send Claudia a message.

Annas and Caiaphas declined to go further into the fortress, something about not defiling themselves before Passover, and asked to be met outside, and so we all waited just outside the door to the reception room.

Pilate, after keeping us waiting for an appropriate length of time to establish his superior position and importance, appeared with his face looking determined but drawn, somewhat preoccupied and annoyed at this early morning intrusion into what everyone must know was a critically busy morning for him, not the time for trivial affairs of some arcane religious nature. He couldn't refuse to see these visitors, but he seemed surprised to see Joshua with these two manipulative high priests. I was sure he thought better of Joshua than to be mixed up with these two at this early hour. Then he noticed ropes around Joshua's hands, and then noticed us women, totally unexpected.

The official greetings and salutations were quick and brusk. "What is your business?" he demanded. As planned, Annas told his story about Joshua committing a religious crime worthy of death, impossible for them to execute the punishment today, so they were here to demand that Pilate execute judgment on behalf of Caesar, since a crime—

"What crime?" Pilate interrupted.

"He claims to be the Son of God, and—"

"Nonsense," barked Pilate. "Why is that punishable by death? Emperors and kings all claim to be gods, themselves. I thought all of you claimed to be children of God."

"But he—" began Caiaphas.

"I was speaking," interrupted Pilate in an icy voice. "Joshua, what do you have to say?"

Caiaphas, not content to be ignored, spat out, "He claims to be King of the Jews!" Joshua smiled and looked at Pilate with sympathetic eyes, a slight shrug, and a nod. Pilate didn't wait, but simply motioned for Joshua to follow him into the reception room. I wanted to follow, but uninvited, it was impossible.

Claudia came into the court just then, and immediately drew me away from the others. "Oh, Miriam," she said softly. "I'm so glad to see you. Everyone is so on edge. I didn't sleep well at all last night. Can you believe that I dreamt about you and Joshua? It was terrible! But why are you here? Are you all right?"

We embraced, and holding hands, I said, "I'm glad to see you, too, Claudia, I—"

"What's wrong? Where's Joshua? Can Pilate help?" she asked in rapid succession, and then following my nod, she took me by the arm, and walked me toward the door.

"Yes, I think he'll help, Claudia," I answered, "but not as you expect. I think that's what Joshua is explaining to Pilate now. Anytime Joshua heals someone, it's necessary to trust him, and difficult as this will be today, I think that's what he's asking, that we trust him."

"I don't understand," she responded, looking back at Judith and Elizabeth. "Who is Joshua healing? Why does he need help from Pilate?"

Joshua and Pilate returned from the reception room just then before we reached the door, not giving me an opportunity to answer. Pilate had a puzzled expression, "So you are King of the Jews?" he asked Joshua in our presence.

"If you say so," Joshua replied with a smile. Then looking at Annas and Caiaphas, he added. "My kingdom is not really political but exists wherever and whenever someone loves God in truth."

"In truth?" Pilate asked with a cynical laugh. "Ah, that's a difficult standard." He smiled, for an instant bemused at such an ethereal, abstract idea worthy of an evening's debate, but not this morning of all mornings. He himself was a man of action. "What is truth?"

Joshua flashed another smile, understanding the question from the perspective of this man who must listen to complaints and allegations, decide disputes, and give orders many times each day. "Good question...the God I'm speaking about is The One who meets us every day, always offering us choice so we can discover whom we really are in our choosing and doing."

That was a sobering, uncomfortable proposition not only for Pilate, but for Annas and Caiaphas as well. "So, you've chosen?" Pilate asked Joshua, then turned to the other two and said, "I find absolutely nothing worthy of death in this man."

"Offer the people the choice," replied Annas, uncomfortable in his role, understanding what Joshua must have explained to Pilate, understanding that Caiaphas and he must now take the consequences of their past manipulations.

"Offer the people the choice and keep Rome satisfied, now that you have a substitute."

Pilate was not accustomed to giving anyone a choice except the emperor, but he understood the situation as briefly described by Joshua, and he could think of no other solution this morning. He felt powerless to bring about a good outcome. Perhaps one would appear as they proceeded. The first step was to go out to face an angry crowd of men gathered around his guards, around his door. "Shall we go?" he asked.

Joshua, his hands still tied together and flanked by Annas and Caiaphas, followed Pilate, who was flanked by his two personal guards, four more Roman guards following behind. We women followed, but remained out of sight, just inside the gate. Claudia understood there had been some negotiations, that something was changing the expected routine of this crucifixion morning, not that crucifixions of criminals and rebels did not occur on a fairly regular basis, but this one was different, of course; this one was to be the three main leaders of the rebellion that had been discovered. "What does Joshua have to do with this?" she whispered as we arrived at our protected spot. "Why are his hands tied?" I motioned for her to listen as Pilate was beginning to speak.

"What charges do you bring against this man?" he asked Caiaphas.

"According to our law, he has blasphemed God and deserves to die," Caiaphas responded, and then as Pilate looked at him as though he hadn't understood their previous discussion, he added, "And he claims to be King of the Jews, which is an offense against Caesar. We demand that he be put to death."

Pilate looked uncomfortable, saying, "On the occasion of your holy days and of this feast, as a special favor from the emperor to you," he paused, and looked like he couldn't believe what he was saying, "I will release one prisoner. I will give you a choice. Whom shall I release, Joshua or Justus Bar-Abbas? Whom do you choose?"

The men closest to the door were those who had come with us. They looked to Caiaphas and then to Annas, who said loudly, "Justus Bar-Abbas; we want Justus Bar-Abbas." Their guards took up the name with a shout, and then as the name of their leader was heard, men in the courtyard crowd took up the chant, "Justus Bar-Abbas, Justus Bar-Abbas, Justus Bar-Abbas..." until it seemed like a roar.

When it diminished slightly, Pilate asked, "What then shall I do with Joshua?"

"Crucify him! Crucify him! Crucify him!" came back the shout quietly begun by Annas and Caiaphas, amplified by their guard, shouted by what seemed to be the entire crowd.

We watched how this transpired, and believed what Joshua told us about the crowd of men hanging around the fortress. They were certainly Zealots, waiting for the opportunity to overpower the crucifixion party as it moved out of the fortress and into the narrow streets. If Pilate stalled, had Joshua lashed in preparation for crucifixion, though I was sure the thought was repugnant, Pilate might allow time for pilgrims to wake up, and he might get another crowd response, though I knew he didn't trust crowds any more than I did. There seemed little else he could do under the circumstances as described by Joshua. He ordered Joshua taken to the dungeon, prepared for crucifixion, and returned with

Justus Bar-Abbas. Sun and heat rose, and the crowd actually swelled with Zealots as news spread to those along the street, prepared to overpower the crucifixion party. Pilate ordered all available men on alert. Marcus looked stunned.

As I watched the crowd gather, I asked myself where our servants and friends were. Where were all of the people who hailed Joshua king last Sunday, who followed him all week, who were healed? Where were their friends and relatives, people who wanted to touch him, to ask one more favor, one more healing? Though Joshua had tried to prepare me for this, I felt overwhelmed with deep grief and saw it reflected in the faces of Judith, Elizabeth, and Claudia, who were beside themselves. All three were distraught by what was happening and the danger threatening beyond the gate.

When Pilate walked past us again, Claudia rushed to him to plead that he not get involved but somehow protect Joshua and me from this mob. Her nightmare, she told him, warned her he mustn't get involved. Pilate responded, "I'm doing my best, Claudia. I'm afraid we have to trust him again and hope for a miracle!"

I could hardly believe my eyes when soldiers marched Joshua back from the dungeon, his face blood-streaked, some beard torn, looking worse, I thought, than when he had returned from the inn on the Jericho Road. He had another strange robe draped over his shoulders, red like his blood, and a crown fashioned from thorn, though why there were thorn branches within the fortress, I couldn't guess. He saw me, smiled faintly through bruised lips, and mouthed, "Don't worry...part of the sacrifice....Trust me." This time I couldn't run to him, prepare a bed and dressings to heal his wounds.

Just then, four guards brought Justus Bar-Abbas into the courtyard. No longer the charismatic, handsome, well-groomed man I knew, nine days of prison had left their mark, but his flashing eyes were wild with defiance when he first saw me, then shocked as he saw Joshua's back and realized Joshua was the one taking the lashes, the taunting, and the beating he'd heard. Our eyes met again as his face changed to horrified disbelief.

Pilate appeared from the reception room again, and not looking right or left, walked straight out the door of the inner court with another centurion and his seasoned guards. Pilate then ordered both Joshua and Justus brought outside the gate with their guards, and asked the same question of the priests and crowd of men now filling the area. "On the occasion of this feast, as the emperor's favor to you, whom shall I release?"

Annas and Caiaphas had had some time to think over their predicament. They had learned through their informers that Joshua's summary of the situation was completely accurate. The area and the streets were filled with men waiting for the signal to begin fighting for better or worse for the honor of their cause with all of the hatred they shared for the Romans, Herod, and the Temple establishment, which must be cooperating with the first two. Much as Annas and Caiaphas, for their own reasons, hated the situation in which they found themselves and hated to play this part in switching Joshua for Justus Bar-Abbas, Elizabeth told me later, they couldn't think of an alternative that might get them and their wives out of this morning alive, caught as they were between the Zealots and the Romans if fighting were to break out.

What had Joshua said? "It's better for one man to die for the nation, than..." but they hated their part in it. They both could see he was dying for them, as well. And so, at Pilate's question, Joshua looked at Annas, nodded, and Annas shouted as he had agreed, "Justus Bar-Abbas! Release Bar-Abbas!" And the crowd was whipped into a frenzy of chanting. "We want Bar-Abbas! We want Bar-Abbas! We want Bar-Abbas!"

Justus Bar-Abbas himself shouted out, "Release Joshua, Son of David!"

I saw Joshua shake his head, and I suspected with a glance that he'd confirmed to his lifelong friend that he was here to take his place.

Pilate looked determined but uncomfortable with his part in this now obviously dangerous situation, the streets full of an armed, excited crowd. Before asking the next agreed-upon question of Annas and Caiaphas, he seemed compelled, perhaps in response to Claudia's warning, to give his own verdict, honestly, but said to the priests, "What do you want me to do with Joshua? Release him?" If they had accepted Joshua's release, Pilate told Claudia later, he wasn't sure what the repercussions would be for crucifying only two of the three rebels. Was he losing his grip? What had he gotten himself into? What would Herod and Rome say? If Justus and Joshua were both free, if Caiaphas and Annas suspected his vulnerability, who knew what chaos might erupt! What had he been thinking? He had to have Justus or Joshua on a cross this morning. And now it could no longer be Justus. Pilate realized Joshua would be dying to save him, too.

Joshua understood; he looked at Annas and smiled, prompting him to do what he had to do, say what he had to say. Annas responded loudly, "Crucify him!" Those nearby took up the chant, following his cue. We looked into the crowd for any dissenters, but saw none of the throngs of people who had followed Joshua all week. This angry, mindless crowd just took up the next chant begun by the priests. "Crucify him! Crucify him! Crucify him!"

Pilate gave the order to bring a table and a basin of water. Ceremonially in front of the priests and the crowd, he said, "I find no fault in this just man. I am washing my hands."

Joshua smiled. Compassion shone in his eyes for these men caught in their own net. Annas and Caiaphas were about to speak when he said quietly, "Let the responsibility rest with me. It's my gift to all of you." They knew they could only say, "So be it."

Pilate said, "So be it!" and without looking at anyone in particular, but knowing he was averting armed chaos, he ordered those guarding Justus Bar-Abbas, "Release him."

The surprised guards untied Justus, who seemed as bewildered as the guards. He started to object, to walk toward Joshua, but was barred by Roman guards, and almost at the same time, intercepted by some of his ardent and enthusiastic supporters who had rushed up to lift him onto their shoulders and carry him out into the shouting crowd; people swarmed the men carrying Justus on their shoulders and serpentined out into the street beyond, shouting, "We want Bar-Abbas! Long Live Bar-Abbas!" Thus the jubilant crowd in front of the gate dissipated, leaving only the men following the high priests and now an ever-growing number of the curious.

Pilate turned to the men guarding Joshua and barked, "Get those ridiculous things off of him. Show him respect. Crucify him; the charge on his cross: 'King of the Jews.' Write it in Latin, Greek, and Aramaic."

Caiaphas, nearby, objected, "No, no. Write only that he claimed to be king of the Jews."

Pilate, with utter disgust in his voice, said, "It shall be written, 'King of the Jews.' He's the most noble man I've ever met. You don't deserve such a king, but king he is."

Pilate ordered the centurion in charge of the crucifixion party to proceed with the crucifixions.

Soon the men taking Gestas and Demas began to march while others formed around Joshua, who was again dressed in his seamless wedding robe. I stepped forward to follow. Pilate, so much on his mind, commanded two of his men to accompany me. Too awkward to say goodbye, with tear-filled eyes, the women each quickly kissed me, and I followed in the procession just after Joshua and two guards, who were between us, then two with me, other guards ahead and behind.

The order to show respect registered with the centurion in charge of the crucifixions. Working his way back to Joshua, carrying the beam for his cross, he stopped the march briefly and ordered the guards to take someone from the street to help Joshua carry the beam. They grabbed a man nearby traveling with two other men and three loaded donkeys. When Joshua saw the man, he greeted him with delight, "Simon... it's you again!"

As if introduced, I knew this was the good Samaritan, Simon of Cyrene, for whom we'd been looking. As we began to move again, I asked his surprised companions, his sons I found out later, to follow. People, beginning to wake and come into the narrow streets from every door and passage, joined the crowd, jostling us as the Roman guards tried to keep our way clear, keep us moving. A short distance later, I saw Mother Mary, Hannah, Salome, and Mary Cleopas, dazed and distraught, shoved up against a wall by the crowd. I reached for them to join me and we continued, protected from the crowd pushing behind us by the guards and Simon's two sons with their three donkeys.

Our sad procession made its way through the crowded streets, out the gate to the great rock outcropping, the place of the skull, where Gestas and Demas were already being fastened to their crosses. Simon dropped the beam as ordered. Joshua embraced him, spoke to him, and directed him to me. When Simon reached me, he said, "He asked me to tell you not to be afraid, to have courage, and to come to him when the soldiers...finish their job."

"I will," I responded...and added barely above a whisper, "with God's help."

Simon's eyes were filled with tears. "Naomi told me about you. We'll do whatever we can to help you when...." He couldn't finish, and went back to his sons and donkeys.

# CHAPTER THIRTY-FIVE

The three men were hung, the crosses set. The soldiers gathered at a comfortable distance to eat, drink, and brag about duty done in spite of danger while they kept the crowd back and began to joke and wager, waiting for the inevitable. My whole being shuddered, but with my arm around Mother Mary, who was bent over in tears, I slowly walked toward Joshua's cross, taking her with me. The guards ignored us, just two women.

Joshua seemed to feel us drawing near and opened his eyes. We stopped a few paces away at a place where he was able to see us easily without moving his head, and where I could easily see his eyes and lips. His mother sank to her knees, sobbing, hands over her face, unable to bring herself to look.

So even in this moment, Joshua and I were alone together.

He silently mouthed, "Thank you. I love you," and my heart breaking, I mouthed in return, "and I love you," shuddering at flies buzzing about his bloody wounds. Demas and Gestas began to curse. Priests—I thought I'd seen Zachariah among others in the crowd following us—began to laugh and compete for the loudest, cruelest insult. The wary guards kept them at a safe distance.

Joshua watched all of this.

I could hardly believe that through all of his pain, his eyes radiated a bemused patience. In spite of difficulty breathing, true to himself, he called out, "Father, forgive them. They don't know what they're doing!" He winced and closed his eyes again. I'd heard his amazing forgiveness before. Not even this could stop him. He opened his eyes, smiled and mouthed, "Sing," and then bit his lips.

It was something I could do for both of us if only I could without my voice breaking with my heart. I would try to comfort him, unite us as long as he lived. He bit his lip again, and I realized he wanted to remain silent in his pain. I remembered a psalm by David, about silence and Job. I tried it. "Let me keep myself from offending with my tongue.'" Joshua nodded slightly and mouthed, "Yes," and closed his eyes again. I continued, "'Let me keep quiet. As long as vicious hecklers are in front of me, I'll be silent; I'll keep still and not say anything, my pain is so intense....Let me know how transient I am."

My voice cracked, "Look at me, a mere man, as insubstantial as breath," and tears streamed down my face. "A man goes about like a shadow, stores, and doesn't know who'll gather. And now, what do I wait for, Lord? My hope is in you," I sang, but we still heard the taunts of the crowd. "For their crimes I'm being punished," I swallowed, amazed at the psalm's relevance. "Turn toward me; stay beside me, until the moment when I fully return to your presence."

I was interrupted by a shout from Gestas who had picked up shouts from the crowd and challenged Joshua to save them now, when it counted. Demas shouted back, "We're getting what we deserve...He tried to stop us...bring peace," he gasped. Gestas cursed and Demas, with another breath, shouted, "He doesn't deserve this...It should be Bar-Abbas."

Gestas let out a scream of pain and shouted, "To hell with Bar-Abbas!"

Demas ignored him, and with another effort, called to Joshua, "Thanks...for my ankle...never forgot." A howl of pain escaped his lips too, but he gasped, "for trying...for peace...remember me...in your kingdom."

Joshua had opened his eyes and turned his head, and called back, "Don't be afraid....Today, you'll be with me in paradise!" Looking down, he found me dissolved in tears, amazed once more at his incredible strength and love. With a slight nod he mouthed, "and I..." giving me the clue that he wanted me to continue with the next psalm of David.

"I rely completely on the Lord. He turned toward me and heard my voice. He lifted me up from the pit of muck and mire. He set me on a high rock and made sure I wouldn't slip." Could any in the crowd see and understand this? I could still hear their taunts to come down from the cross if he were the Son of God, and I sang louder, "How blessed is the one who trusts in the Lord and doesn't seek help from the proud or from liars. You have done so much for us, O Lord our God. No one can match your plans for us. Your primary concern isn't sacrifice and grain-offerings. You make that quite clear to me. You don't ask for burnt sacrifices and sin offerings."

Then why this sacrifice, I wondered and fell silent as I tried to understand.

Joshua opened his eyes, looked at me with sympathy, and I continued. "But then I saw what is written in the scroll pertains to me. I desire to do what pleases you, my God. Your law dominates my thoughts. I have told everyone about your just peace....I spoke of your reliability and deliverance. I did not neglect to tell the great crowds about your unchanging truth."

I knew that Joshua lived this psalm. His mother's sobs subsided as she listened, but I knew what came next and found it difficult to continue, "Lord, don't hold back your compassion from me. Your loyal love and faithfulness always protect me, but crimes have overwhelmed me, more numerous than the hairs of my head."

Joshua hadn't committed any crimes unless they were crimes of omission...that he hadn't cured everyone in the heckling crowd of selfishness or jealousy or fear or hate. This seemed to refer to all of their crimes that were covering him now and weighing down his spirit...crimes of Justus Bar-Abbas, Annas, Joseph Caiaphas, Pilate, and the Zealot crowd; crimes and offenses Joshua had taken on himself when he had forgiven them all.

I continued, "O Lord, hurry to help and save me. May those who are trying to take away my life be surprised." Will these men be embarrassed some day, I wondered. "Let all who seek you rejoice and may those who love your rescue always say, 'God is great.'"

I love God's rescue, but is this it? I wished the ugly shouts from the crowd would stop. "As for me," I continued, "I need you and humbly confess you are the only one who can deliver me. My God do not delay." I kept repeating that plea silently. That *was* my prayer: "My God do not delay. My God do not delay! My God do not delay! We're waiting."

Joshua gasped, winced, tears trickled down his cheeks. He bit his lower lip and then called out in a loud voice, "My God, my God, why have you forsaken me?"

I was flooded with grief and chilled as a shadow passed in front of the sun and then engulfed us in a sudden dark cloud. Joshua had begun the psalm he sang beaten and abandoned for dead on the Jericho Road three years ago. God had heard him then.

I repeated his cry, "My God, my God, why have you forsaken me? Why are you so far from my cry, from my distress? O my God, I cry in day time, but you do not answer, by night as well, but I find no rest."

"Please God," I sobbed. "Please don't let Joshua be put to such shame." Mother Mary, through her sobs, echoed me, "Please God, don't let my son's life end in such shame."

The cloud grew thicker and settled around us. The crowd and the flies stopped buzzing. A strange silence was within the cloud. I found my voice again and continued, "But as for me, I'm not a man, but a disgrace, a mere worm. People insult and despise me. Those who see me laugh at me and taunt me and mock me and say, 'He trusted in the Lord. If the Lord delights in him, let the Lord rescue and deliver him.'"

With the crowd grown silent, I wondered whether some had actually expected a miracle they didn't want to miss.

Joshua opened his eyes, now glistening with tears, mirroring mine as I searched for strength to continue. "You were my God when I was still in my mother's womb and have been my God ever since. Don't be far from me, for trouble is near, and I have no one else to help me." This psalm, written so long ago, described what we were enduring, and how he'd even noticed the soldiers playing dice for his beautiful seamless wedding robe. I shuddered. He was still patient, his faith unshaken, "Oh, Lord, my strength, hurry to my help!"

Was the dense cloud surrounding us God actually coming to our help? It became so thick, with moisture caressing our skin, that no one even as close as Demas and Gestas could see us. In this cloud that enveloped us, I somehow began to feel God's presence and continued to sing. I wondered whether the priests, who had become silent as the cloud descended, were shaken by it. In the Torah, the cloud was the visible sign of God's presence in the Holiest place, in the tent of meeting with Moses. Had they made the connection? Were any of them embarrassed at what they'd said and done?

I continued, "God has not ignored the affliction of the lowly. When he cried out, God *heard*." Amazing! I had just received Joshua's message to me. In crying out, "My God, My God," in singing this psalm, I had just spoken his assurance that God had heard him. They were still in conversation. I said it again, louder. "God *heard* him when he cried out!" and Joshua affirmed it, nodded slightly, and smiled.

Encouraged, I continued, wondering about the rest of Joshua's message to me. "I praise you in the great assembly. I fulfill my vows before those who fear you." He has, I thought. "Those who seek God will praise him with great joy." No matter how it looked, Joshua seemed to be saying, "Fear not, I bring you good news of great joy. Unto you is born a savior. Peace on earth and good will to all!"

This was a very long psalm. Overwhelmed, I closed my eyes, but Joshua got my attention with his shepherd's whistle. I'll never forget the gleam in his eyes. He knew I was beginning to understand and wanted the shepherd psalm next, and so I began again, "The Lord is my shepherd. I have everything I need. You let me lie down in soft grass, and guide me to quiet streams. You refresh my life. You lead me on paths of peace for your name's sake. Though I walk through the valley of death, I'm not afraid for you are with me. Your rod and your staff protect me. You spread out a full table before me in front of my enemies. You anoint my head with oil, my cup overflows. Your goodness and kindness pursue me every day of my life and I shall live sheltered by you forever." I had anointed his head with oil; our love overflowed, God was with us, sheltering us from insults in this moist, dense cloud.

We both sighed.

Joshua's eyes, shining confidently through his tears, were open, looking at me with compassion. Could he still smile in the midst of his agony and still believe that while passing through this shadow of death he could reassure me that goodness and mercy were following us? In response to my unspoken questions, Joshua cried out, "I thirst!"

The soldiers, uneasy with the uncanny darkness, the strangeness of this crucifixion, heard the cry. One of them rushed over with a rag, which he'd wrapped around the end of a pole and dipped into the jug of sour wine they were

drinking. Joshua sighed, refused it, and looked to see whether I could remember the psalm. I did, and began, "As a deer
longs for streams of flowing water, so I long for you, O God."
Our eyes met and he nodded. "I thirst for the living God.
When shall I see God face to face? I weep as they say to me
all day long, 'Where is your God?'" How could we tell the
doubters that we knew God was with us in this cloud-filled
valley of death?

"I will remember and weep for I led the procession of the
great throng to the temple of God, shouting and giving thanks
along with the crowd as we celebrated the holy festival." Was
his jubilant entry into Jerusalem only a few days ago? "Why
are you depressed? Why are you upset? Wait for God! Hope
in God, for I will yet praise Him for rescuing me." Still hope
for God's rescue? I wondered.

"Deep calls to deep, the Lord shows me steady love by day
and sings to me by night. My life is still my prayer to God."

Tears welled up in my eyes. "I ask God, my Rock, 'Why
have you forgotten me? My enemies revile me when they say
to me all day long, 'Where is your God?'

"Why do you ignore me? Why am I weighed down by
despair? Rescuing presence you are my God." Tears streamed
down my face, but I continued, "I trust you to save me and I
will sing to you with great joy. Plead my cause, O God. Why
should I continue in gloom, hard pressed by the enemy?"

Oh, this moment, this day, this chilling gloom....I faltered,
but saw his compassionate glance.

I sang on, "Reveal your light and your faithfulness. They
will guide me and bring me to your holy mountain, to your

dwelling place." Our eyes met again, and I yearned to be in the holy place with him. "Let me come to God's altar, to God who gives me ecstatic joy. Let me praise you, my God." I let his praise and song and silence float in the air, in the cloud.

My mind went back to the opening lines of the psalm and I began to sing again, "As a deer longs for streams of water, so I thirst for you, my God...."

I was interrupted by Mother Mary, whose anguish exploded. "Dear God, it's not supposed to be this way...my promised, wonderful son...the angels, the messages of protection, the promises. How could our cousins, the priests...?" She couldn't finish her question, but then asked others, "How could James or Joseph not stop this? Where is Nicodemus? Where are all of our servants...all of his friends...and all of those people who made such a big parade?" I bent to hold her and calm her sobs, and looked up to see Joshua watching us.

Joshua said, "Mother, look at your son!" At his command, she stopped and did look up, something she'd thus far been unable to do. His compassion for her overcame his difficulty in speaking. "Nothing about me has ever been as you expected...from my conception, to my birth, to this....The Lord acts in unexpected ways.....Listen to Miriam." He was exhausted from the effort, but looked at me and gasped, "Look at your, Mother!" I looked and knew he wanted me to care for her and teach her as my own mother now, not let her be passed on to James and his younger brothers. I knew he wanted me to teach her all I'd learned from him.

He approved my understanding of his request as we held one another's eyes for a few moments. After a grimace, he said, "Father, into your hand I commend my spirit."

I thought for a minute, remembered his quote from another David psalm, and was glad we'd sung them together so often. With something as close to a feeling of confidence as I could manage, I began, "With you, O Lord, I take shelter. Never let me be humiliated. In your generosity, rescue me. Listen and save me quickly. You are my rock solid fortress. Guide me and lead me for the sake of your own reputation."

I sang with a glimmer of hope that God wouldn't turn a deaf ear. "Get me out of the net they have hidden for me, for you are my refuge. *Into your hand I commend my spirit.* You have redeemed me, O Lord, God of truth. I hate those who serve worthless idols, but I trust in you, Lord. Let me rejoice and glory in your kindness. You have noticed my pain and you are aware of how distressed I am. You did not abandon me to the power of the enemy, but you set me free to do your will. Grant me your grace now, Lord, for I am deeply distressed. My eye is worn out as is my throat and my belly."

I sang the rest of the psalm, wondering how I had never really listened to these words before. This was Joshua's song, and it would be my song when I was led away. I finished, "Lord, I trust you. You're my God and my life is in your hand." Then praying for me, our family and followers, a catch in my voice told him I understood. "Hide them in your presence where they will be safe from attacks and quarrels of men....In my haste I thought I was cut off from your presence, but you heard me when I cried to you for help."

Joshua and his Father in Heaven were still in conversation, had been in this conversation all of his life, and through all of this ordeal. The Lord God heard his cries just as I had, and heard me singing just as Joshua had. Looking into his now exhausted eyes, I finished singing the psalm for him. "Love the Lord, all of you faithful followers of his. The Lord keeps you with integrity, and pays back those who disdain you. Be strong and take courage all of you who hope in the Lord." With these last words, our eyes flooded with tears of pain and love, drawing us together in perfect, sacred union, deep tenderly calling to deep, longing to end each other's suffering. We each mouthed, barely above a whisper, "I love you." He heaved a heavy sigh of resignation, said, "It is finished," and stopped breathing.

It was suddenly completely dark. A powerful, blinding flash of lightning struck the cross, hit the ground in front of me. Shaken by the force, Mother Mary and I were jolted but unharmed. Thunder crashed. The earth shook violently in three rumbling waves.

Rocks tumbled. The other two crosses swayed, Demas, Gestas, Mother Mary, the soldiers, and what was left of the crowd screamed, terrified. But I was in a place of perfect calm, in the center, in the eye of the storm, in perfect union with my beloved. Part of me had died with him.

# CHAPTER THIRTY-SIX

In the moments that followed, the cloud instantly evaporated, disappeared. Normal afternoon sunlight suddenly returned. Frightened, almost hysterical, Hannah, Salome, and Aunt Mary ran from the edge of what was left of the crowd to embrace us. A still living part of me asked Hannah, "Please go find Uncle Joseph....Tell him what happened and ask him for help....Ask Pilate for Joshua's body."

"I'll go quickly, Miriam, and then go to tell Lazarus, and Martha and Simon." She kissed me and was off, running.

I thought if Salome could find Nicodemus, he would help, too, so I sent her off with my request. Aunt Mary comforted Mother Mary, and I went to put my arms around the cross and stay at Joshua's feet, guarding his body and bathing his feet again in my tears.

Time has no relevance, no measure adequate for such an experience. I have no idea how long I was there, transfixed by the overwhelming emotion of his messages to me through the Psalms, by the possibility, even until the last minute, that there could be a reprieve, a miracle. The finality of Joshua saying, "It's finished," freely giving himself as an offering, and then God's dramatic acceptance of his sacrifice with the flash of lightning, fire as dramatic as the fire called down from heaven by Elijah, and then the sudden disappearance of the cloud that had protected us in our suffering from taunts and prying eyes, all stunned me.

Clinging to the cross, all background noise seemed to dim; the startled soldiers had hushed and regrouped; his mother and aunt clung together and wailed. I felt empty, amputated, as though part of me had vanished. I remembered Joshua had told me that hope is as hollow as fear because both arise from thinking of myself, from imagining the world as separate from myself. "See the world as yourself," he'd said. "Trust God with the way things are." I had hoped, but I would try very hard to look through his eyes and love the world as myself now.

The centurion and the soldiers who had witnessed this most unusual crucifixion were stunned. After the lightning strike and the earthquake, after the sudden disappearance of the mysterious cloud, the centurion, awestruck, had walked up behind me and said to me, to his men, and to the universe, "This must truly be the son of God."

Uncle Joseph, calm, determined, and ready to take control, arrived after a while with a guard and Pilate's order to release Joshua's body to him. He'd been at the fortress with Claudia and Pilate and sensed what had happened. I heard him talking with the centurion. The order required the centurion to verify that Joshua was dead and then release his body to his uncle.

Knowing he was dead, the centurion commanded one of his men to jab a spear into Joshua's side to prove it beyond a shadow of a doubt. Warm blood and fluid drained from the wound and spilled down onto my head, uniting us again, as I sank further down onto the hard rock altar, his warm blood trickling through my hair, my arms still around the cross. The men were satisfied. Uncle Joseph took me by the shoulders, lifted me to my feet, gently telling me we must let the guards take Joshua's body down so we could give it an honorable burial before sundown.

Uncle Joseph, used to giving orders, found a willing helper in the centurion who had the best of his men carry out those orders. Still frightened at the omens, the men took care in their tasks. The centurion himself found Joshua's robe among their things and presented it to me. As the soldiers were taking Joshua's body down, Nicodemus and Salome arrived with linens and myrrh as well as with James and John to help carry Joshua. Uncle Joseph had purchased a new tomb before his last trip, never dreaming it would be used so soon, but now it seemed to him the place to take the body of his beloved nephew.

Pilate, still uneasy that he had released Justus Bar-Abbas, had ordered that the legs of any of the three still alive be broken at once in order to speed their dying. He was afraid the Zealots might still try some kind of rescue. The cries from the others were wrenching as the order was carried out, while our little burial party left the rock of crucifixion, the altar of sacrifice, with Joshua's sheet-wrapped body on the four men's shoulders. Uncle Joseph led the way to his new tomb in a garden nearby.

Following Joshua's body toward the tomb, I drifted between my overwhelming loss and my desire to remember everything Joshua had said and done. Everything moved swiftly out of my control, and I was at the tomb, wetting his body with my tears, as I rewrapped it hastily with the myrrh, aware of the others trying to be helpful. We must leave before sundown. Now in tears also, Uncle Joseph gently drew me away. The other three men rolled the stone to close the tomb and we left.

Returning home with Mother Mary, Uncle Joseph, Nicodemus, James and John, Aunt Mary and Salome, the eight of us made our way slowly back to the city gate toward home through the crowded streets where everyone talked about the earthquake. Our shock was in some way shared by everyone. "A major quake," they said. "Doors flew open, windows cracked, things tumbled from furniture and shelves, loose stones fell, tops slipped off sarcophagi, and have you heard the news? Pilgrims in the Temple say the great curtain that separates us from the Holy of Holies, from God, was ripped open from top to bottom! Imagine! Torn wide open at the hour of the evening sacrifice!"

In spite of my sorrow, I smiled. Joshua and his heavenly Father had done it, or rather, undone it. Atonement! We are no longer separated from God. A student of Nicodemus saw him and ran to tell him again that the veil was ripped, altars were cracked, tables were turned over, money flew to the pavement, animals were spooked, birds flew from their cages. How could I not smile? It seemed Joshua and God, his Father, were completing unfinished business at the very time lightning had struck and the mysterious cloud had evaporated as suddenly as it had arrived.

Uncle Joseph walked beside me and told me he'd been called to the fortress in the late morning where Pilate told

him what had happened and how helpless he'd felt, even with
the power of Rome, to stop the events that unfolded. He
regretted Joshua sacrificing himself, and he wanted to tell
Joseph personally that he did not condemn his nephew to
crucifixion. They were soon all shaken by the unusual darkness, and then by the earthquake. Claudia was sure these
were omens of disaster, her nightmare come true.

At Joseph's mention of darkness, I felt again the dark
cloud protecting us in our suffering from mocking eyes.
Then I heard Uncle Joseph again, the earthquake at the fortress, conversation interrupted. Uncle Joseph instinctively
knew Joshua had died and asked Pilate for permission to
bury his nephew's body in a new tomb he'd purchased for
himself rather than let the body be thrown into the common
criminal grave. Pilate said it was the least he could do.

I hadn't thought of that possibility. I just knew I needed
Uncle Joseph's help.

As we passed more rubble and pockets of pilgrims huddled together in the streets, Uncle Joseph told me his servant
had been terrified, but still waiting for him at the fortress
gate when Hannah arrived and confirmed Joshua had died.
He sent his servant to Nicodemus, to ask him to bring spices,
linen, and a couple of men to help carry Joshua's body to the
tomb. He, himself, quickly walked, half ran, with the Roman
soldier, around fallen stones, through clusters of hysterical
people wondering what would happen next.

Nicodemus walked with Mother Mary just a few steps
behind us and called for a rest stop for her. Lost in Joseph's
story, we'd begun to walk faster as he told of hurrying with
the soldier as we'd started up the hill toward our house.

After a short breather, Joseph took Mother Mary's arm and led the way at her pace, while Nicodemus walked beside me. Joseph's servant had arrived to confirm the news Salome was telling them incohcrently through her tears. Peter, James, and John had each taken refuge with him and Rachel during the morning. Everyone was on edge.

Joseph's request gave them something to do. Rachel gathered linen and some myrrh. Nicodemus, James, and John hurried past panicked people crowding the narrow streets, passing shops that were in shambles. Nicodemus led them toward the spice merchants' street where he took a bag of myrrh from the jumbled stall of a friend, telling him he would pay him later; he was on his way...Nicodemus' voice faltered. He couldn't finish his sentence.

I pressed his arm. I knew the rest. We were at our gate, my reverie interrupted; Rhoda and Nathan opened the doors and embraced me.

# CHAPTER THIRTY-SEVEN

As I stepped over the threshold, my eyes welled with tears. The house was filled with the aromas of freshly baked unleavened bread and succulent stew prepared for the Sabbath dinner. Life in our home had continued, but Joshua wasn't at my elbow stepping over our threshold. I felt strange stepping into a familiar and now unfamiliar place.

Rachel was waiting just inside the entrance. We held one another for a long while, speaking only with our tears, and eventually made our way arm-in-arm, up the stairs to the upper room where those who were with us the night before had returned to wait for me. As we entered, they came to embrace us, to share their shock, their grief, and then dissolve into small, huddled conversations in hushed tones. Nicodemus, James, and John told the others about the burial in the new tomb. Uncle Joseph collapsed onto a bench, at last able to sit down, and give in to his grief. He simply held his head in his hands and quietly sobbed. The women gathered around Mother Mary, Aunt Mary, Salome, Rachel, and me.

Servants hovered, not knowing quite what to do. After a while, I realized they were waiting for me, so somehow I found my voice. "It must be sundown. I'm sure Joshua would want us to share the Sabbath meal tonight and remember our Passover. He taught me that every moment is a sacred gift to be shared...." I paused. "We shared our love all day. He helped me to stay centered with him in God's love, as impossible as that seems." Tears welled up again.

My words seemed inadequate. I asked that we sing the psalm about God encircling us. "Those who trust in the Unnameable God are like Mount Zion," everyone joined in. "They are as immoveable as God's chosen mountain. Mountains encircle Jerusalem, and God encircles his people, always has and always will. Wrongdoers will not always provoke violence and take what is due others. Be good to your people, Holy One, to those whose hearts are open. Round up the violators and bring justice and mercy and peace to your people and to the world." When we finished, I added with a choked voice, "Today, Joshua said, 'Forgive them...they don't know what they're doing!'"

More tears flowed. I motioned for the servants to bring the food, for everyone to find a place at the table, and for Mother Mary to sit beside me After we had settled, I looked around and asked, "Where is Judas?"

There was grumbling. Peter said, "Miriam, Judas was the one who led the guards to us last night in the garden. He doesn't dare show his face. He's a traitor, he—"

I paled and raised my hand. "Stop, Peter; don't judge, not tonight. You don't know everything. Remember, Joshua forgave everyone and said, 'Let the one without sin cast the first stone.'" I gave a questioning look to Thomas, who said he hadn't seen his brother, either, didn't know what had happened to him. Then looking around the table, I pled, "Make

Judas welcome and hear his story, too." Judging him and excluding him seemed so contrary to everything I had just lived through with Joshua.

After regaining my composure, I began the meal. I lit a lamp as I said again, "Blessed are you Lord God, King of the Universe who brings light out of darkness." And then with still glistening, tear-filled eyes, I lit a second lamp. "Remember, Joshua said, 'I am the light of the world.'"

I asked Uncle Joseph to say the blessing He led us in the traditional prayers as he broke bread and then poured wine. As we remembered what Joshua had said, there wasn't a dry eye around the table. Silent, we were together and yet each alone with memories, shattered hopes, and dreams. We tried to make sense of the words we had heard last night and what had happened since. The women who'd stayed home knew nothing except the darkness, the earthquake, and then the shocking news.

Big bowls of succulent stew were brought to the table along with more bread, but no one had much of an appetite. Conversations full of guilt, frustration, confusion, and fear of further arrests slowly started.

When we heard a loud knock at the door below, everyone fell silent; the tension was palpable. I nodded to Rhoda, who went downstairs to open it. To her relief, she found Lazarus and Hannah, who'd managed to be within a Sabbath day's walking distance before sundown. They came to embrace me and tell me my children were safe. Martha and Simon had put John Mark in charge and sent all three to the cave with provisions. Lazarus had made plans with Simon and Alphaeus to hide them further if any soldiers came looking. I was relieved, thankful our children were wrapped in the love of aunts and uncles. Lazarus and Hannah's message delivered, they found places at the table.

Peter got up from his seat and came to kneel beside me. He told me how in the garden last night and then again in Caiaphas' courtyard early this morning he had been ashamed of himself, but he really hadn't understood or liked what was happening. He'd hoped someone with authority could help, so he'd gone to Nicodemus because he was afraid he might be recognized again and arrested, and then the darkness, the earthquake, and Salome and Joseph's servant came with the news. He had gone to check on Joseph's home and then came here. Poor Peter, I thought, couldn't face Joshua and couldn't face Joshua's dead body. Peter's ambition and his imagined future had been completely shattered.

Peter asked me what he could have done. Actually, everything he'd done seemed so pitiful to him. Disgusted, he said he was a better fisherman than a swordsman and we all laughed through our tears at that declaration. Well, at least he'd tried. The others all seemed so hopeless, but he still didn't understand.

I smiled. "And this morning? I looked for you when I left the courtyard."

Peter closed his eyes, swallowed hard. "I denied I knew him, Miriam...three times, and then the cock crowed. Joshua predicted it! I was scared and ashamed and left the courtyard quickly, but I followed you in the shadows as you went toward the fortress."

Peter stood and walked back to his seat and included the others, "We just weren't prepared, Miriam; even though

Joshua kept talking about being betrayed, suffering, even dying, we didn't want to hear it. We didn't expect anything like this." I nodded in sympathy. But Peter continued, now addressing Nicodemus, "You weren't called to any meeting of the Sanhedrin." Nicodemus nodded in agreement as Peter kept talking. "It was crooked. Caiaphas held a sham trial; everything was done at night in secret. I'll be next if Malchus has anything to say about it."

The others agreed or disagreed among themselves as Peter kept talking. "I haven't slept except when Joshua asked me to stay awake and pray. I was tired and wasn't sure what to pray. We all should have prayed...prayed for courage. Do you know who else betrayed Joshua besides me?" he looked around the table. "And why?"

I couldn't answer his questions. I knew Joshua had offered himself and knew his sacrifice was received by God. None of the others answered either.

Peter persisted, "Did his cousins in the priesthood or the rabbis out of jealousy or indifference betray him? Did Justus and the Zealots with their revolt? Did Judas because of money problems? Or did all of the pilgrims betray him with their festive procession, hailing him Messiah and king without thinking of the consequences...or of how they'd help make it happen? They just stirred up trouble for him with the priests and Herod and the Romans who aren't about to give up their power."

Andrew answered his brother, "Maybe we all did."

But Peter was still troubled. "Last night at dinner, Joshua said one of us would betray him. One of us! Was it Judas, or was it me with my denial and desertion?"

How could we answer?

Peter, tears welling in his eyes again, said, "I did. I can't believe I actually denied that I ever knew him. I should have gone for help, rallied the pilgrims from Galilee, tried to find Joseph, tried to find the rest of you after we slunk off into the dark. No one has clean hands, but I didn't want to come here tonight. We're losers. We deserted him. How could I face you?"

Exhausted, I simply said, "Peter, I forgive you, and I know Joshua forgave you. He even forgave the soldiers and the crowd of hecklers. Don't be afraid, Peter." He heaved a deep sigh, but he couldn't forgive himself yet.

I felt overwhelmed by my husband's absence after so many years of celebrating Sabbath together, side-by-side. I realized his request that I take his mother as my own now somehow helped me fill his empty place. I turned to her and gently reached out my hand. Normally so talkative, words failed us. She took my hand within hers, and I reached out my other hand to grasp both of hers in mine. Our eyes met and mirrored one another's through tears. Our hands, held ever so tightly, expressed better than words that we had gone through our loss together and were bound by it forever.

James and John took turns telling everyone their story. It seemed like an eternity since they'd left the house last night, laughing and singing the Passover songs. Philip interrupted them, saying they all had scattered so sheepishly in the garden last night.

Thomas and he came to look for me. They hadn't been together until each returned here after the earthquake. Bartholomew said he'd gone to find his uncle, a member of the

Sanhedrin. Matthew and James had run to Alphaeus to get help.

Thad spoke softly and hesitantly. Returning from Bethany, he had learned what had happened from a pilgrim, and stumbled off the road. Too late, he couldn't go on, just had to get away and retch until nothing was left, just sobs and tears...first his father, and now Joshua. Deeply moved, I got up and went to him. I gently put my hands on his shoulders, kissed the top of his head, shared his sorrow.

Simon listened to the others, holding back his own tears. He finally choked them down, told us he'd returned to the city, found Zealots, heard what was happening, stayed on the edge of the crowd, troubled that both Joshua and his brother were in the fortress. The crowd began chanting, "Bar-Abbas! Bar-Abbas!" and he had joined in, not knowing why. He had worked his way toward the gate to see Joshua and his brother brought out. The shouts became, "Crucify him! Crucify him!" and he realized what was happening.

Simon, through tears he was no longer able to stop, whispered hoarsely, in a cracked voice. "I've never seen my brother's face look like that."

Complete silence filled the room, broken when he was able to continue. "You all know Justus was so sure he could inspire us to drive out the oppressors and to crown Joshua our rightful king, but here was his peace-loving friend taking his place, giving up his life for him, forgiving him, calmly smiling and nodding to him. I think my brother finally realized the great reversal. Joshua loved him so much he was dying for him, taking the consequences, the punishment he deserved. I don't know, but it seems to me Joshua somehow substituted himself to save Justus."

"That's true, Simon," I reassured him, impressed at his observation and understanding, but there were grumbles around the table at Simon's view. Others were sure that Joshua was betrayed and caught by the priests in some kind of trap. They were glad for Simon that his brother was free until someone else double-crossed him, but they were sure Joshua had many enemies. They'd heard of the plots. The priests and Herod were out to get him. Anyone might be next.

Encouraged by my support, Simon continued, "I followed the men carrying my brother on their shoulders and finally caught up with him. He sent me right back to Joshua, Demas, and Gestas. He wanted to organize and stop the crucifixions." Simon fell silent. "I watched from a distance. The Zealots came too late. I admire you so much, Miriam," he added just above a whisper, "for staying with him, for not deserting him."

The stories were done. Each of us had a different view of what had happened, different expectations, different questions. We were all very tired and needed sleep. I thanked Joseph, Nicodemus, James, and John for helping me with the burial, and I told everyone that it was one of Joshua's last requests that I care for his mother as my own, now. So even though she would be known as the mother of James, her oldest living son, she could live with me as long as she wanted. I asked them to gather again after Sabbath to celebrate the barley harvest together.

Tension and sadness still pervaded the room. I said, "We don't know what's next. Pray for peace for us and for our city, and remember Joshua called you friends and taught you to forgive, and to love your enemies. Blaming ourselves or others, even Judas, doesn't help our grief. We're all God's children, all forgiven. Judgment is God's, not ours."

I paused...and then continued somewhat hesitantly, "Even though we don't understand what happened, Joshua taught us that nothing can separate us from the love of God, and he taught me that God is loving all of us, even in this. I'll tell you more in a few days, but for tonight, remember Joshua taught us the way to live in peace, showed us the way, and asked us to follow."

My voice quavered, "Before we go, let's sing one of the Psalms he shared with me from the cross. 'The Lord is my shepherd,'" I began and the others joined, "I have everything I need..." and finally, "Your goodness and kindness pursue me every day of my life, and I shall live sheltered by you forever." Tears welled in my eyes, in eyes around the table.

Overcome with emotion, I wiped away tears again and stood to help Mother Mary to her feet. We were all exhausted and needed rest. As the others stood, I asked Uncle Joseph for God's blessing. He cleared his throat and repeated the familiar blessing given to Moses and Aaron: "The Lord bless you and watch over you. The Lord make his face shine upon you and be gracious to you. The Lord look kindly on you and give you peace."

# CHAPTER THIRTY-EIGHT

I awoke with a start the next morning. Was it a night-mare? No, the bed beside me was cold and empty, no one was waiting with twinkling eyes and the first line of a psalm. I scrunched my eyes closed. I didn't want to cry again, but the urge swept over me like a wave of nausea. It passed momentarily. I opened my eyes as bravely as I could and took a deep breath, but found myself back at his feet.

"Father God, you are my shepherd. I have everything I need" floated into my mind as if Joshua had started the psalm for me again this morning. Was it from the cross or from sharing it with the others last night? Tears began as I continued, as I had yesterday, struggling to mean every word. "Your goodness and kindness pursue me every day of my life." Shall I live sheltered by you forever? I was in our bed, in our house, which had survived the earthquake without visible cracks. I was still alive, but I wondered about invisible cracks, about all Joshua had told me about his sacrifice, and then mine.

Everything tumbled together in my mind: adulation and desertion, praise and betrayal...the taunting, mocking, and quibbling. So many sins seemed to weigh me down. My muscles tightened in revulsion. Could I continue alone, follow him and face people as he did, love them and say, "Father, forgive them. They don't know what they're doing?"

When we were alone the other evening after I'd anointed him with the precious oil, it had seemed so clear. "This is why we're here, Mim," he'd said. "God is making peace through us. Others will see our way of love and be fearless, too. I'm sure of it."

Rhoda knocked softly and came in to ask whether there was anything she could do or bring me to eat or drink. I must have looked exhausted. Her eyes filled with tears. "Yes, thank you," I responded. "I'm still very tired. I'll stay here and rest this morning. I just need time." I asked whether she'd seen Mother Mary. She hadn't, but she promised to stop in her room on the way to the kitchen. "Tell her I'll come to see her in a little while," I said. Rhoda left before I added to no one in particular, "I just need time..." which is what I told her again when she returned with warm bread, honey, fruit, and her warm herb tea that was very soothing. Finishing it, I slipped back down into the bed, and fell fast asleep.

I dreamed about the wilderness. Tents surrounded me as far as I could see. I was being led to a special tent with Joshua. Our cousins, Annas and Caiaphas, were at the entrance. It was the most beautiful tent, with intricate carving and weaving and brightly colored threads decorating it. Annas and Caiaphas were dressed in beautiful robes, but when we got close, I could see that their robes were all splattered with blood. They smiled invitingly at our approach, anticipating our sacrifice.

It seemed that Moses himself was leading us. We stopped in front of the priests. My nostrils burned with the smell of death. Suddenly, a crowd was around us, chanting, "Kill them! Kill them! Kill them...not us!" Someone shouted, "Save us. We didn't know what we were doing!" Others shouted, "Save us from snakes! Save us from temptations! Save us from dying! The snakes are killing us! Hold him up so we can see him!" Moses spoke in a booming voice, but then it was Pilate, "Silence!"

I couldn't hear a sound except for my heart beating. "Aaron, I bring you two sacrifices for peace with God against whom we have all sinned: two goats, one a blood sacrifice to be sacrificed on the altar for the people's sins, the other a scapegoat to be sent into the wilderness with all of the people's sins piled on it." But it wasn't Aaron. Annas and Caiaphas kept grinning. They took Joshua inside the tent. Not a sound. Then red blood splattered across my face, but no sound came from the beautiful tent. The acrid smoke of death suddenly mixed with the sweet, pungent odors of frankincense and myrrh.

The crowd went wild. I hated crowds. I heard yelling, laughing, poking fun, cruel voices: "Now let's dump everything on the other one," they shouted. It got darker and darker; heavier and heavier. "It's all her fault! It was her idea! She tempted him! He loved her too much! She's too educated! She's too powerful! She doesn't understand us! She's a whore! She stinks! She's just a widow! Take her things and get her out of here! She knows too much! She'll make trouble! She's too smart! She's too dumb! She's too emotional! She's not one of us! She's just a woman! Don't trust her! Don't let her stay in our camp! Get rid of her!"

Before my back was broken, Caiaphas called someone to lead me out of the camp, away from all the discontented people, away from the beautiful tent, away, away, away. I walked past tent after tent after tent, past children playing and women cooking and men working, who all threw dirt and small stones at me as I was led out beyond the last tent into the valley, into the far hills. It was hard walking up the hill carrying all of those burdens: jealousy, greed, hatred, envy, judgment, gossip, lies, complaints, fears. I didn't know where I was going or what I was going to do, and so I just kept going.

I woke in a sweat, my eyes filled with tears. Even though I knew it had been a dream, it was so vivid. I sobbed and sobbed and sobbed myself to sleep again, exhausted without a flicker of a dream I could remember when I woke an hour or so later with the urge to write down the earlier dream as well as the Psalms Joshua had asked me to sing at the cross. I didn't want to forget. Things he'd taught me through the years continued to come to mind...."Let go of your desire to control the past or the future," he'd said. "Live now and welcome whomever or whatever comes." Was that part of my dream? I splashed my face with cold water from a basin, dressed, and sat to write, to record simply, what I had sung for him yesterday. I wondered whether others would want to know what he had taught me from the cross, or if they would prefer to stay in the crowd, a safe distance away.

Yesterday, I had looked for a substitute for Joshua like God had provided for Ishmael and Isaac when Abraham offered them on the altar. Up to the moment Joshua had said, "It's finished," I had hoped. Today, I accepted the reality that Joshua was the substitute for Justus, Annas, Caiaphas, Pilate, and all of us. I let go of my fear of what might come next. "Your will be done," I repeated and repeated and repeated again as I moved through the Sabbath, the rest of the day spent comforting his mother and the others as best I could.

The second night, however, I barely slept. I tossed and turned and waited impatiently for the dawn. Early this morning, I could do something. I could go to the tomb and finish my widow's duties that I'd so hastily begun before sundown. I wanted to put the chain with his golden key, given him in the ceremony when he became a rabbi, around his neck, even though he hadn't worn it since leaving the Sanhedrin. It was a prescribed custom to bury a rabbi with his key, and it seemed right and just that I give our great teacher this token, this simple tribute, after properly cleaning and wrapping his body all before someone came to arrest me, carry me away, or put a guard at my door. I didn't know what would happen. Sleepless, my thoughts wandered. My favorite little oil lamp cast an ever-changing pattern of light and shadow flickering across the ceiling and walls just as scenes from the last few weeks flickered through my mind.

Since the day before his trip to Bethlehem, Joshua had begun to prepare me. I'd anointed him for his task with the precious gift of the Wise Men. I pictured the board nailed to his cross, "King of the Jews." I got out of bed to put the alabaster jar beside the basket I had prepared to take to the tomb. I wanted to empty anything left in the jar onto his head. The sweet, earthy fragrance of myrrh permeated me.

As I returned to bed, another tomb came to mind. I remembered meeting Joshua outside of Bethany near the entrance to the tomb where we had placed Lazarus. Joshua wept with me, and said, "Mim, believe me, I am resurrection and life." I felt again my astonishment when Lazarus hobbled out when Joshua called him.

I almost dozed, relaxed in that feeling of unexpected joy. I don't know for how long, but after a while, the words of a song ran through my head: "Give thanks to the Lord, for he is good; his compassion and kindness endures forever."

It was as if Joshua had given me those beginning lines this morning and it was my turn to continue, "Entangled, I called to the Lord and the Lord disentangled me, set me free. The Lord is with me so I need not fear what anyone can do to me. The Lord is at my side to help me so I can rise above those who hate me. It's better to rely on the Lord than to rely on people or trust in any ruler." This confident belief in the ever present Unnameable True Lord God was how he had moved through these past few days, I thought, and it's the way I can face whatever comes without dread or fear.

I was to be next and almost heard Joshua continue, "The vicious surrounded me; in the name of the Lord I stopped them. They hemmed me in on every side and in the name of the Lord I walked through them. They swarmed about me like bees and blazed like a fire of thorns, but in the name of the Lord I forgave them. I was pressed so hard that I almost fell, but the Lord came to my help." I thought of him battered and bleeding, walking through the jeering crowd, and I remembered Simon of Cyrene. Oh, my God! Thank you! I must try to find him, but I began to cry again. This would be my song, too.

Wiping away the tears, I drew the soft wool blanket around me against the chill of the night and continued the psalm. Where was it taking me? "My strength and my song are from the Lord who sets me free. There is rejoicing wherever people live in peace. The Lord has overcome! I shall not die, but live, and tell what the Lord has done." Overcome, I wondered. Live? How?

"The Lord punished me, but did not hand me over to death." The words seemed to describe what we'd gone through, but not this. I didn't understand, closed my eyes, but seemed to hear him continue the song, "Open the gate of justice for me. The one who is honest and just may enter. I will enter and offer thanks to the Lord. I will give thanks to you, for you answered me and have rescued me."

Puzzled over unbelievably confident words, I continued, "The stone which the builders rejected has become the chief cornerstone. This is the Lord's doing, and it's marvelous in our eyes. The Lord is acting this very day; let's rejoice and be glad." How could I rejoice and be glad? With the morning stars, with dawn, would some light shine on these words that seemed to have come from my husband? Perhaps they were for me and my journey. I finished the song and waited for answers. "Blessed is the one who comes in the name of the Lord to give us light. You are my God, and I will thank you and praise you. The Lord's compassion endures forever."

Through tears that flowed again unbidden, could I still say, "You *are* my God. I will thank you. Your compassion endures forever. They didn't know what they were doing?" Maybe that was enough. I tossed fitfully, waiting for the first rays of light. Hannah, Salome, and Mother Mary had helped me gather together the cloths, the myrrh, and ointments we would need this morning. I was to wake them when I was ready, but I had asked Hannah to stay home with Mother Mary. We were all concerned for her. All afternoon, she had repeated over and over stories of angels at his birth and the Wise Men and miracles and her pride in her son for having helped so many people. He was such a bright and influential rabbi. "What will become of us?" she asked, but she insisted that she wanted to support me in my widow's duties, insisted we four go together.

Half-awake, my mind skipped from person to person, image to image. It was good to have Lazarus here and know he would be here when we returned from the tomb, after properly cleaning and wrapping Joshua's body as I had helped Hannah with Lazarus' body. Joshua's body had felt so cold to my touch. Dazed, half-dead, I had hurried to do what was necessary, closed his eyelids and placed the napkin over his battered face, which seemed at peace. The struggle was finished for him. It continued for me.

Visiting the tomb was a painful repetition of burying Lazarus. This time it was the body of my beloved husband rather than my brother. This time I'd called the Unnameable God to come to my rescue, but He had delayed also. I shuddered as I heard again the sound of nails pounded and nails pulled, felt the blood and water from his side, and remembered wrapping his limp but stiffening body in the shroud Nicodemus had brought. The centurion had shown pity, and with his gloved hands, removed the awful crown of thorns.

I remembered feeling light-headed, stumbling along the path with Mother Mary, helping to steady her as we tried to keep up with James and John, Nicodemus and Uncle Joseph carrying Joshua's body. Four women followed his body, the only mourners in our sad little procession to Uncle Joseph's tomb. What a contrast we were to the joyous, noisy procession a few days ago when the pilgrims wanted to make him King. We'd had no time for grieving, no funeral cortege. All had needed to be done before sundown. Everything had seemed so rushed.

My body shivered involuntarily. In my sleepless state, my mind drifted back and forth between the memories of Lazarus' death and those of these past two days. All of our friends from Jerusalem had come then to mourn with me in Bethany. No one came this time, except Uncle Joseph, Rachel, and Nicodemus, to mourn with me and our family and frightened servants. Of course, Elizabeth and Caiaphas didn't come, and I suspected they kept Mathias at home, too.

Had it been the third or fourth day, I wondered, when Joshua had returned to Bethany and asked me to come to meet him beside the tomb? Maybe Joshua was actually preparing me for this. It all seemed too familiar, except this time it was the Unnameable God who delayed. What had Joshua said to me? It was for the glory of God that he had delayed his return....

Maybe the Unnameable had delayed so we could see more glory, but who could call Joshua from the tomb? Could I do it? Could I, his beloved disciple, the one who sat at his feet, his loving wife and the mother of his children, the one who had anointed him with oil for his mission, the one whom he had baptized and cleansed of the seven ubiquitous sins, the one who had stayed at the cross with him? Was it possible that my love could call him from the tomb? Could it be for the glory of the Lord? If not I, who else? I felt so weak, so inadequate, but I got up out of my rumpled, empty bed and held up my arms and said, "Here I am, Lord. Your will be done. Send me if it will bring you glory."

# CHAPTER THIRTY-NINE

The faint light of my lamp and the light of the full moon coming through the window were enough to find my warm robe and stole lying beside the seamless robe the centurion had given me. Memories flooded back as I picked it up and wrapped it in my arms. The soldiers were visibly shaken and superstitious, I thought, and knew something strange had happened. Hearing me chant at the foot of the cross, they may have imagined I was the priestess of an unknown God. When he gave me the robe, the centurion had said again, "He truly was the Son of God."

But what was I doing, thinking of calling him from the dead? Joshua had been clear that my part of the sacrifice would come. Now that he was gone, who would come to lead me into the wilderness, I wondered. Thoughts tumbled together. Where is Uncle Joseph? What are Annas and Caiaphas thinking? Will our children be safe? Who will care for them? I hadn't asked those questions before.

Our children, descendants of both Saul and David, could be a problem as deeply political and threatening to the current rulers as the announcement of Joshua's birth was to Herod. We had no interest in an earthly kingdom, but those

who did might take advantage of our children's lineage and
make them the focus of a struggle for power. Uncle Joseph
seemed exhausted and uneasy. I wondered what threats he
saw? Joshua had asked Annas and Caiaphas to protect us. I
quieted my mind and wrapped myself in the extra layer of his
robe and settled back into bed, comforted with his familiar
smell.

Inhaling deeply, I pictured the moment I'd gone forward,
taking Mother Mary with me to stand near his feet, listen,
and sing. I was not afraid. He was sacrificed and it was my
turn now to be "forgotten from the mind like the dead, forgotten like a vessel lost at sea, to be surrounded by threats
and to be slandered by many. They will secretly agree to get
rid of me too and plot to take my life," I was sure as I remembered the psalm again.

How had I not paid attention to these words before? This
song he had asked me to sing would be my song when I was
led away. I sang the next lines again, sang alone in the night,
sang quietly, as bravely as I could. "I trust in you, O Lord,"
I sang. "You're my God. My life is in your hands. Rescue me
from my enemies. Shine your face on me; protect me in your
kindness. Lord, let me not be dishonored."

A cock crowed somewhere nearby and I was brought back
into the present with a jolt. Morning at last and time to go to
the tomb, so early that no one but friends would be with me,
no prying or jeering crowd to pass in the street, just women's
work. We could cry again over our linens, ointments, and
spices.

As I put the alabaster jar in my basket and trimmed my
lamp, I remembered again my baptism and the seven levels

of human entanglements. Joshua had taught me to overcome the demons that try to crush our spirit and separate us from God's love. I remembered he had led me through darkness, past desire, past ignorance, past the wish to die, past the desire to live only for my body's fulfillment, past foolishly thinking that I knew best and could tell God what to do, and past being angry with God and others for not doing things my way, past all seven into the light of God's presence. Retracing our path in my mind, I was ready to go into this new day, past all fear and anxiety about what men could or would do to me, loving and trusting God who first loved me.

Carrying my lamp and the basket with the precious alabaster jar, my red shawl around my head and shoulders against the early morning chill, I went down the stairs and woke the others. Rolling the stone away from the entrance would be a problem, but four determined women should be able to do it. We let ourselves out the door, each with a lamp against the deep predawn shadows, and made our way along the familiar, dusty streets. The guards at the city gate paid little attention to us, four women carrying lamps and baskets. Outside the city gate, the sharp smells of wild herbs hit our nostrils as we walked along the dusty, deserted road leading to the garden and the tomb. Uneasy, we said little at this early hour. Determined to move the stone and do what was necessary, we trusted that the cool temperatures and hastily spread spices had kept his body from the smell of death and decay. We would soon find out.

Approaching the garden, we walked into a thick morning mist; we felt confused and began to compare memories. We had been in shock three days ago, but walking toward the tomb I was sure was his, the stone was already rolled back.

The others, frightened, stopped and hesitated before following me as I walked through the gloom with my little lamp
to the door. Eerie. Strange. Unexpected! Who would have
rolled away the stone?

I looked. We all looked and saw linens but that was all.
There wasn't a body! Certain it was his tomb, we panicked
and ran back to the house to get help, to tell the others that
there was no body in the tomb. Who would have done something on Passover Sabbath? Why? Would they come to get us
next? Our heads were down as we hurried past the guards at
the city gate. Reaching home, we found Rhoda giving Peter
and Lazarus an early breakfast. I breathlessly told them what
we'd found, or rather what we hadn't found. Surprised, and
then alarmed, Peter asked whether I was confused. Was I
looking in the wrong tomb?

How shocked but delighted Lazarus looked at the news.
We still didn't fully understand my brother's return from the
dead. Like returning from a war, a battlefield, Lazarus was
glad to be back alive with us, but he didn't have the words to
talk about his experiences, didn't want to try to explain something for which his listeners had no experience.

Peter swore an oath at my assurance that I was looking in
Joseph's tomb; regaining his lost bravado, he vowed to make
anyone pay who'd tampered with his master's body. Lazarus
ran out the door to see for himself. Peter stopped to get a
sharp knife from the table before running out after Lazarus.
They didn't wait for me.

Even though I was out of breath from running, as were
Hannah, Salome, and Mother Mary, I wanted to go back immediately. I put down my lamp and basket, asked Rhoda to

help Mother Mary give others the news, and ask Nathan to guard the door. I had to be sure that Lazarus and Peter found the right tomb. As I left, I asked Rhoda to send a message to Uncle Joseph, Nicodemus, and James with the news and ask them to come quickly. My heart was pounding as I ran out the door and down the street again. I felt no connection to my legs and feet as they moved rapidly over the uneven stones in the road, retracing my early morning steps in more light. I was shocked and bewildered.

Peter and Lazarus met me on the road between the garden and the city gate. They were already returning and told me that Lazarus had reached the tomb first, the only new one. He looked into the dark tomb, saw the empty slab and linen in the predawn light, but instinctively recoiled, couldn't bring himself actually to enter another tomb. Peter caught up, pushed past him and went in to look, and to exclaim, "Oh, dear God! Look, Lazarus!" as he pointed to the folded linen and spices all laid out in good order.

Lazarus had taken courage to join Peter for a minute to confirm the odd circumstance of grave cloths and spices without a body.

They were baffled! And to Peter's question, "What do you think has happened to him?" Lazarus, remembering his own recent experience, had a flicker of hope, but how? He hardly dared voice his faint hope. He simply shook his head and said, "I don't know, Peter. I don't know! He told me he would rise, too, but how? Who could call him back? It's strange. I just don't know."

Peter and Lazarus told me they couldn't find any evidence of grave robbers. Nothing was out of place, no marks of his body being dragged or carried out, no blood on the floor. There had been nothing to steal. They were perplexed and frightened.

# CHAPTER FORTY

Nothing more to see, Lazarus and Peter were hurrying back into the city to get help, to find Joseph and Nicodemus to see whether they'd heard anything. They wondered who would fold things up so neatly and take the body. Why? Where?

They told me I should hurry home immediately. They were afraid of whoever had done this. No matter how or why, it couldn't be good. I wasn't safe and we had to alert the others. Perhaps none of us were safe. Who knew what could happen next? I told them I would go home, but I wasn't afraid and first needed to go back to the tomb, to see it again for myself. Perhaps there was some clue we'd overlooked.

I hurried on toward the tomb, trying to calm myself and think of possibilities. Nothing had happened as I had expected it would, just a month ago. My world had been turned upside down, and I had tried to be brave, but now this. Who would have taken the body I loved, and why? Was there no decency left in the hearts of Caiaphas and his priests, or had it been the Romans? Did someone pressure Pilate to go back on his word with Uncle Joseph? Had he decided it better, after all, to throw the body into the common criminal grave?

It was getting lighter. The sun was almost up behind the Mount of Olives. The dry dust of the road gave way to a few trees now shrouded in thick morning mist. Was there another new tomb? Could we have been looking in the wrong one? No, but a kind of desperation made me try to think of any alternative to an empty tomb with grave cloths and spices neatly laid out, which was beyond my expectation or comprehension. Could Joshua have risen like Lazarus? If so, who could have called him? I couldn't imagine it. Perplexed, I hurried on through the mist-filled garden to the tomb.

Once again, I bent down and looked into the new tomb to see the grave cloths and spices Nicodemus had brought Friday afternoon, now as Peter and Lazarus had said, arranged neatly on the slab where we had laid Joshua's body, where I had washed the blood from his face with my tears and hair, had smoothed his hair, smothering it with kisses where the crown of thorns had punctured his skin, had kissed both of his closed eyes, and then had laid the napkin over his face after tenderly kissing once more his bruised forehead, and his cold lips. My eyes began to blur as I relived those moments of farewell. Then, someone asked me, "Why are you looking for the living among the dead?"

The voice startled me and so did the question. Was I hearing things? Could it possibly be true? Could he be alive? But how? This was not at all like Lazarus.

Stumbling back out of the tomb to look for the person who had asked the question of me, through my tears I saw someone in the thick mist walking toward me through the garden, silhouetted against the sun, which was suddenly dazzlingly bright as it broke over the horizon behind him. He asked, "Who are you looking for?" Blinded by my tears and the brilliant light, I asked him, "Are you the gardener? Do you know what has happened to my husband's body?"

I will never, ever, ever forget the sound of my name on his lips that morning. "Miriam." ...He held open his arms and I rushed into them, gasping, "Rabboni, My Love! How?" Words failed as we held each other and cried together for an eternity. I was safe, at home in his arms where I wanted to be forever. He stroked my hair, and kissed me and kissed me, then held me back a bit and said in his teasing way, "I want to get a good look at you this morning. You look a bit disheveled." His eyes sparkled, and then he drew me close again and began to kiss me as I had kissed his face in the tomb, first along my hairline as he nuzzled his nose into my loose hair tumbled out of my shawl in all of the excitement, in all of my desperate running back and forth. Trembling in spite of my joy, I couldn't help laugh and cry at his comparison between how he looked three days ago and how I looked now.

He calmly held me close again, and when my sobs had subsided, he again gently kissed my forehead, my eyebrows, my now closed eyes, and then the tears that still lingered on my cheeks, softly repeating my special names in between every few kisses, and then he found a tear that had strayed over toward my left ear, kissed it, and took a little nip of my ear lobe, and we both began to laugh softly. I lifted my eyes and tilted my head to look him full in the face, his twinkling eyes, his smile, all traces of Friday's pain gone. "This is certainly not what I expected," I said barely above a whisper. "I never want to let you go, ever, ever, ever again! But how—how is it possible you are alive?"

He smiled, kissed my forehead, and said, "My dearest Mim, there is so much for me to explain, but now is not the time. Explanations will come later. There are dimensions of life you don't know about yet...but for now, know that this is not like Lazarus. I'll always be near you whether or not you can see me, whether or not you know it, just as I was here waiting for you this morning."

I smiled in return and freely admitted, "I certainly didn't know."

He continued, "Don't cling to me, my love. I'm fulfilled now, completely at one with the Unnameable God, Our Father. We wanted to reassure you first, and ask you to take the good news to the others before you make your part of the sacrifice and join us. Be brave, Mim; many won't believe you, won't understand. They'll think you're crazy with grief and exhaustion. They'll want proof, want me to continue on earth as Lazarus has. They'll find some theory, some rational or irrational explanation for my body's disappearance." He smiled broadly and his eyes began to twinkle. I could feel another tease coming, "As fantastic as..." he paused, almost chuckled, "You heard it from me first...that some Essenes have stolen my body for ritual burial."

I couldn't help myself. We both began to laugh softly at the idea. Essene ideas of ritual, separation, and self-denial seemed far from ours. Some of them had come to question him from time to time, and Joshua had welcomed them, but they'd not been among our followers. "You can't be serious! Stop teasing," I said when our laughter subsided. What a relief that I saw no trace of the wounds he'd suffered three days ago.

"Oh, there'll be many explanations, and many more accusations." He kissed the top of my head again. "My dearest one, my dearest student, there will be people from many different groups who'll steal or deny everything about us, our life, our story, our teaching, all for their own purposes, to fit us into their own theories and traditions, their own attempts to insist God and others conform to their view of life. Don't be afraid, Mim, even though our names and lives will be written out of the Temple records."

"Our names out of the records," I asked. "I don't understand. How could they...?"

"They can and will," he answered with a smile. "Just tell our truth and write our truth, my dearest one. You're the one who knows the story of what I've taught and lived, my way of peace. Leave the rest to God. As you're led into the wilderness, exiled, as you will be, don't be afraid. You'll live our truth no matter how many of the world's honors and comforts are taken from you, no matter what others say about you. Have courage, Mim. No matter what comes, remember I love you. We've chosen to give ourselves this way."

He held me quietly, reassuringly in his arms again for a few minutes, then drew back a bit. "Do you remember the passage in Jeremiah that I showed you, the passage where he prophesied about you, too? 'For the Lord has created a new thing on earth: a woman protects a man.' You are that remarkable woman, my love. With your notes and diaries, you can write for John Mark and the others to help them tell our story. From the wilderness, no matter how unlikely or unexpected it seems, you'll protect my memory, my life, and my teaching as you write. I'll be with you. Don't worry; I'll come again to support you. Our way of love and peace has overcome the sting of death."

"But—" I started to ask. He simply kissed me again to quiet my flood of questions as he had quieted my flood of tears. He took my shoulders firmly in his hands, turned me around toward the path, and softly in my right ear, urged me, "Go now, my Dearest One, Go! Tell them that I'm alive, risen from the dead. Death is not the end to be feared, but a new beginning. You can do it! You have wonderful news! I'll see you soon!"

With that said, he was gone, and the thick morning mist vanished as well. Was it again the cloud of God's presence? It felt so familiar, so much like the clouds over the Jordan at our baptisms, like the cloud that protected us at the cross. I suspected Unnameable God, our Father, was with us again in the garden, sharing our joy, and blessing us.

The garden of the dead in that brilliant dawn light had become the new Garden of Eden, the garden of new life. Joshua and God had disappeared from sight, perhaps hidden behind ethereal golden leaves, but we would remain together forever. I felt sure of their presence without knowing how. A joyful new energy flooded through me. No matter what might come, I knew I was not alone as I headed along the path toward Jerusalem in bright morning sunlight with un-imaginable news.

Going along the path for the third time in as many days, I felt as though I were walking on air, alive again myself with his living resurrected body. Together, we would still bring news of peace, forgiveness, healing, and God's love to ev-eryone. I wouldn't fear or forget. I would tell everyone that nothing, absolutely nothing, even suffering and death, could ever separate any of us from the love of God!

As the first witness to that good news, my heart was beating so fast as I approached the city gate. I wanted to shout, "He's risen! He's risen, everyone! Can you believe it? Killing people isn't the end! Dying isn't the end!" Then I thought, who will believe me? What shall I say next? "He came back to tell me that he's just fine, living in God's love. There's still so much I don't know or understand, but I'm not worried. He loves me and has promised to teach me!"

Nearing our door, I wondered where to begin. I was so full of joy, and yet already I began to feel the burden of what waited for me and my news: the accusations and ridicule, the doubts and fears, the blame and shame, the selfishness and guilt, the rituals and sacrifices, people doing again and again what separates them from God and each other.

I would bear that burden and make my part of the sacrifice. I was not afraid. I was thrilled. It seemed to me that all of our lives dissolve into air, as insubstantial and ever-changing as a cloud. There is no imagined past or imagined future to which we can cling. An unimaginable new adventure waited for me. I felt a deep sense of peace, and I still felt the thrill of his touch, his embrace, and the reassurance that he was with me now, and would be with me always, whether or not I or anyone else could see him. I wanted with all of my heart to do what he asked me to do.

# ACKNOWLEDGMENTS

I am deeply grateful to all of the many teachers, scholars, and writers from whose work I have benefited, including: Jim Rayburn, Martha Zimmerman, Margaret Starbird, Jean-Yves Le Loup, Karen King, Elaine Pagels, Marvin Meyer, James Breech, Martin Buber, Rudolf Bultmann, Bart Ehrman, Marcus Borg, John Dominic Crossan, Miriam Feinberg Vamosh, David J. Hamilton, and Tim MacIntosh.

For the translation and paraphrase work on which my versions of the Psalms, prophets, and wisdom books are based, I am indebted to Eugene Peterson's *The Message*, Robert Alter's *The Book of Psalms* (Copyright ©2007 by Robert Alter, published by WW Norton & Company, Inc.), Stephen Mitchell's *A Book of Psalms* and *Tao Te Ching* (Copyright ©1993 and 1988 respectively by Stephen Mitchell, published by HarperCollins Publishers), Biblical Studies Press' NET Bible® (New English Translation) (Copyright ©1996-2006 by Biblical Studies Press, L.L.C. http://biblc.org All rights reserved), and Thomas Nelson's HOLY BIBLE; The New King James Version (Copyright ©1979, 1980, 1982 by Thomas Nelson, Inc.).

I would like to thank professors Edward Hobbs and Peter Lutz for stimulating questions, writing guru James Bonnet for shaping answers, and my friend Morton David Goldberg for guidance. I am especially grateful to architect/artist Roger Katan for drawing the map, and to my wonderful, generous editor, Tyler Tichelaar, without whose careful reading, probing curiosity, and constant encouragement, the story would have been incomplete. For connecting me with Tyler, my gifted book designer, Shiloh Schroeder, and my enthusiastic publisher, Susan Friedman, I am  sincerely grateful to my publishing coach, Patrick Snow, and to creativity consultant, Marilyn Schoeman, for recommending Patrick to me.

My heartfelt appreciation goes again to many people who have encouraged me with their interest through the years, including seat mates on flights, tech supporters at Apple, print assistants at Kinko's and FedEx, and to all those who have read, questioned, researched, responded, and helped in countless ways, including:

Cynnie Salley, Joe Grodin, Marilyn Couch, Diane Stevens, Wayne Thurman, Shirley Bell, Clem Classen, Steve Harms, Joan Raines, Patrick Woodward, Erin McInerney, Diane Bonnet, Linda Knudsen McAusland, Roberta Kennedy, Tim Nuveen, Carolyn Kerr, Carter Mears, David and Cynthia Price, Flo Goldberg, Irene and Bob Fischl, Luci Shaw, Sandol Stoddard, Barbara Janes, Jasmine Locatelli, Rebecca McClain, Stewart Scham, Richard and Liz Caemmerer, Cathy Weldy, Ellen Tausig, Patricia Tall-Takacs, Linda Watten, Joe Hester, Bill Cohn, Rob Salkowitz, Josef Venker, Rita Sperry, Roger Katan, Gerard Thurnauer, John Zimmerman, and my son David Kerr.

# A REFERENCE GUIDE TO PSALMS AS NUMBERED IN MODERN BIBLE TRANSLATIONS

# AN INTERVIEW WITH JUNE KERR

**How did you first become interested in Mary Magdalene and the theories that she may have been Jesus' wife?**

My first contact with the idea was when my sister-in-law told me of reading the book *Holy Blood, Holy Grail* as part of her curiosity about grail stories in English literature. I think she thought she would shock me. I dismissed the possibility at first, but then thought I shouldn't be afraid of any idea that might actually enlighten my faith and make it stronger. Later, I came across Margaret Starbird's books and her same reaction of doubting the possibility that Jesus was married until she began to explore a persistent story hidden through the ages.

**Other authors have written about Mary Magdalene as Jesus' wife but I believe you are the first to write a novel in Mary's voice. How else do you think your book stands apart from other books about Mary Magdalene?**

Combining clues from the Gospels, Acts, and Letters, I think Mary was the loving, supportive partner of Jesus, the first witness to his full humanity and full divinity. I don't think anyone else has made the connection in just this way, grounded their lives in psalms, or explored the consequences of her witness and why she disappeared from Jerusalem. The connection between John Mark, Jesus, and Mary has not been made to my knowledge, though Sarah, according to legend, arrived in the south of France, with Mary Jacobi and Mary Salome and is the patron saint of the "gypsies." Sarah is the child identified by Margaret Starbird and then Dan Brown as the likely daughter of Jesus and Mary.

**In the novel's prologue, Mary is writing from France, but the novel doesn't tell us how she ended up in France. Would you fill us in a little on that?**

Mary is writing from the marvelous cave in the south of France (the wilderness) where Jesus told her she could find refuge. This is explicit in the sequel which will take her on her harrowing journey from Jerusalem into the wilderness (eventually France), to protect the memory and teaching of Jesus.

**I understand you intend both a sequel and a prequel. Again, without giving too much away, what can you tell us about the prequel, and why do you think it's important to write about Mary's life before and after Jesus' recorded ministry?**

There is some mention in The Gospels and Paul's letters to Jesus' life before his public ministry, and there are legends and stories, but none fill the gap in a way that explain the brief public life and profound teaching of Jesus. Neither is there a clear path from the Resurrection to the accounts of Jesus' life and ministry recorded in the New Testament. I believe understanding Mary's role can shed light on both. Without giving away too much, in the sequel, Mary is the one who teaches Paul "in the wilderness." Paul says he went into the desert to learn his "gospel" rather than learn it from Peter and James (Jesus' brother and head of the church in Jerusalem), and only later went to "verify" it with them.

**In the book you state that Jesus and Mary are in their mid-thirties when he begins his ministry, yet traditionally, Jesus is said to have died at age thirty-three. Why did you decide to change his age?**

There is nothing written in the Bible that says Jesus died at age thirty-three. Pilate was Prefect of Judea from 28 to 36 A.D., Caiphas was High Priest from 18 to 36 A.D. I suspect thirty-three was a "special" number, and curiously thirty-three is the number of years Mary is supposed to have lived in a cave in the south of France after the resurrection, having arrived there in 40 A.D. according to legend. Luke reports that Jesus "was about thirty" when he began his teaching ministry in Galilee. I don't know about you, but I was "about thirty" until I was forty. When he was born and when he died is still a matter of scholarly debate. It would be more consistent with patterns in the Torah and Prophets if he lived forty years on earth, but I don't think this timing is as significant as what he taught and how he lived and died.

**One thing I really liked about the book was how you showed real-life events behind many of Jesus' parables, especially the story of the Good Samaritan. What gave you the idea that Jesus' stories might have been drawn from real life?**

With that particular story, I was looking for what might have been the experience that would push an otherwise obscure man into suddenly becoming a public figure, a celebrity teacher/healer. People I listen to tell stories from their own experiences or those of friends and family: carpenters tell stories about building, ball players tell stories about ball games, lawyers tell stories about legal cases, bankers tell stories about banking, parents tell stories about parenting their children, and so on. With these two observations, I suspected that the story of the Good Samaritan was a significant story for Jesus and the experience of it could dramatically change his life and shape his understanding of it.

**Politics are very important in the novel, and I was especially surprised by how you worked in Bar-Abbas and the two thieves crucified beside Jesus into the story. What made you decide to weave them throughout the story of Jesus' life?**

"The Son of The Fathers" is all the man whose place Jesus took is called in the Gospels. I wanted to probe what that title could tell us and flesh out the contrast between the life choices of the two and the consequences of those choices, their relationships to each other and to the other two men who were crucified. I found "Bar-Abbas" bound by traditional thinking of revenge at any cost, bent on doing whatever he could to harass the corrupt government to restore the righteous kingdom of God, not unlike the Taliban in Islam today, while Jesus saw an encounter with another as an opportunity to forgive and create peace.

I was surprised and learned a lot from some of the historical details you included, such as the mention of Elijah coming at Passover, which is not something Christians are familiar with. I felt like you did a lot with such details to illuminate aspects of the story of Jesus which we only have fragments of in the Gospels. Will you tell us a little about the research you did and how you decided what details were important to include or leave out of the novel regarding Jewish traditions and political details of the period?

Jesus was a faithful Jew. The Gospels allude to the fact that he observed the feasts required in Leviticus Chapter 23, though many Christians, unfamiliar with the Torah, the books of Moses, miss the references. While I am not a scholar competent in ancient languages, I have read many translations of the Bible and other writings which illuminate the political and religious world in which Jesus lived. Also I have had the privilege of celebrating the Passover for many years with Jewish friends, and also with Christian friends.

Why do you feel it's important to think that Jesus might have been married and had children?

I think this is an interesting question. From Adam and Eve on, partnering is integral to the human experience. When the sacred relationship was broken or violated, the Bible records dire consequences. The first commandment was "to be fruitful and multiply." Parenting would be part of being "fully human." We have stories of Jesus' relationship and attitude toward children that confirm this. In the book of the Acts, the accounts of John Mark are coherent with the idea that he was traveling with relatives or those who would protect him as he endeavored to carry on his father's legacy, protect his mother, and eventually, be the nominal author of the first widely accepted and distributed summary of his father's life, his teaching, and the meaning of it. As for Sarah, there has been much written about her possible links to the future royal families of Europe, while her other brother Joseph rather disappears in time, though again there are legends of his traveling to England with his father's great-uncle, Joseph of Arimathea. Genealogists and DNA research suggests that if Jesus had children and they traveled to Europe, all Europeans today would most likely be descended from them, as well as many people on other continents. Personally, I rather like the idea that we may all be descended and related, and there may not be any need to compete or exclude, but rather generously to share with one another what we can for everyone's benefit.

**June, I understand you are a practicing Christian yet the Christian Church has never been open to theories that Jesus was married or had children. How did you reconcile writing this controversial story with your Christian faith, or does it even need to be reconciled? Did you feel nervous or worried about people's reactions while writing this book?**

I don't know if several hundred years after the life and death and resurrection of Jesus, the church organized under Constantine had any concern or idea of how or why the story of Mary may have been hidden in the gospels. Even in early house churches where both men and women shared insights and responsibilities according to letters in the New Testament, there were fights between various factions, liberals and conservatives. The faith, hope, and love that Jesus and Mary lived and taught will never die, but unless the organized church can grasp the wisdom of their way and honor both men and women as full partners in the faith, it seems to continue to dissolve in divisiveness. I hope this story of love and faith will help people of all faiths and of no faith understand the power of love. As Jimi Hendrix said, "When the power of love overcomes the love of power, the world will know peace." I hope that day comes soon in each of our lives. I don't understand why anyone would deny that God could give Jesus a mate as God had given one to Adam, or reject the love story of Jesus and Mary seeking peace on earth.

**In writing this book, what do you hope, more than anything else that your readers will come to understand or feel about Mary and Jesus? Why did you feel this story is so important to tell?**

I hope that readers will see Mary and Jesus as role models: honoring their parents, supporting one another with love, patience, and humor in the fulfillment of their lives, and loving, educating, and encouraging all of their children, daughters and sons, to realize their full potential. But equally, I hope that readers will understand that Jesus and Mary showed us the way that love, responding with what we can to the need of those we meet each day, is the way to live in peace.

I feel this is a lost story which is important for our time because, instead of loving and caring for one another with mercy and justice as the diverse and delightful expressions of our "God of Gods and Lord of Lords," we continue to fight one another, to try to force the other into our image rather than to accept the other as created in God's image. Christians fight Christians, Moslems fight Moslems, Jews fight Jews. Horrific conflicts continue among and between people who all claim allegiance to the God of Abraham, the God who commands us to love. I hope that a new view of our common story can help us understand and follow the way of peace

# ABOUT THE AUTHOR

June Kerr lives in the Pacific Northwest and the South of France. In France, she became intrigued with persistent legends that Mary Magdalene, Martha, Lazarus, and others lived in the area after Jesus' crucifixion and resurrection. She found a seminar on the life of Jesus in twentieth century film, held at the Grunewald Guild in Washington's Cascade Mountains, thought provoking

Born in the Midwest, June received a B.A. from Miami University (Ohio) and an M.A. from Northwestern University. At age ten, she began to study with a woman writing a novel based on Genesis, and has continued to study with diverse teachers and scholars ever since, including those at the Young Life Graduate Institute in Colorado, the Graduate Theological Union in Berkeley, California, Seattle University in Washington, and Regent and Carey Colleges at the University of British Columbia.

June has traveled throughout the United States, on both coasts of Canada and Mexico, and extensively in Europe, Asia, Australia, New Zealand, and the Pacific islands. She has traveled in parts of South America, North Africa, and the Middle East, studying and observing art, architecture, and culture with diverse histories and approaches to the Unknown...God and gods by whatever name.


VISIT JUNE AT
WWW.RABBONIMYLOVE.COM